PEACE, LOVE &
PETROL BOMBS

Peace, Love & Petrol Bombs
By D. D. Johnston

This edition © 2011 AK Press (Edinburgh, Oakland, Baltimore)

ISBN-13: 978-1-84935-061-7
Library of Congress Control Number: 2011920479

AK Press
674-A 23rd Street
Oakland, CA 94612
USA
www.akpress.org
akpress@akpress.org

AK Press UK
PO Box 12766
Edinburgh EH8 9YE
Scotland
www.akuk.com
ak@akdin.demon.co.uk

The above addresses would be delighted to provide you with the latest
AK Press distribution catalog, which features several thousand books,
pamphlets, zines, audio and video recordings, and gear, all published or
distributed by AK Press. Alternately, visit our websites to browse the catalog
and find out the latest news from the world of anarchist publishing:
www.akpress.org | www.akuk.com
revolutionbythebook.akpress.org

Printed in Canada on 100% recycled, acid-free paper with union labor.

Cover by Chris Wright | Interior by Kate Khatib

PEACE, LOVE & PETROL BOMBS

A NOVEL BY D.D. JOHNSTON

AK
PRESS
EDINBURGH · OAKLAND · BALTIMORE

★ 1 ★

The way I tell it, I almost die. The train has a metal cow catcher and it's mushrooming steam and it's blasting a fuck-off-angry klaxon and I'm on the tracks and at the last second—when the light's gone bright, when my life's flashed before me—I am pulled to safety.

She says it wasn't like that. She says the train was hardly in view, that it was almost stationary, that we could have sat down and eaten a picnic before it reached us. I like to think she's too modest. I know that she was wrapped in black clothes—black hoodie, black combats—shouting "Allez quoi!" through a black bandana. "Come on! Putain! Viens!" A hundred metres away, beyond the police vans and motorcycles, the black bloc trickled out of view, leaving the pavement rubbled with cobblestones. I remember that she ran into the woodland that banked the road and I followed. She gestured for silence, as if the crack of twigs could be heard above the rattling helicopter, the sirens, the echoing detonations. "Merde. Sprechen sie Deutsch?"

"What?"

"Italiano?"

"No, Scottish."

"Scottish? I tell you to fuckeeng move! Now we are alone to be beaten and raped." She crouched in a rhododendron bush, still wearing her swimming goggles. "Stupide."

"Sorry," I said, considering taking my chances with the police. "You want a cigarette?"

"I have my own. Do you have the fire?" The lighter shook in my hand as I lit her cigarette. When I pulled down my bandanna, she laughed, "You are white as a ghost!"

"We don't get much sun in Scotland."

"You are how old, Petit Fantôme?"

"Twenty."

"Non! I thought you are fifteen! Anarchiste?"

"Kind of."

She pulled her swimming goggles over her head, and her brown eyes spread out like melted chocolate. When she removed her hat, her fringe spiked with sweat. The rest of her hair was clipper short. On her left cheekbone, an inch-long scar curved neat and white, like the scars they paint on the cheeks of Action Men and GI Joes. She smiled and blinked and stuffed her gear into her backpack. All these things were heroic.

After two minutes, she said "On y va" and crawled through the bush, tip-toeing onto the road. "Bon. We find the comrades. We follow the smoke and the helicopter, yes?"

And I thought: We stoned the police; we set them on fire; the people they catch are fucked. So I shrugged as nonchalantly as I could and pointed up the street. "You know, I was just after getting something to eat?"

She looked at me and laughed. "You want to stop for lunch? You are sure you are not from France?"

Prague, September 2000. The day we charged the World Bank Summit, crashing through crowd barriers, smashing folds in police lines. The police dropped their shields and beat flames from their uniforms. They fired more teargas and the crowd pushed back then forward and a water-cannon traversed the road, tumbling protesters down the slope. I ran downhill, out of the gas, to an intersection below the bridge, where the jet from the water cannon trickled between the cobblestones, and I stood, gasping, hands on knees, looking back at the mist of gas and smoke. I had lost Spocky.

There was no fighting at the intersection. People were juggling and twirling ribbons and playing diabolo. When police reinforcements arrived with two armoured personnel carriers, a man in a woollen poncho sat cross-legged on the road; a woman in a raincoat threw flowers. The police formed a new line, thirty metres from the Čiklova intersection, and *then* we built a barricade. We piled logs and branches, street signs, an office chair. A Polish skinhead tried to light it. I helped fill wheelie bins with cobblestones.

Then the police advanced and you could hear stones hitting tanks and the hippies chanting "*No violence—No violence—No violence.*" There was a man lying on the pavement, drooling blood onto his vest. A German punk bowled a bottle across the barricade. "Hey! Provocateur!" shouted an Englishman in a blue pac-a-mac.

"*No violence—No violence—No violence.*"

"Fuck you! Fuck da poleez!"

"People fucking live here, yeah?"

"If the World Bank come to *my* town," said the injured guy, spraying a speech bubble of blood around every syllable, "you burn my grandmother's house!"

"Opá," said his friend, pointing into the gas. "Batsi." The explosions were louder and the air was thicker and it had become harder to breathe. The Englishman in the blue pac-a-mac stood up; then the circle of pacifists stood up; then the medics stood up. Soon everyone was standing, wondering why everyone was standing. Then people were jogging past us, red eyed and gasping—Czech syndicalists in construction helmets, German antifascists wearing balaclavas. They bottled into the yellow underpass below the railway line, and hundreds tried to squeeze behind them. Then the police emerged from the fog, weighed down by armour. Somebody shouted "Come on!" but I was sprinting across the grass verge, by the railway fence. Too late I saw the police emerge from the trees, running down the hill in a line.

The cop who hit me, who chased me into the path of the train, was splashed with white paint and had lost his truncheon. He crashed me into the railway fence, and as I held onto it and tried to climb, he punched me again. I was scrabbling my feet, tearing my hands on the wire, and he was behind me, wheezing through his gas mask. The fence collapsed under my weight and threw me hands first onto the railway line. I pushed off the ground, took one step, two steps, stumbled, tripped and—

In Bar Neviditelný Hněv, old men stood up, gesticulating at the street, arguing as they watched the riots on TV. Otherwise, the room was empty. We sat at a table in the corner, and she fidgeted with the salt shaker, making L-shaped knight moves across the red and white checked tablecloth. "I'm Wayne, by the way."

"You know who made the first cup of tea in Prague?"

"The first cup of tea?"

"Michael Bakunin."

"Aye?"

"Oui. He ask for tea in a restaurant. They do not know, so he go to the kitchen, make the tea."

"He carried tea about with him?"

The barman shuffled to our table and flicked the top page over the edge of his notepad. By 2003, when the G8 met in Evian, the police had learned to commandeer whole towns, so you couldn't even get a bottle of water; in Prague, however, the streets were cobbled, the police force had the crowd control skills of a student P.E. teacher, and the restaurants were so cheap that we almost lived like the delegates. Sure, the low cost of living didn't stop Germans in Exploited t-shirts from scrounging Koruna on every street corner, but nobody cared: you could eat a good meal, wash it down with Pilsener, and still have change to pay off the German anti-fascists. "Eh, can I have the fish. And a beer, please. Big," I said, gesturing something the size of a bucket.

He nodded and scribbled.

"Jeden Staropramen prosim," she said, "et... brambory?"

"Brambory? Huh... hranolky? French fry?"

"Ano, ano."

"Dobrý," he said, accepting the menus.

"Dekuje"—she pronounced it *day-kwee*.

"How d'you say thanks?"

"You eat fish?"

"I've been saying 'Deck-you-jay.'"

"Fuckeeng idiot!"

"How many languages d'you speak?"

"You eat fish?"

"Aye—what's wrong with the fish? You don't like fish?"

"I am vegan."

"Right," I said, unsure how to deal with this. "You ever like... I dinnae ken, like really miss just ordering a steak or something?"

"Non. You know what I miss, what I really fuckeeng miss? I miss, maybe, just once, to eat dinner with no imbécile tell me I want some meat."

"Sorry. What made you become vegan?"

"Now you want to start an argument because you feel insecure. Because in there," she pushed her finger against my forehead, "you do not really understand why you think it is wrong to kick a dog, when you think it is okay to eat a cow."

"No, I—"

"You want to tell me how much I miss meat, yes?"

"No."

"You want to pick what ever fuckeeng badly cooked shit is on your plate and you want to put it in my face, yes?"

"No!"

"And then I want to be polite so... je m'en fous: 'It look nice,' I say. But this will only encourage you. And next you will tell me it is un-natural to be vegan, yes?" I laughed because it was true. "And maybe I really do not want to argue. So I shrug—peut-être—is opinion. Then you will keep on and fuckeeng on. Until eventually I say, 'But people did not eat dairy until the last few thousand year.' Then you will be very angry, look at me and say, 'This is what I cannot stand about you fuckeeng vegans. You have always to shove your view down everyone else's mouth.'"

I laughed. "No, I dinnae think any of that."

She smiled and lit a cigarette like a movie star.

She told me King Wenceslas was never a king. She told me Wenceslas Square is one of those places history won't leave alone. Think about the dates, she said. It kicked off here in 1848; in 1948, it witnessed the Communist coup. In 1918, crowds celebrated an independent Czechoslovakia; in 1968, they returned to fight the Tankies. The Nazis invaded in 1939—fifty years later, where did the people gather during the Velvet Revolution? Here. Night after night, until the Jakeš leadership resigned, and Havel and Dubček stood together, just up there. And at the top of the square, Národní Muzeum, shot at by Soviet troops, its steps where Jan Palach set fire to himself: a box seat on the century.

We started from where we had last seen the black bloc and followed the graffiti, the broken windows and smouldering barricades, until the trail faded and the streets we walked through had a quiet normality. We passed a middle-aged couple in matching Jubilee 2000 anti-debt t-shirts, and a group of Italian disobidienti wearing white boiler suits stuffed with padding. We followed the tramlines back to Náměstí Míru but found the square empty except for the International Socialist contingent, their placards drooping as they traipsed in the shadow of the charcoal-coloured church. A helicopter swung over the church and a black kitten ran across the tramlines, through the trampled flower beds, where it stopped, looking up at us with a pet-me meow. "Le chat," she said, dropping onto one knee and extending a finger. The cat padded forward, sniffed her finger, and then rubbed the side of its face against the back of her hand. It rolled on the ground so she could tickle its belly and then, suddenly bored with this, stood up and stretched, arching its back before bounding across the square scattering pigeons. As we walked on, she said, "When I am sixteen, I buy a cat."

"Aye?"

"I was a cleaner. In Paris. This was 1993, and I live in a tower block, on floor eleven. One day my friend telephone me and ask do I want a cat. In my appartement? I do not think so. But then she tell me that her brother want to drown the cat, so, okay. When I get there the cat is in a bag with some stones. It was very small, and beautiful, with big blue eyes and silly fur, and the brother of my friend say it cost one-hundred-Francs. I say, fuck off—you want to drown this cat! He say, there were six of these cats and he sell five and nobody want this cat. He say—vraiment—he say, it is not fair on his other customer if he give me the cat for free. I say, 'Ta mere elle suce des ours!' And he shrug and drop the cat back in the bag. But its eyes! Putain, I could not leave it. So I buy this stupide cat. And all the way to the appartement, it… I do not know in English, the happy noise of the cat?"

"Purring?"

"How do you say?"

"Purring, it purred."

"Yes, it purred. It was very thin beneath the fur. I carry it up eleven floor of stairs, and I say, 'Ça va, ma petite chatte? Mignonne friponne.' I knew nothing about cats except they like milk, so I pour it milk and then I go to sleep, very tired. And when I wake up, when I wake up, the stupide fuckeeng cat has piss on my floor."

"So what did you do with it?"

She stopped to look at a church, circling it with her eyes. "You know why it is like this, this city? Emil Hácha surrender Tchècoslovaquie to the Nazis so these buildings would not be destroyed." She heeled 360 degrees, put a cigarette to her mouth, and mimed for the lighter. "Why did you come here?"

"Why did I come to Prague?" I said, lighting her cigarette. "I was at a football match in Germany."

"You have gone to *Germany* to watch a *football match*?"

"Aye. My mate Spocky said I should come here."

"Why?"

"It was the UEFA Cup."

"No, stupide, why does he say you are to come here?"

"You ken, for the demonstration and that."

She started to walk again. "Spocky? You have a friend who is called *Spocky*?"

"It's kind of like a nickname. We work together, in the fast food industry, Benny's—"

"Benny's Burgers?"

"We ken it's a shite job, that's why we've—"

"Lentement."

"What?"

"Slow, slow."

"Sorry. Ken means know."

"I like your accent."

"Aye? Barry means good. If you had a friend called Ken you could say 'D'you ken Ken? He's barry, eh? Radge means—'"

"You are working at Benny's Burgers?"

"Aye. We've started this group, like a trade union."

"Ah. This is in Scotland?"

"Aye.'

"Glasgow? Édimbourg?"

"Dundule. It's kind of between the two."

"Ah. And *Spocky*, he is also at the football match?" The way she asked these questions made my story sound like an absurd lie.

"No, he doesn't like football. He came for this." We passed a boutique with a jagged hole in its window and "NO WB" and "FUCK IMF" sprayed across its walls in red and black.

"And now he is where?"

"Who?"

"Your fuckeeng friend."

"Oh, Spocky. I Dinnae ke— I don't know. I lost him in the tear gas."

"So maybe he is arrested?"

"I dinnae ken. I was looking for him when I met you."

"Non—when you met me, you were asleep on the railway." Then we reached Wenceslas Square and girls cobblestoned McDonald's and skinheads kicked the glass out of Deutsche Bank and local kids threw furniture out of KFC. It was there that she told me King Wenceslas was never a king, that history won't leave Wenceslas Square alone; she was shouting above the applause of shattering glass. Then the police formed lines in front of the museum and burst the night with gas canisters and firecrackers. We ran forward throwing bottles and cobblestones, and somewhere in the back and forward, between our nervous advances and panicked retreats, I lost her in the crowd.

★ 2 ★

Whenever you question how something came to be the way it is, and especially if you try to change it, someone will tell you, "The world is just that way." But the world is not *just that way*; there are reasons why things are the way they are. Take Benny's Burgers. At Benny's Burgers there is a procedure for everything—I mean *everything*. There is a procedure for how you wash your hands; there is a procedure for how you fill a mop bucket; there are procedures stipulating which side of your shirt you wear your name badge on and how you tie your apron. There are prohibitions on certain colours of socks and regulations on how high you can stack boxes (boxes of fries should be piled five high; boxes of fruit pies should only be piled three high). You're allowed to cook nine hamburgers in a batch but no more than six chicken burgers. Why? Because that's the procedure. Why? Because it's just that way.

Wrong. Benny's Burgers is not *just that way*; there are reasons why a small chain of Italian ristorantes became a multinational burger conglomerate. Benny's began life in the Bronx borough of New York City. In those days it was Benito's: a family place where the pizzas were cooked in a stone oven, the carbonara was recommended, and the seafood was surprisingly good. Sonny Alligarta ate there in 1958 (he had the spaghetti marinara) and he liked everything about it. He liked the precooked sauces and the pre-boiled pasta. He especially liked the teenage girls who served him from a numbered menu. In fact, he liked Benito's so much, he bought it.

Sonny dreamed of expanding Benito's across the continent, envisaging a time when basil and red wine would be indispensable to the diet of every American, but in 1963, a snapped fan belt left him stranded and hungry in Codicioso. As far as Sonny could figure, Codicioso only had one eatery. The burger he bought cost fifteen cents and was ready made when he ordered; served on a toasted bun, with a slice of cheese from a packet, it tasted like it had been sitting in a hot cabinet since before the Civil War. They were serving this shit and people were queuing up to buy it—the future, he decided, was burgers.

Sonny didn't mean to disrespect his Italian heritage but *Benito's?* It was a bit... un-American. So he changed the name to Benny's. He replaced the chefs and waiters with children, college students, single mothers, and first-generation immigrants. He bought the cheapest ingredients and for two years he undercut every greasy spoon in New York. Soon you could get a Benny's Burger in Chicago, Sydney, Shanghai, Islamabad—even Dundule—and with his fortune, Sonny found celebrity. Like McDonald's chief Ray Kroc, Sonny was moved to publish his autobiography, but while Kroc's legacy is illustrated in poetic quotes that capture the Zeitgeist of post-war America, Alligarta's statements have proved more controversial. Where "We sold them a dream and paid them as little as possible" is attributed to Kroc discussing McDonald's staff, Alligarta is reported to have said of Benny's employees, "We worked them like dogs and paid them like monkeys." Kroc's autobiography is filled with insights such as "It was not her sex appeal but the obvious relish with which she devoured the hamburger that made my pulse begin to hammer with excitement," while Alligarta's memoirs bluntly recollect, "The ketchup dribbled on her considerable cleavage, and it really gave me the horn."

D.D. JOHNSTON

And yet, by 1998, Benny's employed over a million people in over a hundred countries and annually spent over two billion dollars beaming Big Benny's twisted world-view into toddlers' underdeveloped minds. When we say something is *just that way*, what we're really saying is that we don't know, or can't be bothered to explain, why it is the way it is. To try to understand McDonaldization (and Benny's hated the term, preferring to describe McDonald's as "Bennyized") we'd need to consider the logic of capitalist production, investors' demands for profit, and the resultant urge to maximise the extraction of surplus value from labour. We'd also need to consider the genealogies of Fordism and centralised scientific management, how the Fordist method of production was implemented to break the power of the organised working class, how the State turned machine guns on the unemployed during the 1932 Ford Hunger March, and so on.

But these are not the sort of events that corporate historiography records. Every year, Benny's marks the anniversary of Alligarta's investment by sending each restaurant a frozen cake. Senior managers make morale-boosting visits to the shop floor, and in the evening they organise team quizzes where all the questions are about the optimum temperature for cooking fish burgers or how high boxes of fries may be piled. For Kieran Hunter, Second Assistant Manager, Founder's Day was better than Christmas.

The day I met Spocky, Kieran stood pondering his wristwatch, sweating in the late-morning heat. Benny's divided their staff into those they trusted to tie a neat Windsor and those who would forever need to wear a company-issued clip-on strip of polyester. Whatever ignominies the rest of life might inflict on him, Kieran would always belong to that stratum of the corporation trusted to tie their own ties. "PACE, yeah?" he said as I opened the door. "Punctuality. Attitude. Customer focus. Enthusiasm. Yeah?" The store was quiet and the tables had been wiped streaky with anti-bacterial spray. "You are... seven minutes late, yeah?"

"Am I?"

"Yes," he said, exhibiting his watch. "*And*, I've checked your file. This is your third late arrival and you know what that means, yeah?"

"I get to keep your watch?"

"It means a formal written warning." He wore a new cap with a high dome that made him look like an extraterrestrial cone head. Above his mouth, his freckly face was decorated with a light ginger down. These few wispy centipede legs were the only evidence of his ongoing attempts to produce a moustache (facial hair was banned at Benny's, but they permitted groomed moustaches). "Well, what you waiting for? You're now eight minutes late. Yeah?" He took a heavy set of keys from his pocket and lobbed them in his right hand.

The staff room was a small square box that contained thirty lockers and a table for two. There was an ironing board (someone had stolen the iron), a broken video player, and a television that was trapped on BBC One. The floor was strewn with plastic cups, polystyrene foams, and cardboard fry cartons, and the room had a strange smell, as if a diseased animal had died in one of the lockers. There was only one other guy in the room; I didn't recognise him, and he didn't acknowledge me. He appeared to be reading a book. "Is the TV knackered again?"

"I don't know," he said, turning the page. He wore a black trench coat, stone-washed jeans, and cheap trainers. His head was shaved and he wore spectacles with a thin black frame.

"What you reading?"

"It's just a novel."

"Let's see," I said, grabbing it from him. "*The Dispossessed*," I read, making it sound stupid. There was a picture of a planet on the front. "What's this, *Star Trek* or something?"

"No, it's about this alternative civilisation. These people set up a utopian society on the moon of—"

"Sounds shite," I said, throwing my jacket in an empty locker.

He reached for his book, thumbed to his page, and scratched his neck. That was when Raj crashed the door against the lockers. "Wayne, motherfucker!" He made to punch fists but I messed up the timing and his knuckles landed in my open palm. "Alright?" he said as we clasped hands. "What sort of time is this? Listen man, we're gonnae be busy as fuck the day so I'm gonnae need you tae work your ass off, aye?"

I tugged my cap on and saluted. "No bothers, chief."

Raj's real name was Rajiv, or Rajesh, or Rajani. We called him Raj because it was easier. Raj wasn't allowed his own tie, but he did get to wear trousers with pockets (a licence denied to regular staff). He was alright, Raj—alright for a Paki. That's probably what they'll put on his gravestone: "Here lies Rajesh (or whatever his name was). He was alright for a Paki." Although he had contended with it all his life, at times you could see that Raj still struggled to accept the Dundule understanding of geography: the population of Dundule maintained that Pakistan was a massive country, starting near Bucharest and stretching across Turkey, North Africa, much of the former Soviet Union, the Middle East, the Indian Subcontinent, and Sri Lanka. "Hoy, who the fuck are you?"

The new guy looked up from his book. "I'm Owen Noonan. I just started today."

"Well, shit, get your uniform on!"

"They never gave me one."

"Machod, were you gonnae sit there till one grew on you?"

"Nope, I'm off at five."

"Oh Wayne, we've got a smart one here. What you reading?"

"Star Trek or something," I said.

The new guy showed Raj the cover. "No, it's about these people go to live on the moon and—" He bent over the table with a phlegmy cough.

"Can you speak Klingon?"

"Captain Spock, eh?"

"I'll get you a uniform. I'll send it to you in the transporter beam." You could hear Raj laughing as the door swung closed.

"He's awright for a Paki, eh?" said Gordon, crashing the grill tongs onto the grease trap.

"What?"

"I says Raj is awright for a Paki."

"Aye, suppose."

Gordon had started at Benny's two months after I had, but we'd known each other since school. He'd been planning to follow his uncle into the jewellery trade, but when that didn't work out, I persuaded him to join me in the burger game. I enjoyed working with Gordon even if it was hard to talk above the background noise—metal trays cymballed steel surfaces, grills hissed, bun spatulas clattered, fry baskets crashed through the automatic racking machine. "Someone hit that fuckin' timer!" shouted Raj because the "Time to wash your hands" beeper had been ring-ing for two minutes—*preep preep, preep preep, preep preep*—like a phone call that nobody wants to answer.

"Woah, where you going?" said Raj, stopping Lucy as she walked through the kitchen.

She paused by the milkshake machine, holding her apron. "Kieran says I've to count a float."

"Kieran!"

"What?"

"Did you tell Lucy to count a float?"

"Yeah, she's going on tills."

"Fuck off," said Raj, brandishing the floor plan. "I've got Lucy and you've got Captain Picard through there."

Kieran studied the plan and stroked his tie. "Okay, but whose shift is it, yeah?"

"It doesnae matter whose shift it is; you cannae steal my staff just cause you fancy them."

Lucy looked embarrassed, and Kieran pulled the keys from his pocket, tossing them from one hand to the other. *Everybody* fancied Lucy. "If you'd ever been on the ABC shift supervisors course then you'd know about PROSE—Plan, Review, Organise, Supervise, Encourage. There's the plan, yeah? Here's me review-ing it, 'Hmmm.' And here's me organising: 'Lucy, you're on tills today.' Okay?"

The milkshake machine had been making an enteric growling noise, and now Raj removed the lid and peered inside. "Buzz!" he said. "Get us some shake mix!" He turned back to Kieran, wield-ing the lid like a shield. "No danger are you swapping Lucy for that prick. No danger."

"Raj, at the end of the day, I'm the shift runner, so all the staff, including you, are under my jurisprudence, yeah? It's not about any one area; it's about maximising sales and improving the performance of the whole team. Yeah?" Kieran tossed his keys higher, caught them, and slipped them into his pocket. "Go on, love," he said, patting the small of Lucy's back. "Put your apron away for me." So Lucy strolled past the chicken vats and paused by the backroom sinks, where Spocky was attempting to clock in. I watched as she said something, took his card from between his fingers, swiped it, pressed yes, and left him to survey his new environment.

Spocky was so slightly built that at a casual glance he appeared taller than he really was. Perhaps this was why he'd been given enormous polyester slacks that trailed in the seeping sink water. Holding up these circus clown trousers, Spocky stood in his red and white striped uniform, gazing at the swamps of grease beneath the fry station. He studied the polished white walls, the cascading faces of stainless steel, and the mayonnaise-crusted ceiling tiles. Meanwhile, above a stack of defrosted buns, the electric fly trap sparked blue, incinerating another victim with a short *fizz-crackle*.

★ 3 ★

Listen, the only good thing about Benny's was the craic you could have with your colleagues. Now, looking back from beyond a train wreck of friendships, I'm nostalgic for this teenage camaraderie. When I think about Dundule, I think about Gordon: Gordon, aged thirteen, swaggering into school with tramlines shaved into his head; Gordon, on his first shift at Benny's, returning from B&Q having failed to buy a tub of tartan paint; Gordon, in full Highland dress, marrying a girl who was, technically, his sister (I know! I know!); and Gordon, departing on some mad odyssey, leaving me to deal with the police. I think about Kit, too. I met Kit at work, but she soon became my girlfriend. The last time I saw her, she was pregnant with someone else's child, but at one point, Kit and I thought we were going to get married. I think about Buzz, who could get you any drugs you wanted, and Spocky, whose real name, Owen, I almost never used. But most of all, perhaps, when I think about Dundule, I think about Lucy.

Like me, Lucy only scooped fries part time. During my second year at Benny's, I was re-sitting my school exams at Dundule College of Further Education, while Lucy was already at university, halfway through a sociology degree. It was Lucy who persuaded me onto the politics course at the University of Central Scotland. At that time, Lucy could have persuaded me to do just about anything.

The first class I ever attended was halfway through my first term. My arm was in a sling (I'd been stabbed the week before), and though I was late, the class hadn't started. We were in room 7G in James McPherson Tower, Melvyn Macveigh's room, where, because Melvyn Macveigh taught Marxism, the desk-graffiti said stuff like: "Dyslexics of the world untie"; "Academics of the world unite: you have a world to win and nothing to lose but your chairs." At ten past the hour, Macveigh strode in without apology and slapped his briefcase on the table nearest the door. "It amazes me that they entrust a train company to a man who considers a hot air balloon a desirable mode of transport. Right, what are we supposed to be doing? Ah, I think I'm supposed to stimulate you with this handout." In brown cords and salmon shirt, he slithered around the rectangle of desks, placing an A4 sheet before each student. When he reached me, he paused and whispered, "Politics and society?" as if circulating profiteroles. I nodded and he affected surprise, rubbing his head as he returned to his desk. "Miles Austin? No? Ashley Zechstein? Wayne Foster?"

"Aye."

"Ahhh!" he said, as though a long-standing mystery had been contentedly resolved. "*Bene qui latuit bene vixit*, I suppose. Shall we have a moment to digest this handout?"

> After the fall of the Berlin Wall, revolution in Romania and celebrations in Wenceslas Square, the USSR ceased to exist at midnight on the 31st December 1991. With the categorical refutation of Communism in Eastern Europe, has the spectre of Marxism finally been exorcised? In 1991, the *Wall Street Journal* was less sure: "Marx's analysis can be applied to the amazing disintegration of communist regimes built on the foundations of his thought but unfaithful to his prescriptions."

"Well?"

"   "

...

"   "

...

A plump girl in a stripy sweater clutched her *Beginner's Marx*; a mature student sighed, rubbed his beard, and squeezed the bridge of his nose; a boy in a rugby shirt thumbed that month's *Economist*. With every moment that passed, the chair creaking, heating humming, background noise grew louder, until you imagined you could hear breaths and heartbeats, and you looked at Melvyn Macveigh, who continued to stare out the window, happy to wait for the silence to crescendo.

"   "

...

"   "

...

It was a freckly boy who cracked first. "It's like, it doesn't really matter, you know?"

"Really?" said Macveigh, distracted from the world outside.

"It's like, kind of basic and old fashioned? Like it's stuck in all this worldly... you know? It's like we're all talking capitalism and communism, and none of that matters, none of that's... Is it? Like Buddhism, you know?"

The older student leant forward. "So are you saying Marxism's an inherently homogenous doctrine? A modernist metanarrative grounded in Enlightenment epistemological certainties and incompatible with a pluralistic world?"

"No. I'm saying, it's like... I spent my gap year in Nepal, right—"

"Woah-kay. Thank you," said Melvyn Macveigh.

The heating changed gears.

"You can get this book from Waterstone's," said the plump girl, exhibiting her *Beginners Guide*, "but I still can't see how this is relevant to the modern world? Like, which employer's going to care whether you understand 'Historical Materialism'?" She mouthed the phrase as though there was a chance the words would give way and plummet her into a valley of ridicule. "Besides," she continued, "there are definitely easier topics for the exam; I mean, it's in the same unit as the transformation of the Labour Party, isn't it?"

Melvyn Macveigh was trying to fix something on his watch.

"And it's never going to happen again, is it?" said the boy in the rugby shirt.

"Oh no. Not here at least," said Macveigh. "The climate's too inclement for marching and demonstrating and all that." As if to prove his point, a gust of wind shook the pre-fabricated tower, triggering an avalanche of plaster.

"I still think his ideas are important to discuss," said the mature student, stroking his chin. "I mean Marxism, more than anything else in the philosophical canon, sort of shapes contemporary discourse, doesn't it? It's like Derrida says: 'We are all heirs of Marx.'"

This began a pattern which lasted throughout the academic year: every week, the mature student was distinguished from his classmates, the tutor, and the creaking post-war tower, in that he looked like he wanted to be there. As the only person who had done the reading, or had any interest in discussing the topic, the mature student was often driven to internal debate: he would raise a question, listen to the silence for two minutes, and eventually answer himself. On other occasions, provoked by boredom, perhaps, Macveigh would pick on the person who was trying hardest to avoid eye contact. "Mr. Foster, do you wish to contribute to this vibrant debate?"

"..."

"Prospects for Marxism in the twenty-first century?"

"Well... pretty shabby, I suppose."

"'Pretty shabby, *I suppose.*' *Cadit quaestio*. I shall endeavour to include this erudite contribution in the year exam paper: 'Prospects for Marxism in the twenty-first century are *pretty shabby, I suppose*. Discuss.'"

It seemed that people got very emotional about this Marx guy. Melvyn Macveigh appeared to consider my disinterest unforgivably rude, as though Marx was in the room and I was refusing to pass him the cashew nuts. On one occasion, in Benny's staff room, I overheard Lucy and Spocky discussing Marx as if he was an intimate friend who might at any moment arrive with their ice cream sundaes. What was the big deal?

At five o'clock, I was due to meet Lucy in the Student Union (she said she had "news"), which gave me three hours for research. In the University Library, I found the first book on Melvyn Macveigh's reading list: *Capital: Volume One*. It was a bit slow to start with, certainly not a page-turner. I persevered but there was no discernible plot and there were too many formulae. This Marx guy was no John Grisham. Disillusioned, I put it back. What I needed was some perspective, a human angle; who was this guy? I returned to the catalogue and entered Marx as a title. This time it suggested *Karl Marx: A Biography*.

This was more like it. It turned out that Marx was a total chancer. Famous for theorising the emancipation of the working class, Marx spent all day drinking port at the expense of some Engels bloke who had inherited a factory. It seemed to me that Marx must have been sleeping with the Engels guy, because why else would Engels give him all that money? And get this: Marx had his bread buttered on both sides—he married Jenny von West-phalen, whose dad was a baron or something. One of the best bits in the book was when they could no longer afford their middle-class lifestyle and Marx sent his wife to scrounge off her parents. While she was away, he knocked up the servant.

At five o'clock, I explained all this to Lucy's chest. Fortunately, Lucy didn't notice that I spoke to her chest any more than she noticed that barmen always served her first, or that men walked backwards after they passed her in the street, or that women swore at their husbands and hissed "Marry her then!" as if she'd jump at the chance to bed down with their hairy-backed, bald-headed mates. "It's quite a sad story," I said. "All the children from his marriage died tragically."

"Yeah, I heard that."

"You wouldn't believe it: Jennychen got cancer and died just before her dad. Laura Marx, she went and married this Paul Laf-argue guy and they committed suicide together in 1911. The wee boy Edgar died of tuberculosis when he was just eight. Another two died as babies, a third before it could even be named, and get this: Eleanor Marx, she shacked up with this Edward Aveling guy—"

"Is this the suicide pact that wasn't a suicide pact?"

"Aye," I said, a bit pissed off to have my story spoiled. "I guess brains aren't genetic. I mean, surely it's the first rule of suicide pacts: if he hands you the prussic acid and insists you go first, don't do it."

Lucy laughed, lips red from the blackcurrant cordial in her snakebite. "Do you know about Marx's bastard child? Not Lenin,

I mean the one he had with the servant?" Lucy was originally from the North West and she spoke with a Gaelic lull that sort of lingered, so that my replies always seemed delayed, as if we were talking on a satellite link.

"Aye, I read that too."

"How *is* the arm?" she asked, her expression changing as she watched me struggle to get a fag out with one hand.

"Alright. I'm supposed to get the stitches out tomorrow."

She shook her head and touched my knee as three students cheered, *The Simpsons* tune jingled, lights fizzed and sparked, and coins rattled out of a fruit machine.

"Just cause, cause... I've no really done it before?"
She laughs and laughs and laughs.

I start by describing the Southfield Fry, its own story will be [be]nging. Why did Grandpa Salvatori leave Parma to sell deep-[fo]od in a Scottish housing scheme? Whatever the reasons, the [fi]eld Fry was probably the best chip shop in the world. Even [opening] the door felt like you were releasing a genie: all the pent up [w]ould push past you and soar, liberated in the cold air. [After] swimming, we'd warm our paws on the hot cabinet, and [Fran]co would yell "Dinnae put yer honds on the cabinet, ye [wee] bastards." We'd pull our pink wrinkled fingers from [behi]nd press them on the stainless steel and watch as our [print]s faded then disappeared.

[Fra]nco's menu, a yellowing fat-speckled piece of card, was [not] his customer service skills. You could have chips, chip [and] sausage, haggis, or pie. In 1993, he introduced deep-[fried] but these were never added to the grease-stained [card; th]ere the cigarettes and chocolate bars, or the big glass [of Irn] Bru and ginger beer. These sat on shelves behind [him,] wearing their prices on star-shaped orange badges. [The] only other decoration was a fixtures chart from the [local] cup, a picture of Rossi, and a framed photograph of [fr]om the seventies. The Southfield Fry was only two [metr]es wide by six metres long. There were no seats and [; you] you bought your food, you fucked off outside, [you]r hands greasy.

[Except] for the Salvatori family's legendary frying skills, [there'd] been no reason to patronise the place; and if

★ 4 ★

The stabbing? Okay.

A canal runs through Dundule. There's no lighting—not many people would choose to walk there on a November night—but in 1998, I always went home that way. I liked its cavernous stone cul-de-sacs and the rusty rings on its overgrown mooring plinths. I used to think, what an effort, what labour, to have built all this only for it to be replaced by the railway. It runs for eight miles, and then it just stops.

Under the bridge, where the road passes overhead, I heard shouting and laughing and saw three boys—fourteen year olds? Fifteen year olds? They were arranged in order of height, swaggering to fill the track. One of them whispered, "That's that cunt that jumps aboot wi that Jason radge."

"Fuckin bawbag!"

I kept walking, pretending I couldn't hear them.

"Here, cunto! Dickheid, we're talkin tae you." In the distance there were fireworks, shot up a mile or two away, bursting red, amber, and green. I turned, just as the middle-sized guy shoved me. Then I was stumbling backwards and he was following me, fists clenched, shouting "You mind Giorgio, eh? You mind Giorgio, eh? Ya fuckin radge cunt." He was leaning into my face and shouting and I could feel his breath. And the world bleached white because when I lose my temper I get this— it's not a red mist, it's more like white dots that merge together until I can't see, like a blizzard that gets faster and faster until—

The only thing I can tell you is that I would have expected more pain. At first I thought someone had punched me. Then my whole side was warm and I saw the blood running oily thick from my fist and the kids saw the blood and for a moment we all stood there and stared. Then they ran towards the road and I remember being on my haunches, jeans soaking up puddle water. Then I stood up, dizzy and sick, alone but conscious of how this looked—the blood, the fireworks, the whole composition of the scene. I wrapped my jumper around the wound and stumbled towards the street lights.

On the main road, the taxi drivers swerved towards me, saw the blood, and accelerated. I had to jump in front of a black cab, place my hands on the bonnet. "Please, I really need to get to hospital?"

At A&E, the receptionist took my details. A mop diluted my blood on the plastic floor. They slammed me on a trolley and crashed me through swinging doors. "Okay, he's nineteen, lacerations on the upper arm."

They wanted to know what had happened.

But how far back do you go? Should I start with the blowjob in the Railway Inn? With Deanne? With her butterfly tattoo, short skirts, and ripped stockings? Jerry the Fence's daughter, Gordon's cousin, and briefly, *briefly,* my girlfriend, Deanne was eighteen when eighteen was impossibly old. When I met her in the summer of '96, Deanne was already old enough to work in a bar. She was old enough to know how to slam tequila with salt and lemon. She was old enough to have a stud in her tongue.

When Gordon introduced us, we were drinking illegally in his uncle's pub. Joop perfume buzzed around Deanne like an en-

tourage. She had big lips and acne and a brow[...] a neat border with a white neck; she had big[...] coopers' hoops, trussed in her platinum blon[...]

When it was late and we were drunk, s[...] the gents, shoved me into the cubicle, and[...] my head, crashing our teeth. She kissed a[...] slimy wet tongue—she kissed like a Labra[...] buckled my belt. Imagine it: I've spent th[...] hide my erection, but just when I need it[...] small. She takes it in her mouth (kneel[...] heels pressed against the foot of the d[...] her waist, but all I can think about is t[...] lock might have been, the toilet seat[...] dowsill, the gang names carved int[...] roll holder, the bloody bogeys sme[...] other side of the door, some guy's[...] urinal. He farts and exhales in sat[...]

She stops. "What's wrong?"[...] her hand.

"Nothing."

"Nothin?" She throws the[...]

"..."

"Are you queer or somet[...]

"No! Fuck no."

"Do you no fancy me?[...]

"Oh aye, totally, you'r[...]

"Can you no get stiff[...]

"Aye, course I can. I[...]

"What?"

"Well, I'm a wee b[...]

"What the fuck h[...]

Or, if[...] left ha[...] fried fo[...] Southf[...] to open[...] steam w[...]
After[...] Gianfran[...] mucky w[...] the glass[...] fuzzy prin[...] Gianfr[...] as limited a[...] butty, fish,[...] fried pizzas[...] menu, nor w[...] bottles of Ir[...] the counter,[...] In 1996, the[...] 1986 world c[...] a Parma side f[...] and a half metr[...] no "chip-forks'[...] and you got you[...] In short, bu[...] there would hav[...]

you frequented Salvatori's in the mid-nineties, chances are you would have heard Gianfranco lament his son's refusal to fry. "The boy can dae it, ken? He jist wilnae. And it's no suttin you can teach any doss cunt; it's in here," he'd say, beating his chest. But though he was about as Italian as the food his father served, Giorgio Salvatori had reinvented himself as a Sicilian entrepreneur. He had the name, the dark eyes and Mediterranean features; it was nothing to affect a thick Italian-American accent. In 1996, he was nineteen and had started to traffic fake or stolen designer clothes. As an aspiring Mafioso, he had acquired a Vauxhall Astra, a fake Rolex, and one of the biggest gold chains in Dundule.

And then he met Deanne.

I won't pretend that I wasn't upset when she dumped me in favour of Giorgio, but I certainly wasn't bitter. He was older and better looking than I was. He had a car and a fake Rolex. For her to have done anything else would have been a sign that she was crazy.

The day I chose to say goodbye was the warmest of the year. On Deanne's street, an ice-cream van Popeye jingle drifted from two blocks away. A boy practised wheelies. On a small square of grass, a bare-chested man putted golf balls, while a wasp crawled round and round on his beer can, tilting its bottom up before disappearing inside. Between cars, three girls in football shirts clapped and swung a rope:

"*Ah wet ma hole, wet ma hole, wet ma holidays,*
Tae see the cunt, tae see the cunt, tae see the cuntary.
Fuck you! Fuck you! Fu-curiosity,
Ah wet ma hole, wet ma hole, wet ma holidays."

And a girl on a plastic tricycle, mouth sticky and purple from ice poles, pedalled the pavement, singing "*Wet mole, wet mole, wet moley say, you a cunt, you a cunt, you dee-dee-da-day.*"

Deanne's gate was rusty and it scratched a curved groove on the first slab of the concrete path. The grass was long and yellow and trance music bounced through an open window. She answered the door in her dressing gown. "Wayne, what the fuck are you doin here?"

"Well, thing is see, I know you're seeing Giorgio and that but—"

"Wayne, ah telt ye before: it's over between us."

"Aye, I ken, but—"

"No buts, Wayne. Over. Finished. Goodbye."

"I'm no trying to get back with you, I just wanted—"

"You shouldnae be comin roond like this. Come on, clear off."

"No until I get a chance to talk with you."

"Wayne? Do yersel a favour—" There were thuds on the stairs. A pair of Lacoste shoes. New Levis. A fake Rolex. A Henri Lloyd polo shirt. A big gold chain. "Whadda fuck are you doin here, ah?"

"Alright Giorgio."

"Alright? Am I alright? Look in my eyes. Are these the eyes of a man who is alright?"

"I'm only here to get my CD back."

"You came for a CD? What fuckin CD?"

"Bonkers."

"Did I fuckin ask you? Bonkers, where's that? Is that in your room?" He bounded back up the stairs.

"Wayne," whispered Deanne, stroking my cheek, "dinnae come roond again."

The girls had stopped skipping and were leaning on the fence. "Are yous gonnae start swedgin?"

"Giorgio will kick yer heid in."

"Fuck off and play," said Deanne.

"This fuckin CD?" Giorgio ran down the stairs and threw the box onto the concrete path. It bounced and landed in the long grass, so he ran up the path and stamped on it. Then he dragged the disk out, holding it flashing in the sun. "This fuckin CD?" He tried to snap it.

"Dinnae!"

It buckled but wouldn't break, so he frisbeed it into the street. As I turned to watch its flight, Giorgio kicked me hard up the arse.

Jerry the Fence's shop, below the tenements, at the far end of Lanark Road, with the sign promising "Cash paid for jewellery, antiques, scrap gold and other valuables," and the dusty windows, and the wire mesh, was the sort of place where you thought seriously before you entered, where you studied the chain you wanted while mustering your courage, where you stood at the door, breathed deeply, and pushed.

The day after my altercation with Giorgio, I found Jerry berating a customer. "I dinnae gie a fuck what yer mother paid for it. That's nine-carat gold and cubic fuckin zirconia. If yer mother bought that thinkin they were diamonds then she was as stupid as you are."

"Well at Cash Creator..."

"Cash Creator! Those fuckin bandits, they wouldnae pay ye a price even if they *were* fuckin diamonds. You could walk in there with Tutankhamun's Tomb and the bastards would offer ye twenty quid: 'Well knowin the second hand business like I do, there's no much demand for Tutankhamun's tomb.' Offer the bastards a Fabergé egg and they'll tell ye it's worth a fiver and they've already got three up the stair!" The man shrugged and gathered his things. Jerry watched him stoop over the counter. "Yer rabbit there. Quite a nice piece."

"Aye?"

"Aye. How did ye get hold of this? Royal Worcester Porcelain. Dates fae about the time of the First World War, that. They didnae make many of these brown ones. Quite a nice piece... I might be able to sell yer rabbit, and I suppose I could take the rest off yer hands as a favour. Say," he exhaled, "eighty quid?"

The man shrugged again. "Aye," he said, but with his eyes closed.

"Right, let me nip tae ma safe." The man lay the ring in his palm, tracing its circumference with a dirty finger. Jerry returned with a grin and started to count. "Twenty, forty, sixty." You could hear the notes whispering between his fingers. "And that's eighty. Pleasure doin business with you." The man shuffled past me; he stank of piss and booze. "Wayne," said Jerry, "how are you?"

"No bad, Jerry."

"Aye," he said, showing those yellow teeth. "Come through, come through." He pressed a button and the wire gate pushed open. "Gordon's in the back. Let Uncle Jerry put these things away and I'll be through for a spraff. Tell Gordon tae put the kettle on."

No matter how short Gordon cropped his hair, you could still tell he was ginger. That summer he was supposed to be learning the retail trade from Jerry, but I found him slouched in an armchair, trying to ignore Jason. Jason was kneeling on a large square cushion, punching it. He pulled a corner to his contorted face and head-butted it. "Stitch: like fuckin that." It was a demonstration of what he'd done to someone, or what he was going to do to someone, or what he would do if he ever met someone—if, just supposing, those fucking Gallagher twats came in here trying to act hard, giving it, "Alright ahr kid, let's fuckin ave it," then Jason would be like, "Right you English cunts," and he'd leather them, get on top of Liam and smack his nose so it went back into his brain. Stitch: like fucking that. He stopped and looked at me. "Fuck are you lookin at?"

"Alright Jason."

"Naw. Ah'm fuckin no."

"Jerry says you're tae put the kettle on, by the way."

"Dinnae fuckin ignore me, ya tube."

Gordon shuffled to the kettle.

"You're a fuckin wide-o, by the way, goin aboot sayin ye can have me and aw this."

"..."

Jason ran across the floor and bored his forehead into mine. "Fuck are ye smilin at?" We stood head to head and you could hear his leather jacket creak.

"Anybody else wantin tea?" asked Gordon.

"Aye, ah'll take one. Fuck sake, Wayne. Nae need tae get aw humpty; ah wis only huvin a laugh wi ye."

As I smiled and tried to laugh, Gordon opened the door to the toilet cubicle and a cloud of smell floated across the back room—a stench of shit that wore lemon air freshener like earrings. "What's that stink?" said Jason. "Were ye that feart ye shat yer keks, Wayne?" Jerry had permanent diarrhoea, something to do with the drugs he took for his HIV, and sometimes we'd hear rasping, splattering excretions, that were violent and thrashing like a fight in a swimming pool.

Gordon turned the tap. The pipes groaned and the trickle clattered the metal wash basin. "You huvin tea, Wayne?"

"Nah, no thanks," I said, sitting on Jerry's footstool.

Jason crossed the room to spit in the sink. He dredged for more phlegm, spat again, dredged again. He was always dredging for phlegm and spitting clear saliva. It was like someone had put something horrible inside him and he couldn't get it out. After a minute, he slumped into the armchair and rested his feet on my lap. I shook them off. "Dick," he said, kicking my shin, but he didn't put his feet back. "No danger ah'm sittin aboot here aw day, by the way."

The backroom *was* a grim place to spend a sunny afternoon: it had one small barred window and a bare light bulb and cracks crawled across the dark corners of its ceiling. The shelves were cluttered with broken electrics and equipment for examining or repairing jewellery. There were a few books and some yellowing copies of the Daily Mail. We had long ago decided that all the excitement happened in Jerry's office, where we weren't allowed. In Jerry's office, deals were concluded with international art thieves, or so we liked to think.

"Is that kettle boiled?" called Jerry (Jason jumped out of the armchair). "Ahhh, there we go. Aye." Jerry sat down, sighing in chorus with the chair. "So Wayne, have you and Deanne patched things up yet?" He noticed something in the Daily Mail and lost interest in his own question.

"Aye and no. No and aye. I seen her, but just to get my Bonkers CD. You ken how it is; we've just grown apart. We'll definitely stay friends."

"Aye" said Jerry. "I told her, Wayne. I said no lass of mine's gonnae marry a wop. You know? I said the bastard will change sides in the time it takes ye tae walk up the aisle. Abscond wi the minister or something."

"Did you get it?" asked Gordon.

"What?"

"The CD."

"Aye, well. No. He broke it."

"I told her, an Eyetie's only a bit better than a nigger."

"Who?"

"Fuckin Giorgio."

"Fenian bastard," said Jason.

"How?" said Gordon.

"Well, I was talking to Deanne and he was hanging about like a bad smell. So I was like, 'Look mate, make yourself useful: nip upstairs and get my CD.' When he brings it down, it's broken. So I'm like, 'What the fuck's with this?' He's all like, 'Oh I don't know anything about it.' And I'm just like, 'You're fuckin sad mate.' Then he starts going radio, so I'm like, 'Let's fucking go.' And he slams the door, bolts it, and starts shouting through the letterbox that he's gonnae get a posse to kick my head in."

"Aye?" said Gordon, not totally convinced by this version of events.

"That's oot ae order," said Jason. "That prick thinks he runs this toon."

"And he's been treatin Deanne like shite. I've heard he's goin aboot callin her a whore and that."

"Fuckin Brussels," said Jerry, shaking his head at the paper.

I remember us on Giorgio's street: three long shadows like something from a western. I remember us at his door. Gordon and Jason are hiding against the wall. Gordon is patting a pudgy palm with a knuckle of medallion rings, and Jason is holding a hammer. I chap the letterbox. "Dae it fuckin properly," says Jason. He spits on the path and rattles the flap as hard as he can.

An internal door opens. A television audience applauds. The lock clunks. Giorgio stands in a white Yves Saint Laurent shirt. "Whadda fuck? Whad'I fuckin tell you, ah?" Jason leaps from behind the door and cracks Giorgio's thigh with the hammer. He thumps the hammer into his ribs—like he's chopping a tree. Giorgio falls into the hallway and Jason jumps on him, punching his face, again and again. Giorgio's head is whiplashing, bouncing off the ground, and Deanne's running down the stairs with her nightgown open.

★ 5 ★

I didn't see Deanne until November 1997, by which time she had given birth to a small golem-like creature. She called it David and spoke to it as if it were a person. Sometimes she paraded it, as though the pram was an open-topped bus and the creature was the Scottish Cup. "Is he no just gorgeous?"

"Aye," I said, wondering how such a thing could have happened in so brief a time. A few years later, when Gordon told me Deanne was dead, I had the same reaction. "I saw her in town only last Monday!" I said, like I was amazed the Grim Reaper hadn't been carrying her shopping.

Deanne had found Giorgio in bed with a sixteen-year-old hairdresser from Stirling and had immediately forgiven Gordon and me. The one time I mentioned Jason, she shrugged and said "That's in the past." Meanwhile, I'd met Kit at work. Kit, with her blonde pigtails and pale face, had started working at Benny's in March '97. When you live in a small town, everyone is the friend of someone you know; the local papers are full of tales of serendipity, of long lost brothers who lived next door to each other and men who found their mother in law's wallet on the High Street; we all live like celebrities, worrying who will recognise us if we go to the shops in old clothes. So it shouldn't have surprised me that Kit and Deanne had grown up on the same street, and had, at one time, been best friends. Kit knew that Deanne and I had slept together, but was satisfied that *all that* was in the past. Time had moved on: Deanne was now a single parent, living in a three bedroom council house and struggling for cash; Kit and I were keen to cohabit... living together made sense at the time, but it turned out to be a disaster.

All through the summer of '98, David screamed. He screamed every morning, with admirable regularity, the way some adults go jogging or watch Breakfast TV. "Look, David! It's the Teletubbies! Look, David!" You'd have thought he'd need to pause, draw breath, review what this tactic had achieved. "Gonnae shut the fuck up! I'm fuckin sick ae you!" shouted Deanne.

I don't know how Kit slept through this shit. On the day I met Spocky, I sat on the edge of our bed, and she rolled away, trying to smother the morning with our duvet, as the heat broke through the curtains. "Have you no got work?" she said.

"I'm just going now."

"Stupid work." Even in the summer, Deanne's flat was so wet that mould grew on furniture and wallpaper peeled. One time, the council sent a workman. He painted the bathroom and then watched with us as white drops of watery paint plopped from the ceiling, drawing a polka-dot pattern on the carpet.

"Fuckin shut up!" I heard Deanne's footsteps and the bathroom door slammed and the walls shook and a bottle of CK Be tumbled onto the carpet. There wasn't much in our room: an old television with an indoor aerial sat on a Formica-covered chest of drawers; an unstable shelf supported a cluster of toiletries and a singed plastic rose. The rose was the first thing I ever bought Kit, but one night, during an argument, I burned it with my lighter. It takes time to accumulate possessions. Eventually, the past sticks to you like fluff to Sellotape dragged across a dusty suit.

In the living room, a packet of Super Kings lay on the coffee table, and an American woman shouted about sun protection on GMTV. David was harnessed in his bouncer, hanging in the kitchen doorway. His pink face trembled as the sun bounced through the windows, greenhousing the room. I started to tiptoe across the carpet, as though I was an art thief and the naked baby was a security system, but when I got halfway to the kitchen, his mouth opened. I stopped and smiled but the mouth opened wider, until I could see the whole dark passage, so I stood there, grinning. David filled his lungs, held his breath, and screamed. "David, dinnae. Fuck. Please don't. D'you want this?" I offered him a plastic toy with a squeaky button and a mirror. He threw it at me and screamed louder.

"What ye done tae him?" asked Deanne, when she returned from the bathroom.

"Sorry," I said. "I was just after a glass of water."

"David! David! Wee man. Ssshh. Bouncy, bouncy. There you go. Shhh. Shut up!" She unclipped him from his harness and laid him naked on his mat, sprawled helpless like a crab on its back.

"Right, Wayne, you're on buns. Buzz is dressing, Gordon's on grill. And train Captain Picard here, aye?"

"Owen. My name's Owen."

"Doddy! I've two chicken burgers left! Gie me three runs of six, two beanies, two fish, start holding two trays of chicken." It was the hottest day of the year and the kitchen already stank of sweat. "Wayne, I need a continuous pull on Big Bens and Cheese. Come on, cook me some food or I'm gonnae get in shit." This is how Benny's works: the "I'm going to get in shit" effect. The business functions because everybody is held responsible for those below him. If it's your second week and a new starter is sweeping the floor with her apron on, you have to correct her. If you don't then the store manager will complain to the shift runner, the shift runner will take it out on the floor manager, the floor manager will shout at the team leader, and the team leader will bitch at you. Belatedly, you'll ask the new start to take off her apron. "Sorry," you'll say, "it's just that if you keep it on then I'm going to get in shit."

"Why?"

"Dinnae ken. It's just the procedure." The next time she has to sweep the floor, she'll anticipate rebuke from even her lowliest colleagues. She'll self-censor. In this way, the surveillance becomes panoptical.

Raj exemplified the most successful management strategy practised in Benny's: he divided the plebs into a favoured section of predominantly experienced workers and a sub-class of inexperienced or socially-compromised novices. The favoured section was privileged with lenient discipline and exemption from the most awful cleaning tasks; the sub-class was universally pissed on. When Raj said "Cook me some food or I'm gonnae get in shit," the favoured section philanthropically policed the sub-class. In these times of disposable labour, the relatively unproductive sub-class can do little to disturb this mechanism.

When recruiting managers, Benny's had traditionally favoured ex-military personnel. By the turn of the millennium, however, the totalitarian style of management was losing favour. Although the old regimes *appeared* to be in control, they were actually more susceptible to rebellion than the modern, comparatively liberal systems built on division. There may be truths about society contained somewhere in these observations. At

Benny's, however, it was hard to develop such a train of thought. For example, consider the life of a bun man. A beeper decrees when toasting should start, a buzzer stipulates when it should end. There are two toasters to be worked on overlapping cycles, and the bun man's timing is sometimes regulated by a corporate apparatchik with a stopwatch and an Obsessive Compulsive Disorder. And yet, at Benny's, bun toaster is as good as it gets. Take the poor dressings guy: he's got eighteen seconds to apply condiments to nine buns—a wet slice of pickle, squirts of ketchup and mustard, and a pinch of the onions that come dry in a packet. And the dressings guy is a labour aristocrat next to the grill man. Every time the bun toaster sounds, the grill man must squeeze on a plastic glove and place the frozen discs of meat in the patterns demanded by a plaque above his head. Then he needs to close the grill, initiate the timer, and remove the glove before the lid of his other grill starts to rise. In four seconds, he's supposed to sprinkle salt on every slab of meat and shovel the meat onto the dressed buns; then he's supposed to scrape, squeegee, and wipe the grill, retrieve the plastic glove, and lay another pattern of meat. He has forty-six seconds to complete this cycle.

The only escape from this is to cook so much food that the production caller yells, "Enough!"

"Gie me a hold on everything," said Raj, whose table was now congested with trays of unboxed burgers. "Clean the place up, come on!"

So much lettuce had been strewn on the floor that it looked like a lawn was forcing its way through the tiles. White cloths were dyed yellow with mustard, and every surface was smeared gory with ketchup. On the finger-marked stanchion of the bun stand, a slice of cheese was peeling from its right corner, and somehow a sliver of pickle had stuck to an overhead strip light (where it slowly dried, threatening to launch a kamikaze bombing mission). Raj surveyed the devastation. "Hang on, where the fuck's Captain Spock?"

At Benny's, the stock areas are called The Cave. It's where you go for a private conversation or a five-minute skive. You stand in the stock room with one hand in a condiment box, ready to remove something as soon as the door opens, and if you really don't want to be found, you go to the back of The Cave, past the bulk Coke and syrup lines, and into the chiller. That's where I found Spocky. He was sitting on a box of shredded lettuce, reading his book in the sulphurous light. He didn't hear me open the door, but as I pushed through the curtain of overlapping plastic slats, he stood up, leaving an incriminating dent impressed on the cardboard box. "What th—"

"It's s–so hot out there."

"Are you not cold in here?"

"It's not too–too b–bad actually. I was getting a b–b–bit worried about the oxygen."

"You're not right in the head."

He nodded in vague agreement and coughed into his hand.

"Get your arse back in there."

"Wh–why?"

"Why? Cause you've gottae do some work."

"Wh–why?"

"Cause that's just the way shit is."

After work, I said to Kit, "Let's climb Breast Mountain. Come on, it'll be quality." From our window, the hill looked rubbery in the shimmering heat. "Come on, we'll take the cider; we'll watch the sunset." It was one of those rare hot days, when radios play outdoors and men in shorts wash cars. Parents cleaned mud from paddling pools. Sweaty kids rested bikes against shady walls. In the sunshine, teenage girls lazed in bikini tops, wearing beach towels like sarongs.

Breast Mountain was a sort of no man's land. It was a border zone between city and country, between this time and the past. Weeds colonised bags of sand and gravel. Slugs burrowed in the slashed foam seat of an abandoned JCB. A woodpigeon took off, exploding balsam pods and downing helicopters as it beat through the branches of a sycamore tree. We crawled through a gap in the fence, ran through nettles—hands up so they didn't get stung—and then we followed the old train line to where it met the canal.

The canal was filled with bottles and overrun by chickweed; you could fall into it if you didn't know it was there. The mooring bollards were camouflaged in the undergrowth, and rosebay willow-herb sprouted purple through the loading stage. A bit of everything that ever happened in Dundule was buried here. Refrigerators were dug into the hillside, and burned out cages of cars were charred with rust. There was a roofless warehouse, layered with graffiti, and an industrial chimney stack, poking through a tumble of its own bricks. There were limestone steps curved by generations of walking, and overlooking it all, the big wheel of Brandon Colliery remained suspended, still in the sky.

The "Mountain" was a conical slag heap half-covered with hogweed and docken. Your feet left impressions in the rubble, as if you were climbing a sand dune. Kit told me that she once had sex on the far side, near the bottom, where the gorse bushes had found enough soil to grow. I told her that I smoked my first joint at the top; I recalled leaning back to watch the street lights shiver over Dundule, pretending I was having fun. We agreed that neither extreme skiers nor ice climbers know the risks of sledging Breast Mountain on a plastic tray.

But from the bottom, we could see that a group of boys had already claimed the summit. They were shouting and kicking each other and laughing and acting angry and kicking each other and laughing again. Their shirts were open and they stared razor-eyed into the sunshine. Bottles of Becks flashed in their hands. We stopped and waited for a minute, not yet ready for home but not sure what else to do. That's the thing with these rare hot days: everybody agrees you must make the most of the weather, but nobody's sure how. The beer dehydrates us, the sun burns our shoulders, the insects crawl on our picnics; by five o'clock, the day has betrayed us.

★ 6 ★

"What d'you make of that new guy? I think he's mental."

"Who?" said Buzz. "That Doddy guy?"

"The cunt wi the stutter?" asked Gordon.

"Nah, no him. That guy with the glasses."

"..."

"..."

"He started about a month ago. The fucking *Star Trek* guy."

"Oh, *that* cunt," said Gordon.

"That guy's funny," said Buzz.

"Funny? He's fucking lazy."

"He takes no shit."

"Ever since he's started, I've kept finding him hiding in The Cave."

"It's always the same mugs dae aw the work," said Gordon, shaking his head.

We were in the Railway Arms, Jerry the Fence's pub, where two years earlier, Gordon had introduced me to Deanne. The Railway was a dingy bar with long burgundy curtains and nicotine-stained walls. The leather upholstery on the wooden benches was tough and cracked like the surface of cricket balls. The air was always so thick with smoke and dust that you imagined you were exploring a new planet, whose alien atmosphere might not support life. Guarding a half of cider in the lounge area, a bag lady attempted to initiate conversations with real and imagined passers by. Alcoholic Tam crashed between tables, singing "What a Wonderful World." And an old man hunched over a horse racing paper, his pipe unlit as his half of eighty evaporated. The only other customer, a stocky Teddy Boy, stood fumbling and cursing at the jukebox. "Whose round is it?" I asked.

"It's true," said Buzz. "We do that much work and get no reward. Like, remember that all-night close last week? Man, we were there till when? Like, ten o'clock the next morning. What did they promise us? Twenty quid each, yeah? Check your pay slips. Seriously guys, it's not there." Buzz's glasses were held together with Sellotape and his jumper belonged to someone older and fatter; even by the standards of the Railway Arms, even next to a bag lady obese with layers of clothes, Buzz managed to look noticeably unkempt.

"I got the last one," I said.

"Well, fuckin, yous both owe me drinks," said Gordon.

"And it keeps happening. D'you remember the extra shifts when Andy Duke came from head office?"

"Oh aye, fifteen bar I shouldae got for that."

"It's your round, Buzz."

"Damnit man," he said, kicking back his stool.

The setting sun poked through the windows, illuminating the swirling clouds of smoke and dust, spearing a shaft of light towards the old pipe smoker. I never saw anyone die in the Railway Arms, but that being remarkable tells you it wasn't the sort of place where you went to pick up girls or have fun. "There's other places for that sort of thing," Deborah, the bartender, used to say if anyone sang or fought or danced or kissed.

As she poured our drinks, the old Teddy Boy touched me on the shoulder with fingers that had swollen around gold signet rings. "Gie me a hand wi this, són." Maybe he'd had a stroke at some time because one quarter of his pockmarked face was frozen, with the corner of his mouth held down in a way that made you think of a sad clown. "I'm a bit shaky, shaky," he said, pushing fifty pence into my hand. "Elvis, son. Elvis and one for yersel." I selected the Elvis CD and invited him to pick, but he looked tired from standing and sat down beside the jukebox. "Anything son. Anything by Elvis." I was unsure what to play but I chose "Hound Dog" and "Jailhouse Rock," and I chose "Tubthumping" for myself. The Teddy Boy closed his eyes, tapped his foot, and hummed.

Meanwhile, Buzz lowered a triangle of pints and slapped on the table four pound notes, eighty-six pence, and a sweaty bus ticket. "Guys, it's six o'clock on payday, and in a few hours I'm going to be skint."

"We should huv a union," said Gordon, and we all laughed.

"You know that Doddy with the stutter? New guy, been trained on chicken?"

"Oh aye."

"He was saying that he used to work on this building site where they had a union."

"Oh fuck," I said, "he told me the same story. It takes the guy fifteen minutes to tell you his name. 'We had a you-you-you, a you-you-you, a youn— a youn—' It's embarrassing; you dinnae ken whether to finish his sentences or what."

Gordon laughed. "And?"

"Well," said Buzz, "that was it, really. They had a health and safety officer and got paid five-fifty an hour with time-and-a-half for overtime."

"Cause of the union?"

"So he reckons."

"Nah, see, the question *I* asked him was this: if the job was so great, how come he's not still working there?" Gordon nodded at the salience of this inquiry. "And he says, 'Cause I got sacked.' So I asks, 'What did the union do about that?' 'Nothing,' he says. So what happened to all the money he paid in, eh? I'll tell you what: they spent it on a plush conference and a campaign about lesbians in the construction industry." There was nothing more to say on that topic so we sat and sipped our pints.

"Magic," said the Teddy Boy. "The King—fuckin magic."

He died later that year, the Teddy Boy, in our work. He was waiting to buy his burger and the service was so slow that he died before he ever had a chance to order. You saw the queue step away from him as he clutched the counter with those fat fingers, and then, almost with a look of release, like someone who has heard the punch line to a long joke, he timbered, falling so big and heavy that other customers moved out of his way. You expected him to cry out when he hit the floor, but the only noise was the *beep beep—beep beep—beep beep* of the fry timers. Then, as if she'd been waiting for this, LeAnn Rimes started to sing.

You almost expected more from a dead person, like you wanted him to do more than just lie there. I mean, if he *was* going to die then you wanted it to have some weight—to be less... *silly*.

"Fuck," said Raj, kneeling beside the body. "Come on, stand back. Ah bollocks. Can you hear me mate? Mate? Phone a fuckin ambulance!"

"Take his pulse," said a man in the queue.

"Just gies a bit of space, please. Mate? Hello sir, can you hear me?"

"He can't hear you," said the man in the queue.

Kit appeared from the office, with the phone cord stretching taut from her neck. "Is he breathing?" she asked.

Raj put his ear to the Teddy Boy's chest. "Dinnae think so."

"Oh dear," said the man in the queue.

"Here, put this under his heid," said an old lady, offering her coat.

"Has he got a pulse?" shouted Kit.

"Yes," said Raj. "No. I Dinnae ken. I cannae find it!"

"He's dead," said the man in the queue.

"He's no dead," said Raj, wedging the coat beneath the Teddy Boy's head.

"How auld is he?" shouted Kit.

"How the fuck would I ken? Fuck man. Have we got a doctor? Any doctors in the house?" But you find doctors in concert halls, on international flights, and onboard cruise ships, not in burger bars in small Scottish towns. "Ah fuck," said Raj. "Okay. Alright. Here we go."

"Give him the kiss of life," said the man in the queue.

"Would you shut the fuck up? Here we go. Come on. Wake up, damnit." He pounded the Teddy Boy's chest with both hands and forced air into his lungs (if the heart attack hadn't killed him then that would have finished him off), and as time passed, and the man in the queue looked increasingly satisfied, Raj pushed the Teddy's Boy's chest harder and harder, until the noise it made was like someone beating a dusty carpet with a stick. When the spectacle became grotesque, Gordon draped his arm on Raj's shoulders, the way nurses comfort doctors when a patient dies on *ER*, and he said, "Raj man, we've lost him. Ye've done aw ye can." Raj stood up, maybe a little watery in the eyes, and the Teddy Boy stayed where he had fallen. "Mate, there was nuttin ye could dae."

"Bhenchod, I couldnae mind the course."

"It wasnae yer fault. Fuck, you'd've had mair chance tryin tae resuscitate one of our quarter pounders." Gordon pulled the coat from under the Teddy Boy's head and draped it over the body (the old lady crossed herself and looked at her coat, as though wondering when it would be appropriate to ask for it back). "Alright," announced Kieran. "Come on now. Let's see a bit of service, yeah?"

It's difficult to say why the death affected us; the customers straightened themselves and shuffled forward, gaping at the menu as they readied their cash, but some unknown glitch prevented us from taking their orders. "We need more fries down," said Kieran, because the ones in the baskets, neglected during the resuscitation attempt, had turned hard and brown. "Ps and Qs, yeah? People, procedures, profitability. Quick, quality, quantity."

"..."

"Guys? Come on. Let's do this, yeah?"

Kit looked at me and I looked at Gordon and Gordon looked at Lucy and nobody moved. "Dude, this isn't cool," said Buzz.

"Alright, no more Mr. Nice Guy, yeah? Work. Now."

"No," said Kit.

"*Work.*"

"Nu."

"Work or you're sacked."

"All of us?" asked Buzz.

That was when the new guy spoke up. As usual, Spocky was out in the dining area (the only place where he didn't compromise the whole shift), where he should have been wiping tables or sweeping the floor. Instead, he walked up to the Teddy Boy's corpse. "Hey, can someone give me a hand? Let's get this body into the freezer." The customers looked at him, unsure if he was for real, while Kieran gestured for him to shut up. "I'm serious. Come on, we can't leave him here."

"Okay, fine. You know what? For that, you're on a final warning."

"Think about the food costs. We can get three boxes of meat out of this guy."

"Okay, done. Finished. You just talked yourself out of a job."

Then Buzz sheathed his grill spatula and shouted from the kitchen. "If he's out of a job, so are the rest of us."

"Aye, fuck this," said Gordon.

Kieran strained his muscles in a disorientated attempt to smile. "What is this, a strike?" And in the silence that followed, at more or less the same time, Kieran realised, and we realised—aye, it was.

And what a feeling it is to have your time unexpectedly reimbursed. It was like when the school heating broke or the pipes burst or the teachers went on strike. We paused on our way to the Railway because through the window, beneath an advertisement for "Buy one get one free" chicken burgers, we could see Kieran stocking the condiment trays as the paramedics shocked the Teddy Boy's corpse. When they gave up and loaded him onto a stretcher, Kieran mopped the tiles and marked the spot with a "Caution! Wet Floor" sign.

"D'you think we're gonnae get in shit for this?" asked Kit, pressing up to me for warmth. She picked up the smell of grease like the rest of us but there was a space at her nape, especially when she wore her hair down, where you could sniff out a lemony shampoo smell.

"Probably," I said.

"Aw man," said Buzz.

Gordon shrugged. "If we aw stick together then they cannae touch us."

A few metres from us, Spocky stood alone, trying to form a shelter in which to roll a cigarette. In the border, between the knee-high shrubs, the wind was swirling litter and strips of bark. This eddy of woodchip and rubbish invaded Spocky's shelter, flapping his Rizzla and scattering his tobacco. "Hey," shouted Lucy, "Do you want one of these?" Her hair whipped around her face as she held out a cigarette.

Spocky looked a bit suspicious, but he shuffled forward and took the fag. "Okay, thanks."

"It's Owen, isn't it?"

"Yeah, Owen."

"Some of us are going for a drink, if you fancy it?"

"I don't really drink."

"Well, have a coffee or something?"

He looked at his watch. "Okay, yeah. Alright."

Now, as you can probably guess, the Railway Arms was not the sort of bar that served coffee. There was no family area or smoke-free zone, traditional bar meals were not served all day, and there was no wine list. There *was* a quiz night every Monday, and it was the sort of quiz where all the rounds were about horse racing or the filmography of Clint Eastwood, where any question about the periodic table or South American geography was met with cries of, "It's no University Challenge!" and, "Come on, Paxman, this is a working man's pub."

However, Spocky didn't know this. Spocky joined us, and this slight deviation, this jolt, would veer us into the future, reminding us that stories can be retold, that we don't always have to follow the tracks, that sometimes people like Owen can make a difference.

"Jerry? Gordon's here," called Deborah as we entered the bar. "Drinking in the afternoon again, Gordon? Hi Wayne. Jesus, who's died?"

"One of our customers," said Lucy.

"Oh, I'm sorry," said Deborah. "I thought yous were looking glum."

"He used tae drink in here sometimes," said Gordon.

"Oh, really? Here, Jerry, listen to this—one of the punters has passed on."

"Oh aye, who's that then?" asked Jerry without looking up from his paperwork.

"Old bloke," I said. "Big guy. Lot of gold rings."

"What was he called?" asked Deborah.

"Dinnae ken," said Gordon.

"He had a frozen face, kind of like—" Buzz girned an impersonation of the Teddy Boy's paralysed face.

"Who would that be, Jerry?"

Jerry peered over his half moons. "Naebody ah ken; looks like the Queen Mum."

"His face was kind of pockmarked," said Kit.

Deborah shook her head.

"He liked Elvis," I said.

"You sure he drank in here?" asked Deborah.

A man with a big moustache, who'd been listening to the conversation from his seat at the end of the bar, now put down his newspaper. "Sure, that's yer man. What did ye call him—Jesus, hang on. He had a tattoo of Elvis, so he did. Gary... Gary Thompson his name was."

"Oh aye," said the old man with the pipe, "he's always playing that bloody jukebox. The boy's a pain in the arse. What aboot him, anyway?"

"He's passed on," said the guy with the moustache.

"No he hasnae."

"According to these young ones he has."

"Havers—he was here not forty-five minutes ago."

"Aye," said Gordon, "then he went across the road and died."

"Well, fancy that. It's this wind, I tell you; it's the Devil," said Deborah. "I ken who you mean now. Gary... Are you sure his name was Gary?"

The old man looked sceptical. "Across the road where?"

"That burger shop," said Deborah.

"Ach no. That's no place tae die."

Deborah shook her head. "Well, it just goes to show, doesn't it?" She smiled at Lucy. "What can I get you love?"

★ 7 ★

Nobody knows *exactly* how Benny's Resistance Army started. Conventional history focuses on Spocky for introducing the idea and on Buzz for suggesting the name; Marxist interpretations point to a developing conflict between material productive forces and existing relations of production; the feminist analysis contends that Kit and Lucy's contributions have traditionally been under-theorised. The truth is that nobody remembers: Spocky had gone home and the rest of us were pissed. This isn't a problem if you're writing about the Warsaw Pact or the Declaration of Independence. Nowhere in Robert Service's three-volume biography of Lenin will you find "The Politburo was divided over whose idea it had been to introduce War Communism: Trotsky blamed Stalin, who pointed to Kamenev, who insisted it had been Comrade Lenin himself. The truth is that nobody remembered; they had all been absolutely steamboats." But such were our inauspicious beginnings.

However, regardless of the ins and outs of the matter, by December '98, Kieran was convinced that a plot existed, that some kind of intrigue was being spirited by some sort of... cabal. Although his understanding of the conspiracy was vague, he was certain he'd identified at least some of the conspirators. In Kieran's version, Spocky was the commander-in-chief, while Buzz, Gordon, and I were his lieutenants. Kieran wrote lengthy reports with titles such as "Staff refuse orders and vote for who should empty the bin," or "Plug from sink missing, theft suspected." He always included the full names of suspects and witnesses, along with the exact times and dates. When he finished a report he would read it back to us and close by musing "Dawn's going to be very interested to read this. Oh yeah."

But Dawn, the restaurant manager, wasn't interested in much that happened at Benny's. She referred to items of equipment as "The thingummyjig... you know, the big thing that makes that loud noise." The only work she had any enthusiasm for was typing signs—she enjoyed typing signs. Maybe she'd have continued to ignore Kieran's paranoid intelligence reports had several of her signs not been defaced. In Kieran's reports, this vandalism, like the power cut in November, like the time the drains blocked and the kitchen flooded with faeces, like the time he lost his fucking car keys, was attributed to conspiratorial sabotage.

"Have you, or have you not, been drawing penises on official company notices?" Dawn had a scrotum beneath her chin, and it swayed from side to side when she spoke. Face up on her desk, next to a bumper book of puzzles, lay a freshly printed notice:

IMPORTANT: ALL STAFF!!!

THE NOTICEBOARDS AND NOTICES ON THEM ARE **COMPANY PROPERTY!!**

ANYBODY **TAMPERING** WITH OR **REMOVING** OR **DEFACING** COMPANY NOTICES WILL BE DISCIPLINED!!

YOU HAVE BEEN WARNED!!!!!!!

The office was little bigger than a telephone kiosk: Dawn sat on a revolving office chair; Kieran leant on the safe; Spocky, Buzz, and I squeezed into a tight line, as though about to dance the Dashing White Sergeant. We all shook our heads.

"You are asking me to believe that you know nothing about this?" She reached into a drawer and produced exhibit A:

**FAO - ALL STAFF -
UNIFORM!!**

YOU <u>MUST</u> IRON YOUR
UNIFORMS AND APPEAR
PRESENTABLE AT ALL TIMES.
TIES AND **NAME BADGES
MUST BE WORN** ON THE
LEFT SIDE OF YOUR SHIRT.
SHOES <u>MUST</u> **BE BLACK
AND SHINED.** SLOPPY
APPEARANCE WILL BE
<u>**PUNISHED**</u> AS OF
20/12/1998!!!!

"I like it," said Spocky. "An early Matisse, perhaps?"

Dawn dredged some anger from the back of her throat. "Button it, sunshine. You can take this as a formal verbal warning. You three jokers are walking a tightrope, literally."

"I'm not wearing it," said Lucy, pushing the suit across the table.

Gordon pushed it back. "Ye have tae." He was already sporting a red felt hat and a candy floss beard.

"I'm not wearing a beard."

"Of course you don't wear the beard. You're Missy Clause."

"*Missy Clause?*" asked Buzz, distracted from Macaulay Culkin's silent struggle on the Railway's sixteen inch corner TV (they hadn't had satellite at the Railway Arms since the people from Sky caught them using a black-market decoding device).

"Santa's wife," said Gordon.

"And what's her role?" asked Lucy. "What does 'Missy Clause' do while Santa's bringing joy to children everywhere?"

"Makes the tea," said Gordon.

Lucy shoved the suit back across the table. "No thanks."

It was Christmas Eve and paper chains stretched across the Railway, their multicoloured links bearing dark stains where Deborah had licked the adhesive the previous year. The chain above the bar was especially sad looking, the way it sagged in an uneven W. Spocky shook his head at his Dalek costume, for out of the packet it had revealed itself to be a hand-held plastic thing and a grey sheet suspended from a round frame—essentially, Spocky's costume was a toilet plunger and a shower curtain. "Can't I be a Santa?" he asked.

"Sorry man," said Buzz. "There was only three suits left in Pound Stretcher."

"I don't know," said Spocky, "I'm beginning to question this whole plan."

Lucy laughed. "You can be Missy Clause if you want?"

"Is that what you're intae?"

"To be honest, mate," I said, "we're doing you a favour. These beards are itchy."

"But a Dalek? It's not very... festive. And what if I have to run? I'll not be able to see where I'm going."

"The dude's got a point," said Buzz. "You can't make him wear the thing if he doesn't want to." Behind Buzz, a woman whirled between tables, trying to recruit a dancing partner. She had tied a straggle of tinsel around her neck, and when she laughed, her calves shook where the weight of her legs bottle-necked at her ankles.

Gordon rocked back in his chair. "I dinnae ken, Buzz. We're supposed tae be an undergroond army. The whole plan depends on disguise."

"I'll buy you a pint if you wear it."

"You know I don't really drink," said Spocky.

"Aye, but it's Christmas Eve, Spocky. You've gottae have a drink on Christmas Eve."

"Dude's got a point, man."

"Aye, have a drink."

"Go on, get a pint down you."

Even Lucy joined in. She looked up at him puppy-dog style, all lashes and glitter, overdoing it a bit to show some self-awareness. "Go on," she said, "one drink won't hurt?" I saw him look at her chest then. She was wearing a top that was in two halves: two criss-crossed sails of black material. Spocky's gaze slid downwards, like the wrinkled helium-filled Santa balloons that Deborah had put up a week too early. "Well?" she said.

"Yeah, okay," said Spocky. "One drink can't hurt."

Everybody cheered, and from his position sprawled on the puggy, alcoholic Tam heard the noise and roared a desperate "Merry Christmas!"

"Come on, Tam," said Deborah. "There's other places for that sort of thing." She had dressed up for the occasion with a set of disco-ball dilly boppers, but as the springs had lost tension, the boppers had flopped into her eyes, until she resembled a dying insect. Behind her, someone had taped a scrap of cardboard, on which "Merry Xmas to all our customers" had been scribbled between red and green sprigs of holly. Where they usually piled the empty glasses, there stood a small plastic tree. The tree was decorated with half-a-dozen shimmering bobbles and clumps of cotton wool stretched cobweb-like between its branches. And then it started to snow.

It snowed and the Railway regulars stared through the windows, as they might have stared had the Grim Reaper stood outside, waving his scythe and cackling "Eenie-meanie-minie-mo." Snow. A retired electrician, who stayed in the block adjacent to Kit's mum, died of hypothermia after his gas was cut off over a seventy-pound debt. That's snow: it gets your hands cold, smacks you in the face, immobilises your car, and eventually kills you. And we love it. After a few more pints, it was real snow, like snow was when we were kids. Big fluffy crystals swirled up and down, as if searching for a special place to land, or laid themselves out to melt on windowpanes. And in the middle of it, wrapped up in it, dizzy and drunk from it, they danced and twisted and held their hands up in praise of it. They wore bright hats and colourful scarves. They stroked white cars with mitten hands.

We laughed as we ran out of the pub, grabbed fistfuls of snow, and threw them at point-blank range; and then we spread out, blowing air on our pink tingling fingers, or holding our palms outstretched, like landing strips. Spocky tripped on his Dalek costume and Gordon shoved snow down his back. Buzz shielded an old lady from the crossfire. Lucy giggled and screamed and ran into the doorway of the pub. Her face was pink and frosted pigtails hung from her bobble hat. In the light of the doorway, toggled up in a grey duffle coat, she could have been a carol singer—a wee angel stamping her feet and panting big clouds of steam. "I'm going," she said. "I've still got presents to wrap."

"You're going?" said Spocky. "Oh, alright." The Dalek costume trailed in the snow like a wedding dress. "So... Happy Christmas."

"Come here," she said.

"What?" His toilet plunger drooped at his side.

She looked up past her eyebrows. "Mistletoe," she said. Then she leant forward, so that just for a second she kissed his lips through the small gap in his costume. "See you." She waved to us as the snow erased her step by step. Long after she'd disappeared, Spocky stayed in the doorway, standing still, holding that toilet plunger so it stuck out like an erection. Sometimes, Spocky could be such a twat.

Later, we bought a crate of Tennent's, and from the far side of Elmore Road, we hurled snowballs at anybody who attempted to enter Benny's. It had been calm when it started to snow, but now the flakes vortexed around us, cutting our lips, stinging our cheeks, blizzarding westwards. After ten minutes of snowballing, Kieran Hunter, Second Assistant Manager, emerged from the restaurant. He stood in the doorway, blustering in his shirt-sleeves, gasping at the sting of the evening. The wind was swooshing down Elmore Road, arrowing the snow in horizontal lines. It flapped Kieran's tie out and forced him to hold onto his cap. "What d'you think you're doing, you crowd of idiots?"

"Fire!" He dived for cover as the snow splattered around the door. Then, sensing a pause in our attack, he stepped out. There was something of the Captain Oates about his determined advance. A snowball hit Kieran's chest and another one got him in the face. When we ran out of snowballs, Gordon grabbed an empty beer bottle and hurled it, more up than along, so that it tumbled out of sight then reappeared, seeming to hang in the air as the snow zipped past much faster. When it finally did come down, it exploded, not on Kieran's head, but about a metre in front of him, on the hard-packed tyre-tracked road snow. This *did* make Kieran stop. In fact, he flinched and let go of his cap. The cap seized the moment to escape and spun off his head, scampering onto the pavement and tumbling towards the town centre. We stood on the far side of the road, cheering it on—the way it paused, letting him get close before bouncing away; the way it seemed to say "You can't catch me."

★ 8 ★

February, 2004. Five years later and the rain swooped across London, emptying Trafalgar Square. It had been Buzz's idea to meet under Nelson's Column, but he couldn't have known the weather would be like this. Two Japanese women had stayed out, splashing in puddles and posing for photographs, trying to find some fun in the moment. I watched as big drops of water meandered down the backs of their see-through plastic raincoats.

Kieran was a lowly target, no getting away from that, but Andrew Duke, the director of Benny's UK, the man you saw in the staff magazine—photographed with politicians at the launch of a recycling scheme, or shaking hands with a minor royal at the start of Road Safety Week—a man you imagined getting corporate tickets for the World Cup Final and not using them, he was a proper target. It took us five years to go after Duke, and by then we'd stopped working at Benny's. I suppose we were motivated by nostalgia and a sense of unfinished business, but standing in the rain, I felt exhausted. I'm not trying to make excuses for what happened, but I think by then I was depressed.

It was a year since the biggest of the anti-war demonstrations—the biggest popular protest *ever*. What a waste of time that had been. The old Muslim men with beards, the girls with peace signs painted on their cheeks, the middle-aged women holding cardboard notices above their heads. They spilled off the pavements and jammed up on side streets; they climbed phone boxes, trying to get a sense of it all. On Lisle Street, where the road was tiled with footprint-trampled placards—"DON'T ATTACK IRAQ"; "NOT IN MY NAME"; "NO WAR FOR OIL."—I heard a man strumming a guitar, singing "Give Peace A Chance," as people joined in, laughing at themselves as they sang. You couldn't see the march, but you could hear the refracted echo of whistles and drums. You could hear the high-pitched chants— "*One-two-three-four, we don't want your bloody war*"—shuffling backwards and forwards in big waves of noise.

Near Piccadilly Circus, a ginger boy in a duffel coat had come to be on the opposite side of the crowd barriers from his mum. The toes of his left foot were on the road, while his mittened hand crawled along the barrier, searching for a hold. Locked in struggle with a younger child, his mum could only shout. "Anthony! Come here, Anthony!"

My comrade Hristos said, "You want a help over, my friend?" and scooped the child under his arm. However, a Forward Intelligence Team had snagged us at Leicester Square, and now they moved forward, as if Hristos might eat the kid. The mum ("Labour voters against the war") saw the police and looked at Hristos and looked at the police. But the child was on Hristos' shoulders, laughing so his freckles were pushed into one brown band. "How many people is on the march? Can you see?"

The kid started to count: "One, two, three… a billion!"

"You want to fly to your mother?" Hristos took the child from his shoulders, tossed him in the air, and caught him with both arms. "You are having a good day?"

"Yes," said the boy, still laughing from being thrown and caught. "No way will they start a war now, no way!" You could see what Hristos was thinking, but he just smiled at the mum and patted the boy on the shoulder. We left them and tried to find a channel to the centre of the march. The FIT team followed, churning the crowd up. People saw the police—pushing, prodding earpieces, panting for breath—and thought they were caught in a riot. They tried to push out of the way but there was nowhere to go. You had to keep shuffling, sticking to the guy in front, hoping the current was taking you forward. But when people saw the police, they panicked. They picked up their children and sent them surfing over to friends. At the same time, a roar passed through the march—*"One-two-three-four, we don't want your bloody war!"*—and people squeezed each other's hands for reassurance. They were getting knocked about by people who'd been scared by people who'd been scared by people who'd been scared by— And it opened a sort of undertow that dragged us to where the march was streaming, on either side of the crowd barriers, thirty, forty people wide. They were coming line after line, with balloons tied to pushchairs, with flowers painted on their cheeks, with placards slumped on their shoulders, and seeing the ebb and sway of bodies on the right, they slowed and pushed towards the far bank. The regular police, the ones lining the march, sensed something was happening and started to jog. They gathered near the Eros Statue and the marchers slowed, rubbernecking. Stewards in orange bibs shouted, "Keep going, folks. Move along. Speeches in Hyde Park," but people wanted to see what would happen. A few rows back, not knowing why the march had stopped, a man with a beard seized the opportunity to set down his end of the banner and open a thermos. The small bloc behind him—the staff of a secondary school, or a university classics department, or an amateur dramatics group—slowed up against his back, sharing a joke. And this parenthesis rippled backwards, so that looking towards Trafalgar Square, you could see banner after banner slowing to a stop. You could imagine this break dominoing back to Embankment, so that long after the bearded man had closed his flask and continued, the march would stop, and this would be why.

Want to know how big this march was? When we'd handed out our leaflets, we left the demonstration and walked to the Wetherspoon's in Leicester Square. It was full of protesters eating lunch and using the toilets. The police waited in their vans but sometimes came inside to check on us. We kept them waiting for hours. When we finally left, the marchers were still coming thirty-abreast. It was five hours after the first protesters had left Embankment, but still they came, in winter coats and ski jackets, in wheelchairs, eating sandwiches out of Tupperware tubs, holding hands, carrying flags and umbrellas—it was beyond estimates.

But one year later, Trafalgar Square was almost empty. A girl with a sketchbook bounded up the steps of the National Gallery; umbrella'd business types searched for lunch. I had twenty minutes to wait and reminisce before I saw Buzz shuffling behind the lions. He had a sleeping bag escaping from his army surplus rucksack and his jeans clung to his buttocks as though summoning the courage to jump. "You're late," I shouted.

But there were more memories as we walked down Whitehall. "See that souvenir place?" I said. "It got smashed up on May Day 2000. And that's the McDonald's that got turned over."

"Yeah," said Buzz, "when Winston Churchill had that mohican."

We walked past the pub, towards the Cenotaph and Downing Street. "Why d'you think people got so pissed off about that?"

Buzz shrugged. "*Were* people pissed off? The papers were pissed off but—"

"Reclaim The Streets got thousands of pieces of hate mail."

"But who's writing that stuff? That's what you've got to ask yourself. I mean, that's coming from guys who vote BNP and shag their sisters."

"Like Gordon?"

"Man, Gordon would never vote BNP."

"All I'm saying is that June the 18th never got such a reaction and it proper kicked off."

"But do you *personally* know anyone who was pissed off about Churchill?"

When I thought about it: no, I didn't. "More likely people were pissed off about the Cenotaph."

"Well, that *was* stupid. I mean, seriously, that's one erection you want to leave alone."

At that moment, the preceding years seemed punctuated by marches and sit downs and riots, none of which had achieved anything, and most of which had ambled through Whitehall and Trafalgar Square. Still, the past is inescapable, and I began to think about the people with whom I'd shared these punctutative events. I remembered something that Spocky had said to me years previously. He and I had attended the Mayday 2000 demonstration, and on the train home, as we read the newspapers, he said that every regime, from the pharaohs to Stalin, has had to create its own "Symbolic Order." He said that this was at least as important as power's physical manifestation. According to Spocky, that's why during revolutions people pull down monuments and cut off the heads of statues. "Think about it," he said, "the statues always get it first." Then he said something about the pigeons understanding stuff better than we do because they remember to shit on dead leaders' heads. Sometimes Spocky had a dismissive way of talking, as if his point was so fucking obvious he couldn't believe he had to explain it.

Parliament Square had also been cleared by the rain. There were two policemen, stamping their feet beneath Big Ben, looking across to the peace vigil on the pavement. You could hear the rain hitting the line of tents as the cardboard denunciations of violence turned soggy and the rainbow flags hung heavy with the wet.

Buzz said "Why don't you come home? I'm worried about you." We were waiting at the traffic lights, as an open-topped tourist bus, empty except for the driver, revved its engine in front of Churchill's statue.

"I don't think I can."

We crossed the road, watching Churchill's bald head sweat rainwater.

"Wayne, it's pissing with rain and I really need a pint."

"Give me one minute."

He let out a massive sigh, like a big kite being released into the wind. "Dude, I'm fucking soaking."

"I want to show you one more thing."

"Don't you want to see Spocky?"

"Spocky hates me—"

"What about Kit and Gordon?"

"I haven't seen them since Deanne's funeral."

Buzz laughed and slapped my back. "At least you won't have to see Lucy."

I stood, looking across to Westminster Abbey, finding it hard to believe that this was the same place. The wind was dragging the rain, whipping lines across the square, and all around me abandoned umbrellas slumped against walls, lying in gutters or stretched on the pavements, their spokes twisted and bent by the wind.

When Spocky and I had been in Westminster on the morning of May Day 2000, the ground had been baked dry, except in Parliament Square, where the police had—for obscure reasons—decided to flood the grass. Hundreds of anti-capitalists arrived on bicycles, ringing their bells and blowing whistles. People stood up, cheering and clapping. They blocked the road with green tape that screeched as it unwound. A man in khaki shouted, "It's about opposing car culture! It's about sustainable, communal, ecological alternatives to the car! What's the bloody point of blocking buses?" There was a *rat-a-tat-tat* drum roll, and a samba band swayed onto the road. Dressed in tinfoil and pink crepe paper, they shook plastic bottles filled with stones and lentils, puffing out the rhythm. Meanwhile, punks uprooted the lawn. They turfed the road, levered up paving stones, trowelled in flowers, wiped their hands on their jeans and laughed about it. There were banners suspended between lampposts—"Let London sprout"; "Resistance is fertile"; "The earth is a common treasury for all." A guy—no shirt, facial tattoos—pushed a shopping trolley filled with a rock, a traffic cone, an empty wine bottle.

Spocky and I walked round and round, trying to make sense of it all. There were people dancing around a maypole. There were boys throwing a frisbee. On a public address system, a woman—naked except for knickers and ivy-leaf body paint—talked about Beltane and fire and spring shoots and magic, as a punk—big Mohawk and Conflict patches—listened with his mouth open.

A girl with green ribbons in her hair danced through the crowd, handing out fliers. One contained legal information with advice and phone numbers in case of arrest; the other told us to watch for flags of different colours. Red flags meant "flow through the streets", green flags indicated it was time to "guerilla garden", and black flags warned of danger. We were beside a black skull and crossbones, and there was a red banner on the far side of the square. As we cut across the wet grass, we passed this amazing pond—you had to stop and see this pond. A man and a woman in matching rainbow jumpers, aided by a little girl with pink fairy wings strapped to her back, had sculpted a miniature landscape of rivers and islands and hills. The mud was the colour and texture of clay, and they were working it like potters. The hacky-sack girl, the man with the trumpet, the boys with bandannas covering their faces, the man in cords who'd been collecting rubbish, the woman dressed as a horse, *everybody* stopped to see this pond.

When we reached the red flag, we realised that it belonged to the Iranian Communist Party. It was mostly in Farsi, and it had a picture of a man waving another red flag. While we were thinking about this, a guy with a T-shirt over his face sprayed "SOUS LES PAVÉS, LA PLAGE" on the pavement. Meanwhile, behind a game of football, you could see riot police climbing out of vans, shiny and blue with round shields. A man in a balaclava waved a stick at them, and someone threw a plastic bottle that floated, gentle as a paper aeroplane, and landed far short. Two empty beer cans followed, and the police started to beat their shields with their truncheons, like some ancient Polynesian invitation to war.

Later, I noticed a tramp lying in a flowerbed, and he seemed to have got the joke. His can had fallen on its side, sputtering into the dry earth, but he was laughing up at the sun. Behind him, the trampled square was as muddy as the penalty box at a second division ground in January. I could see a naked guy holding his hands up, announcing something. He ran and jumped into the pond, making his friends laugh the way he thrashed and wallowed in the muddy water, and then he emerged, comical and horrific, like a B-movie monster. The tattooed guy was now crashing the trolley against the curb, pulling it back then shoving it forward, so the wheels lifted off the ground and it spun backwards, the whole cage of it vibrating from the impact. He did this again and again, until it flipped in the air and landed on its front, wheels spinning; then he turned it over and battered the curb once more. The whole day had become a celebration of the pointless. The negation of something or other. A boy in an Atticus T-shirt trotted along the pavement, hopped onto his skateboard, and punted forward. He attempted to ollie onto the wall but the skateboard clattered on its back. He stumbled, regained his balance, pulled his jeans up, and flicked the skateboard into his hand.

★ 9 ★

Lives are shaped like asterisks. At any point, lines intersect in a multitude of directions. You can be diverted, driven down tangents, and then made to reverse. It's the same when telling a story. You start off talking about one thing, then you have to describe another thing, and if you follow that track then you'll forget about the thing you were talking about in the first place. Then, somewhere down the line, you have to stop yourself and wander back to the point where you got redirected. I was telling you about 1999, when Lucy and I were in the Students' Union. She said she had "news." We talked about Marx. Her lips were red from the blackcurrant cordial in her snakebite. This is somewhere we have been before, right?

"How *is* the arm?" she asked.

"Alright. I'm supposed to get the stitches out tomorrow."

She shook her head and touched my knee as The Simpsons tune jingled and coins rattled out of a fruit machine.

"Anyway, what's this news you wanted to tell me?"

"Oh God," she said, gasping and hiding behind her hands. Then she leant forward, closing the space around us, so that I imagined she was moving to kiss me. "Well," she whispered, "you know Owen—Spocky? Well, I think I like him."

"Like him?"

"Yeah, I mean, I think I *like* him."

Spocky? *Spocky?* She liked Spocky? She *liked* Spocky? Lucy liked *Spocky?* How the— what— how— Spocky? How could this have happened? How could Lucy— *Spocky*, the same Spocky who— let me tell you things about Spocky. I'll tell you things about Spocky. I'll tell you about Spocky and you'll understand why—

Spocky only worked at Benny's Burgers because the DSS insisted he applied. On his application form he claimed to have a qualification in capnomancy, and when that didn't put them off, he arrived at his interview with a stuffed elephant whom he introduced as Godfrey. When Kieran asked about his unusual qualification, Spocky soberly explained that capnomancy was the science of foretelling through careful examination of smoke. He added that he also practised palmistry, though it had been some time since he'd achieved divination through studying the entrails of an animal. Of course, Benny's were so short of staff they'd have happily employed the Manson Family, but Lucy? Lucy wasn't desperate, Lucy was—

You want more? The guy was into war gaming—seriously. About a month before Lucy told me she *liked* him, I helped Spocky collect a computer from his dad's house. His dad lived in one of those new shoebox-shaped houses on the edge of town; he had a shiny black cab in the driveway and a birdfeeder on the lawn and a line of roses that had been weeded that morning. The doorbell chimed "Für Elise" and Spocky's dad appeared in the hall, his head mutated through the mottled glass so it looked as wide as the door. A short potbellied man in a red Pringle cardigan and big oval glasses, he ushered us into the living room and pulled the remote control out of the leather sofa to mute John McCririck's preview of the runners and riders. A copy of the *Radio Times* was folded on the coffee table, cacti were spaced equidistantly on the windowsill, and dusted photographs of dead people watched every corner of the room. Everything was immaculate except for the stench of faeces. "I'm sorry about the smell, boys. Bit of a problem with my pipes."

"…"

"It's a blocked toilet," explained Spocky.

"Yes, aye, I've been guddling away all morning and it's no doing any good. You don't know anything about plumbing, do you Wayne?"

"Afraid no."

"Ach well. I'll put the tea on, shall I?"

"Okay, Dad."

"The computer's through here," said Spocky, leading me past an ugly porcelain child who waved his cap at us. The toilet door was open, so you couldn't miss the string of shitty wire coat hangers lying on the purple carpet, or the toilet seat with its fluffy violet wig, or the lilac walls, or the lavender air-freshener that wrestled with the stink of faeces. "In here," said Spocky. Painted aeroplane kits swung from the roof, and two armies of miniature orcs and goblins invaded the carpet. "Does the train set work?" I asked.

"Should do," said Spocky. He knelt under the table and struggled with the plug. The Intercity 125 sparked, rolled forward, and derailed. Spocky realigned the track, blew dust from underneath the engine, and tried again. This time the train spun around the circuit, shining its headlights as it emerged from a plastic tunnel. A miniature man walked across the station platform, bowler hat in hand. "That's about it," said Spocky, slowing the train until it stopped at the station.

We lugged the computer back to his bedsit and used it to start the Benny's Resistance Army website. Spocky's digs had one window that overlooked the concrete wall of a multi-storey car park. The ceiling was half-covered with a partially removed layer of Styrofoam. There was a big opening in the wall where an extractor fan should have been, and the carpet stretched over a hole in the floorboards, creating a kind of booby trap. It was a dump. But Spocky made you take your shoes off, and he regularly polished the broken door handles with Brasso. The guy was weird.

You want more? In December 1999, he made me join the Socialist Workers' Party—seriously, it was his fault. He asked me to take him to the university library so he could borrow some books on my card. It was just after the Seattle demonstrations, when university campuses were haunted by the spectre of rickety trestles and amiable men in tank tops. "Support the Seattle demonstrations... Sign the petition... Build the movement... Copy of *Socialist Worker*, mate?" Spocky hesitated, pulling the collar of his trench coat up while he read the posters: "Turn Dundule into Seattle"; "People before profit." "Want to sign a petition in support of the anti-WTO protests?" It was drizzling and the books and pamphlets were slated beneath a transparent tarpaulin. I could read "What Socialists say about..." but the last word was obscured by the overlapping pamphlet ("Building the Socialist Movement"). The petition was fixed to a clipboard and a string dangled without a pencil on the end. With an apologetic cough, the apparatchik rummaged through the pockets of his raincoat and produced a "Marxism 1996" pen with a chewed lid. Spocky printed his details in his angriest handwriting and then passed the thing to me. As I tried to push it away, I realised that my signature was now *expected*, that I was obligated by a kind of social pressure. I wasn't sure what WTO stood for, but I thought the protests had something to do with dolphins. To not sign would now mean that I was *against* the protests, in *favour* of killing dolphins. And so, feeling it was an inconsequential act, I printed my name and number, declined the opportunity to buy a copy of *Socialist Worker*, and walked on.

Two days later, I woke to Deanne shouting my name. "Wayne—Wayne! Phone call." David had crawled onto the bed and was bouncing and tumbling like some pissed-up trampolinist. He was attacking me with Mr. Potato Head, shouting "Bastard. Bastard."

"Dinnae say that," said Deanne, laughing and slapping his training nappy. When she leant over, scooping him with one arm, her dressing gown opened right down to the curve of her belly. As she tied it closed, I wondered if it bothered Kit that Deanne and I had once slept together and now I often saw her half-dressed. "Come on," she said. "Some dick's on the phone."

"Daddy! Daddy!"

"Wayne's no yer daddy, ya wee tube!"

"Who is it?"

"Eh?"

"On the phone, who's on the phone?"

"Some guy called Stan."

"Stan?" Who the fuck calls himself Stan? "Tell him to fuck off."

"You tell him tae fuck off!" She grabbed David under his armpits and held him to her face. "Uncle Wayne's hungover again. Cause he's a pish-heid."

"Pish-heid!" said David, dropping Mr. Potato Head between Deanne's boobs. While she reached into her dressing gown to retrieve him, I crashed out of bed fully clothed. My jeans were so sweaty I thought I might have pissed myself. "What time's it?"

"It's after ten. I've been up wi him since six!"

"Bollocks." In the TV room, past the stuffed Tinky Winky, the telephone receiver lay face down on the plastic side table. I picked it up just as Richard Madely told Christine from Southampton that she'd won a thousand pounds. She thought it was unbelievable, just amazing. "Hello?"

"Hi, it's Stan here, from the Socialist Workers' Party." Thing is, these petitions are never sent to anyone, and if they are, they're immediately chucked away. The purpose of the petition is to collect the contact details of potential recruits; Stan was a Leninist cold caller offering the chance to join the most revolutionary section of the working class for a mere two pounds. Two pounds was the cost of a pint but it seemed a fair price if it meant I could go back to bed. This was my second mistake: I thought that if I paid up, Stan would go away. I thought that was the deal: you pay the guy, he goes away—like men who want 50p for the bus. But the party's appetite would never be satisfied with two measly pounds; they wanted me to attend meetings, sell their paper, and read distorted histories of the Russian Revolution. They hoped that in time I'd become a full member, who would surrender most of his disposable income, and all of his sense of humour, in order to bring about the dictatorship of the proletariat.

Spocky and I had tripped over the self-appointed vanguard on its quickstep to the end of history, and within a week we'd been persuaded to attend the "People Not Profit" meeting at Dundule University. It was held in James McPherson Tower, the building in which Melvyn Macveigh lectured, the one that swayed in high winds and hosted a heating system that sounded like the battle of Verdun; it was the shabbiest of all the university buildings, and it was probably the most proletarian. The panel featured an SWP speaker, someone from the World Development Movement, and a councillor from the Green Party. It was an example of the Trotsky-ist tactic of the popular front: you create coalitions with Labour MPs, NGOs, and other people next to whom you'll appear radi-cal. It's basically the political equivalent of going clubbing with less-attractive friends in order to increase your chances of pulling.

The room was being decorated with posters when we arrived: "Grants Not Fees"; "Build the Socialist Alternative to New La-bour"; and "The World is NOT for Sale" were all affixed but Stan jumped off the desk leaving "They Say Cut Back, We Say Fight Back" dangling from one corner of blue-tack. Stan was about twenty with a goatee beard and some sort of spasm. "I'm the pres-ident of the Socialist Workers Student Society at the University of Central Scotland. Swsucs, as we like to call it." He chortled at this but admitted, "There's only three of us just now, but the anti-globalisation movement is a real opportunity to build a socialist fight back on the campus. Do you have a copy of this week's pa-per? It's black and white and red all over." He paused, released his unnerving laugh, and then he excused himself to help two men in their struggle to assemble a line of desks. The smaller man tried to pull the desk one way, and Stan tried to pull it the other way, and the larger apparatchik said, "I think we need to turn it around."

"This way or that way?"

"That way."

"This way?"

"Here, let me," said the Green Party woman, seeing the slap-stick efforts of her new friends.

"I think it needs to go round that way," said the World Development Movement guy.

"Like that?" said Stan.

"No," said the big apparatchik. "You go this way; you go that way, yes?" Excluding the panellists, the chair, and Stan, the audience—including Spocky and me—numbered three. The third man was perusing a table of books, picking them up one at a time before throwing each one down with a snort. He spent some moments considering *Marx and the Young Hegelians* before something between its covers provoked an angry "Pah!" and it too was thrown back on the table. Eventually, he purchased a copy of *Plekhanov and Dialectical Materialism*, still muttering to himself as he stashed it inside his jacket.

Someone had drawn a large cock on the blackboard, and Stan searched for a duster before wiping it off with his sleeve. "Okay, looks like that's everyone who's coming. Thank you for coming to this meeting about the amazing popular protest movement that has been started by the magnificent demonstrations in Seattle. My name's Douglas, Douglas Tukhachevski, and I'm delighted to be chairing this meeting." The larger apparatchik enunciated every word: So. As. Not. To. Lose. Anybody. And, worryingly, he settled into his monologue with the air of a person who intended to talk for a very long time.

★ 10 ★

So get this. Back in 1998, Gordon's mum meets this guy. She has a teenage son. He has a teenage daughter. He always holidays in Gran Canaria and has never been to Florida. Her ex-husband plays a lot of golf. He knows there is a Disney Land near Paris but has never been there either. She loves musicals. He drives coaches for Citylink. She smokes B&H Silvers. Sometimes he does European tours. First World War battlefields, that's a good one. You buy cheap cigarettes and get a collection at the end.

They talk about these things, and it turns into a love affair, of sorts. Next thing you know, the registry office is booked.

Afterwards, at a reception in the local pub, a wee bridesmaid twirls for the camcorder but spoils it by pissing her dress; an alcoholic granddad needs carrying home. Gordon's mum is enjoying being the centre of attention for the first time since her last wedding, the DJ is searching for his copy of "Time of My Life," and Gordon's new step-dad is stumbling across the dance floor, scowling with that paranoid aggression stiff men big on self-discipline assume when they're pissed. Gordon's slumped on the bar—he's eighteen and he's getting less action than his mum. The only women who come near him are Aunt Mave, who is famous for her moustache, and Julie, who is now technically his sister. "Here Gordon," she says, "we should really get tae ken each other... Now we're all family and that."

Gordon agrees to walk with her; at least it will get him away from Aunt Mave. Everything changes when they get to the car park. Julie kisses him and places his hand in the warmth between her big white thighs. You can imagine them getting it on in that wedding gear, his sporran bouncing as she wanks him under his kilt. At some point, she must have leant over the wall and pulled the back of her dress up because when the groom goes for a stroll to compose himself—

Imagine it. He's not had a bevvy in a while and it's all caught up with him quicker than he'd expected. He's trying to get his head together—married again, who'd have thought it—and there's his fifteen-year-old daughter, bent over a wall, her face screwed up in pursuit of an elusive climax. And poor Gordon! He's shagging her *recklessly*; his orgasm's building like a fucking NASA rocket launch; he opens his eyes to appreciate her big arse, her purple satin dress, her— her— her dad. "Oh fuck, oh fuck! Dinnae stop, Gordon. Dinnae stop!" This is too much: Julie's dad thumps Gordon on the jaw and slaps Julie as she's pulling up her knickers.

When word spreads that there's a fight outside, the pub cheers. Gordon's mum totters to the car park and throws a glass of gin at her new husband. The gin makes him so wet, you think it might diffuse the situation. Instead, he slaps his new wife pink across the cheek. Gordon folds his kilt down and knocks his new dad onto the tarmac. Julie's uncle sees Gordon deck his brother and takes a swing at Gordon. And when Jerry the Fence glasses Uncle Steve, we've got a full-scale inter-family feud on our hands. The police arrive to separate the Montagues and Capulets, and that was the start of the divorce proceedings.

Well, Gordon was probably alone in thinking that the wedding reception had been a great success. He was desperate to see his

Juliet, his love, his sister, and in spite of the difficulties such star-crossed lovers were destined to face, their secret rendezvous continued until after her sixteenth birthday.

This was in December 1999, when, you may remember, the world was about to end. The millennium bug was going to down aeroplanes, launch nuclear missiles, spring supermarket doors open before crowds of looters. Doomsday was foreseen by ufologists, pyramidologists, televangelists, Seventh-Day Adventists, and a Native American called Sun Bear. Crowds gathered in Jerusalem hoping to witness rapture. Members of the Stella Maris Gnostic Church marched into Colombia's Sierra Nevada, believing a UFO would pick them up and save them from the apocalypse. We were told to fear giant comets, stars falling from heaven, seals opening, all-consuming rains of fire, and a thousand years of tyranny at the hands of the Antichrist. Perhaps most terribly, in Edinburgh's Princes Street Gardens, Moby was scheduled to play a melancholic, ambient, open-air concert.

On New Year's Eve, we took the train to Edinburgh. Walking out of Haymarket Station, it seemed we were already in the middle of the Hogmanay celebrations. There were house parties with open windows surfing music across the street. There were kids smashing the top windows of a double-decker, beating so hard they rocked the bus. There were families with rugs and flasks. There were men pissing up walls. There was an Australian girl, bouncing an inflatable kangaroo all around the streets. "Yay!" she said, "Happy New Year!"

A man in a jester's hat weaved through the revellers, selling glow-sticks (*Revellers* is a strange word: "City expects 300,000 revellers"; "Police ready as Hogmanay revellers arrive"; "Revellers come from all over the world"). On West Maitland Street, a black cab tried to U-turn, beeping as the crowd cheered and blew whistles. Girls rode on piggyback, laughing in uncontrollable ticklish screams. A man in a leather jacket pedalled street party tickets for forty quid each.

"No danger," said Raj, "fuck that."

"You need them to get in," said the man, showing the holographic pass on his wrist.

"No shit, Sherlock."

The man raised his hands—suit yourself—as a small boy tugged his mum's sleeve and pointed at the sky. "Look!" Look at the cones of light, raking the night, and the firework, up, up, up, exploding into golden streamers. Hear the cheer! From here to the Bridges. People cheered for the firework; people cheered because other people had cheered. The noise drowned out Raj's fiancée, Priyanka, but whatever she said made Raj take out his wallet. "Give us two then, aye?" The man smiled—women, eh?—but Raj grabbed the wristbands, glanced at the holograms, and handed them both to Priyanka.

"What about the rest of yous?" asked the man.

"Aye, fuck off," said Kit, shaking her head. I laughed and took a swig of vodka—cheap stuff that burns your throat.

"I need two and aw," said Gordon, "but I've only got thirty bar—"

"Sorry mate, forty each."

"Dinnae be tight. Ye got them for free, ya bam." He was holding Julie round the waist, as though afraid she might dissolve into the party.

The man turned away, bumping a tinsel-haired girl who was laughing as she chased a guy in a kilt.

"Fuck it," said Gordon. "Fuck aw these English wankers. Fuck it aw."

"That's the spirit," I said.

"And fuck you too."

"See, told you this would be fun," said Raj, patting Priyanka's bum. Her hair swung as she reached to push away his hand.

"So how we gonna get in?" asked Buzz.

"We're gonnae Hampden passes offae this kilty cunt when we kick his fud in." Gordon clenched his fists as he stared at the kilted man's holographic wristband.

Julie wagged her finger. "Gordon, you better no be thinkin about fighting; you ken yer bound over."

"Aye, behave yourself," said Kit, placing her hand on his shoulder. "Dinnae worry; it'll still be special."

The revellers were strolling up Lothian Road, wearing their flags as capes: Rampant Lions and Saltires, Irish Tricolours, Stars and Stripes, Welsh Dragons, Maple Leaves. They were crushing at the barriers. The barriers are the worst thing they could do to us. The crowd wants to be one. We want open windows, open doors, and open mouths; we want to be carried and held and pressed and kissed. We do! If you don't then you're not the crowd. Look at the tourists, chubby with clothes, smiling and showing their wrists as they pass through security; they may be *caught up in* the crowd, kidnapped by its momentum, but they won't give themselves to it. Look at the flags—why do they carry them?

The century was ending, the millennium was turning, and sometime after eleven, when Kit and Gordon were in a sort of consultation, amidst all the local people who weren't allowed into the party—the paramedics attending to the girl who had cut her hand, the bald junkie slavering about Hibs, the old man shouting at the security guards ("Listen, son. I've been celebrating Hogmanay in this toon for over fifty years. How can I no go in when aw these English pricks can?")—I found myself in a quiet space, and I thought, *This is it.* The time of my life. It wasn't a moment of clarity; it was a moment of saturation, perhaps.

If you climbed the railings of St. John's Church, you could see the others packed tight along the length of Princess Street and up the Mound—wearing kilts and tinsel wigs, waving flags and glowsticks, looking at the sky or looking at a stage—and you wondered whether the barriers were keeping us out or them in, because we weren't interested in fire jugglers or jazz bands; we were nostalgic for the muscular spontaneity of doing. You could see the steps of the art gallery crammed with bodies and flags. You could see the top of a sparkling Ferris wheel. You could see the Scott Monument, lit up and pointing into the sky. You could see trees draped snowflake-pretty in white lights, and search-beams patterning the night. You could see the castle, glowing above its black rock, so that it looked like something from a fairy tale, floating up there in the dark.

"Wayne," said Gordon, "I need tae talk!"

"Gordon mate, where's the fucking—"

"It's aboot Julie."

"The fucking spirit of the thing?"

"Aye, listen, Wayne—"

"Its balls, its heart, Gordon? Where's its fucking soul?"

"I'm serious, Wayne. I'm dead nervous aboot this."

"Remember the year Kit spewed in the doorway of Deacon Brodie's?"

"Wayne," said Gordon. "Aw fuck!" He'd heard the countdown.

Unsure of itself at first, the countdown gathered momentum with each number. At ten you heard it, at seven you believed it, at six you joined in. You knew they were shouting this from here to the Tron, louder and louder, blasting the boundaries away—"*Five*"—and everything, everything, everything was in this moment—"*Four*"—and you had to make the most of it—"*Three*"—like you'd trained for some super-short Olympic event—"*Two*"—and you had one chance—"*One*"—to be here now.

But having planned for it, you wanted to remember it, to hold onto it, to film it. You wanted to do the right thing and see yourself doing it and frame it all. You heard the fireworks *crack-whizz* the night. You saw the corks shoot way up and fall back down and maybe, for a subliminal moment, hang still at the top of their arcs. You saw the fireworks melting golden across the sky, and you wanted to be able to say, "We went crazy in that moment."

Then Kit pulled back and said, "Where's Gordon? Where's Gordon?" All around us they were holding hands and singing "Auld Lang Syne," or throwing hats and bottles, or shaking beer and cava above our heads. And then I saw him. He was on the ground, amidst the crushed cans and empty bottles of Grants. He was on one knee, holding a ring out to Julie. More people saw and the happiness spread and everyone wanted to share it. "She said yes! She said yes!" We were hugging and bouncing in a circle. We were having the time of our lives.

And what of the parents? No such happy ending. The divorce went through and they never saw each other again...

...Until, they were persuaded to attend their children's wedding. There was an awkward moment when they saw each other in the registry office, and then Julie's dad said "We really must stop meeting like this."

If this was a romantic comedy then here would be the end. Unfortunately, life keeps going. Julie quickly got bored and started to sleep around. She was shagging everybody—old flames, new flames, boys in bars, guys with cars, postmen, most men, fucking strangers she met on the bus. Gordon couldn't see it, and how do you tell a guy something like that? By the end of the year, she'd left him.

It went like this: Gordon separated from his sister, I broke up with Kit, and Spocky was still living in that awful bedsit; in 2001, somehow we got the idea that the three of us should rent a flat together. From the start, this arrangement was problematic. We had three CD players but none of the things a house really needs: a vacuum cleaner, a cheese grater, a toilet brush. Besides furniture, all we inherited was a fibre optic lamp, which lurked jellyfish-like in the corner, a clay pot of dried soil that had once been a house plant, an impotent candle that had been left on the radiator, and an out-of-date chicken and mushroom Pot Noodle. In the whole time he lived with us, Gordon's only domestic contribution was to blue-tack promotional posters for *Pulp Fiction* and *Trainspotting* to the living room wall. But, as I said to Spocky, you couldn't really blame him—the guy was depressed. He would have been more uplifting had he hung himself and rotted in the corner. All his conversation was about how he really wanted to do something, like something really big, but all he actually did was sit on the couch, eating food we'd stolen from work (most things in the house, from mayonnaise to toilet roll, had been stolen from work).

Meanwhile, the Benny's Resistance Army website was clocking hits from all over the world. We had workers writing to us about entitlement to maternity leave in Denmark, youth employment legislation in Canada, how to steal from the tills and not get caught; soon there were branches in New Zealand, in Ireland, in English towns we'd never heard of. It became like a full-time job and, to give him his due, Spocky did most of the work. Don't get me wrong, I liked Spocky well enough to chum him to London and Prague, but the guy wasn't much easier to live with than Gordon. When he wasn't *tap-tap-tapping* on the PC, Spocky was usually reading in his room. You could smell his lamp overheating and some days we only saw him when he emerged to make cups of economy tea. He used each teabag twice, leaving the bags bleeding in a saucer between cups, and he chain-smoked wispy roll-ups, extinguishing each one halfway down so that he could smoke the remainder a few minutes later. Perhaps smoking was the cause of his phlegmy cough, which we endured, minute after minute, hour after hour, day after day. Sometimes, he'd run out of phlegm, and then he would splutter and wheeze, apparently not satisfied until he'd coughed up his very self.

It was hard for Gordon and me to accept that this guy—*Spocky*—was the only one of us who ever had sex. Worse still, we had to listen to it. We'd turn the music up or the TV louder, but we could still hear the springs creaking and, saddest of all, Lucy's stifled, scared-sounding orgasms. "Fake," Gordon would say. "That one was definitely a fake. De-fi-net-ly."

We'd be listening to Lucy's noises, maybe getting a bit turned on, and then we'd hear a grunt from Spocky—it was horrible. If the living room door was open we'd maybe see Lucy bare-footing across the hall, half-dressed with her hair all tousled, and sometimes Spocky would come through for a glass of water, affecting this mature man-of-the-world air; he'd see us sprawling in Gordon's filth, and he'd ask, "How are you two doing?" Not as good as you, you jammy fucker.

Spocky and Lucy progressed through the same stages as every other couple I've known: at first they wanted us around to defuse whatever tension they felt in each other's company, next was the era of splendid isolation during which we hardly saw them, and eventually they re-emerged in the public sphere, presumably having run out of things to say to each other. When Lucy visited we usually sat in the living room and often watched television, but Spocky didn't seem to understand television and would stare at the set as a person might gaze at a minimalist artwork—guiltily aware that it should mean something but unable to see anything except a box. This meant he had a tendency to talk over it. You'd be watching Ewan McGregor prise that sports bag from Robert Carlyle, or Leonardo DiCaprio facing death in the North Atlantic, and Spocky would start lecturing you about the 1912 Lawrence Textile Workers' Strike, or the reds, the whites, the Makhnovists, and post-Russian Revolution agricultural production in the Ukraine. When we watched *The Crying Game*, Spocky was boring us with stories about how the Iron Column was formed in 1936 by—

"Fuck me!" said Gordon. "She's a he!" He kicked a can over in surprise and scrabbled to set it upright before too much was wasted.

"I didn't see that coming," said Lucy.

"Neither did he!"

Spocky nudged his glasses. "They had no permanent hierarchy. Officers were elected and instantly recallable. There was no saluting."

"Fuck, imagine that," said Gordon.

"What," said Spocky, "no saluting?"

"No, ya teuchter: findin oot yer burd's got a tadger." Gordon pointed at his crotch, then at the TV screen, and then at his crotch again.

Spocky focused on the television with his thumb trapped between the pages of his pamphlet. "Oh. What was it you were saying the other day, Lucy? About hermaphrodites or something?"

"It's like, if a child's raised the 'wrong' gender, like a child born chromosomally male but with ostensibly female genitalia or something, yeah? Then it's accepted medical opinion, right, that by the age of four, it's already too destructive to try to realign their gender identity with their biological sex."

"Aye?" said Gordon, flicking his cigarette into an empty beer can. "So?"

"Well, it shows how intense gender socialisation is even amongst very young children. It suggests that gender's overwhelmingly social, not biological, and hence infinitely malleable."

Gordon, now stumbling through an enormous darkness, sunk back into the sofa. "Fair point, I suppose." He rubbed the spilled froth of beer into the carpet with the bare sole of his foot.

The day they put the CCTV camera in The Cave was also the day that Spocky devised the hand wash scam. "We can't have a camera in The Cave," he said as we waited at the sink—everybody was waiting at the sink—"what the fuck are we going to eat?" He was right: at Benny's Burgers, The Cave was where you went to steal some stock or to interfere with the fuse box. It was where Spocky performed an elaborate explanation of capitalism that he liked to call "the Money Trick."

"Why is everybody standing at the sink?" asked Kieran Hunter, Second Assistant Manager.

"We're waiting to wash our hands," said Spocky.

"You can't all need to wash your hands. Not all at the same time."

"Well, I've just been to the toilet."

"It's been thirty minutes since I last washed."

Kieran pointed at Spocky. "You're supposed to be doing fries, yeah?"

"I touched my face."

"Well, how long can it take to wash your hands, yeah?"

"Ah," said Spocky, "good question. See, you have to walk to the sink and probably queue, right? Then you have to place your hands, here. So it sprays a few seconds of water... Here's the soap and wait for it... more water. Then comes the drying stage. The most important stage, what with bacteria multiplying with moisture and all that. It's against procedure to wipe your hands on your apron, right? Now, this hand dryer, you'd be as well to get someone to fart on your palms. See? Not nearly dry. You have to press the thing at least five times."

"What's your point?" said Kieran, tossing his keys from hand to hand.

"Well, having done several time trials, I can tell you that on average a hand wash takes three-minutes-and-twenty-eight seconds."

"That's ridiculous," said Kieran.

"Absurd," said Spocky. "Especially if you work in kitchen. We're supposed to wash our hands when we start, after returning from a break, handling money, touching our faces, performing a cleaning task, or going to the toilet, *and* every half-hour regardless. Right? So, once when you start and once after your break; say you do five cleaning tasks during an eight-hour shift; you probably go to the toilet twice and wash your hands on the half-hour thirteen times—that's already twenty-two hand washes. Then, most people will probably touch their face at least five times an hour—every sneeze, cough or snivel, every time your hair falls, your nose itches, or something gets in your eye—so that's potentially another thirty-five hand washes. Fifty-seven hand washes multiplied by three-minutes-and-twenty-eight seconds results in a minimum of three hours, seventeen minutes, and thirty-six seconds spent washing your hands in the course of an eight hour shift."

"Enough. Everybody back to work, yeah?"

"What about our hands?"

"Now!"

We walked through kitchen and Spocky leant against the milkshake machine, waiting to reclaim his fry scoop.

"There's no fuckin fries! You're off fries, mate. I mean it; you're going to spend the rest of the day cleaning the fuckin toilets, yeah? Someone put more fries down. Come on. Come on. Ps and Qs, yeah?" A new girl was fumbling a cardboard box between her greasy fingers. "No fries, no service, yeah?" Kieran snatched the fry scoop and started filling boxes with Stakhanovite enthusiasm.

Most of the time, they sent Spocky somewhere he could do less harm. They'd tell him to clean the walls in the dining area, something like that. But Spocky would splash water around the skirting boards and then hide behind a bin reading a book. He'd dip his cloth in the potting soil of the dragon tree plant, swirl the muddy rag around his bucket, and then return to the sinks to change his water. "When were those tiles last cleaned?" he'd say. "Absolutely filthy they were—look at the state of my water."

They'd send him to do a rubbish trek and as soon as he was out of view, he'd wander across to the flats on the far side of Elmore Road, lift two full black bags out of their wheelie bin, and drag them back to Benny's rubbish area. He'd slip his tobacco and papers from the lining of his clip-on tie, and when he'd had a smoke, he'd carry the bags past the front window, puffing and shaking his head. "Bloody Hell," he'd say, "when was the last rubbish trek done? Two bags I've filled up already." Sometimes, Spocky's scams seemed to involve more effort than the job he was avoiding; I suppose you could say he was a conscientious objector.

Want to hear Spocky's explanation of capitalism? Of course you don't. Nobody wanted to hear Spocky's explanation of capitalism. Still, once he got talking, it was impossible to shut him up. In his "money trick," he used chocolate flakes to represent the world's raw materials and a discarded tomato slicer to represent the technology that industry uses to turn those raw materials into commodities. Lucy and I were the global proletariat, and he was supposed to represent the entire capitalist class. As such, he owned all the raw materials and all the machinery used to turn those raw materials into commodities.

Because Lucy and I were wage labourers, we needed jobs if we were to share in the wealth of the world. Spocky said he would pay me to work in his factory, and so, at his instruction, I put a chocolate flake between the blades of the tomato slicer and cut the flake into five chunks. Lucy also needed a job, and Spocky agreed to employ her in the accounts department of his office—bear with us, I know the guy was no David Blaine. At Spocky's instruction, Lucy gave ten pence to me and twelve pence to herself. This is where it got tricky. Spocky agreed to sell us the chocolate for twelve pence a morsel, and when I complained that I only had ten pence, he said I could buy the chocolate on my credit card.

So while Lucy and I each ate a morsel of chocolate, Spocky reclaimed his twenty-two pence, ate two morsels, and told us to chop another flake. Same thing happened. Lucy gave me ten pence, she and I each ate a chunk of chocolate, and Spocky, after eating two chunks, reminded me that my debt was now four pence, plus one penny interest. You can see where this is going: by the time we'd chopped another five flakes, Spocky, representing the entire capitalist class, had acquired a reserve of seven morsels of chocolate. He also had all the money he'd started with and was owed an additional thirty-two pence that the global proletariat had incurred in debt. He then declared that Lucy and I were redundant since his warehouse was full and production had exceeded demand. However, since I was now unemployed and unable to meet the interest repayments on my debts, Spocky employed Lucy to repossess my flat. When I asked where I was supposed to live, he said he was prepared to let me my old flat for five pence a week. When I asked how I was supposed to afford rent, he said he'd employ me to build a new house for Lucy. When Lucy asked how she was supposed to pay for it, he said he'd lend her the money at a very reasonable rate. Soon, with each round of chocolate cutting, Lucy and I could afford only crumbs of the chunks we were producing.

The truth is that Spocky's explanation of capitalism was like death: you could only avoid it for so long. He explained capitalism to everybody—taxi drivers, hairdressers, outbound telesales agents. It got to the stage where the Jehovah's Witnesses were afraid to knock at our door: if Spocky caught them in the stair, they'd start making excuses why they couldn't stay and talk. Worst of all, he had an answer to everything. "Okay," you would say, "if you don't like being a wage labourer, why don't you start your own business?" And this would only set him off again.

"Let us suppose," he'd say, "that Lucy tires of working for wages and decides to open a wine bar. This is great news for Wayne," said Spocky, "because in opening the wine bar, Lucy will be creating employment. However, Wayne will have to admit that he is in no position to help Lucy with the start up costs. Now, let us suppose that after viewing her business proposal, the Bank of Scotland is prepared to lend Lucy sufficient funds to launch her brasserie. This is very good news for the economy, which was, frankly, in danger of stagnating. One problem, however, is that because of the interest charged on loans, the amount of money owed is greater than the amount of money in circulation. The global proletariat and the petite bourgeoisie now have combined debts of fifty-two pence, yet only twenty-two pence exists. And the only way to make new money without sparking hyper-inflation is to encourage economic growth."

In other words, according to Spocky, every year, globally and nationally the economy has to grow. Otherwise, he said, businesses (such as Lucy's wine bar) will be unable to repay their investors, workers will be made redundant, and bankers will transfer funds to other economies. If some workers are made redundant then all workers are affected. The unemployed workers have less money to spend, so more businesses go bust. People worry about losing their jobs, consumer confidence collapses, and the economy stagnates; no growth means poverty, recession, negative equity, plagues of locusts, etc. Meanwhile, a growing population means more people are competing for fewer jobs. No wonder everybody wants to see jobs created. It doesn't matter whether we need or want more jobs doing; all that matters is that we find new ways of making money out of each other. This is why so much money needs to be spent on advertising and telesales, so that we want to buy shit, which ultimately we're going to have to produce. So, in the UK, despite all our technological advances, we're working longer hours today than forty years ago.

The paradox is that we're facing an ecological crisis caused by production levels that are already unsustainable. Globally and nationally, we're not short of resources: people starve while food they've produced is thrown away on the other side of the world; in Britain, people sleep on the streets while 800,000 homes sit empty. The planet can't sustain the indefinite production of more stuff and we don't want to have to make it. Right now, according to Spocky, it's like we're on a runaway train and the guard is shouting at the stoker to work harder and harder. We can keep grafting until we hit the end of the line; or, with a collective leap of imagination, maybe we can jump off the train.

The morning after they installed CCTV in The Cave, Gordon was supposed to put the delivery away. It was 8:30; Raj was cooking breakfast, and Dawn wasn't due in until nine. Gordon had stacked and rotated the frozen produce and was lugging crates of shake mix towards the chiller when he noticed the camera—staring right fucking at him. Gordon came up with a plan. Not a good plan, but a plan.

First, he wandered into kitchen and observed that Raj was busy cooking eggs. Next, he hurried outside to the rubbish area and returned with the car park brush. Then, inside The Cave, he unscrewed the head of the brush and lifted the pole towards the giant eye on the wall. He thrust it into the camera, shattering the glass.

Unfortunately, Dawn had come early and seen the whole thing on the office monitor. By the time Gordon emerged sheepishly from The Cave, she was waiting for him, pointing a rosy finger. "You," she said.

"If we can't get your job back," said Buzz, "can I get your uniform?"

"Aye, how many hats have you got?"

"Fuck off," said Gordon.

"At least you'll have more time for the housework." Spocky had a point—plates were piled around the sink, rubbish bags overflowed, dank towels were draped on chairs, and an unfinished plate of pasta had become an ashtray in which fag butts mingled with farfalle.

"Seriously man," said Buzz, "no danger are we gonnae let them get away with this. Right?" He was sitting near the fibre optic lamp, skewering a morsel of resin on the pin of my name badge. "Who's got my lighter?"

Spocky stuck his hand into the couch and guddled beneath the lining (since the demise of its springs, the couch had become a kind of lucky dip, liable to produce anything from a pound coin to a dead mouse).

"This has to call for an all out strike," he said.

"Dinnae bother," said Gordon. "It's no worth the hassle."

I said, "Fucking right it's worth the hassle; I'm not paying your rent."

"You'll get yer money," said Gordon, hauling himself out of the couch and kicking his cap against the wall.

"Come on, just cause you lost your job, you don't have to lose your sense of humour."

Gordon shrugged and checked that the dishtowel was taped over the smoke alarm because otherwise it sounded anytime that anyone made toast. He thumped into the kitchen and you could hear cupboard doors banging and Gordon shouting, "Fucksake! The fuckin bread's fuckin mouldy!"

"Scrape it off," said Spocky.

"Fuck you! That's fuckin rank. Clarty fuckin minger."

"How many folk d'you think we could rely on to strike?" asked Buzz, without looking up from his rolling.

"Fuckin boggin!"

"Maybe ten certainties and the rest would depend on how persuasive we are. It won't be easy—Benny's will put pressure on any waverers and sack all the strikers outright." The kettle was boiling in the kitchen, and Gordon was still kicking and slamming the cupboards.

"So we're all going to lose our jobs?"

"Doesn't matter guys," said Buzz. "We've got to make a stand. If we do nothing now then what's the point? It's like that saying about the Nazis, you know? First they came for the gingers and I did not speak out because I was not a ginger."

"Suck ma boaby," said Gordon, emerging from the kitchen, having finally been driven to prepare the out-of-date chicken and mushroom pot noodle.

"We can win this," I said. "What we've gottae do is convince Benny's that it's more trouble than it's worth to fire Gordon. Think about how much grief we can cause them? If we picket the store every hour it's open. Not just the staff but the customers—we can picket them too."

Gordon sat on the arm of the sofa, slurping his noodles.

"Yeah," said Buzz, "Remember how we shut the place down with a few snowballs?"

Spocky nodded. "We can get help from the other branches of BRA. Maybe political comrades will do solidarity actions?"

"Yeah man," said Buzz. "Come on, Gordon dude, we're going to win this!"

"Nah, we're no," said Gordon. "Fuckin, if we go on strike then they'll sack us aw. If we try tae blockade the place then they'll get the polis in. Get yer mates, yer comrades, their cousins, Jackie

Chan, and the fuckin A-Team—it doesnae fuckin matter. They'll send mair and mair filth, as many as it takes. Ah ken it, yous ken it, and fuckin Dawn and Kieran ken it." He dropped what he was eating, and his fork rattled and bounced and rolled across the carpet, still attached to a wisp of noodle. "I'm goin doon the hotel."

★ 12 ★

On 20th July 2001, Raj married Priyanka, twice. The first time was in Dundule Registry Office; the second time was a few hours later in Hotel Corso Rostóva. The first ceremony took ten minutes; the second, three hours. The first wedding was a civil ceremony for the benefit of the law; the second was a Hindu ceremony for the benefit of Vishnu and various elderly relatives. When we arrived at the hotel, Raj and Priyanka were posing for photographs in the entrance. Priyanka's hands and forearms were decorated with mehndi and from a distance I thought she'd developed a skin condition. Her hair was flat on her head and tied tight at the back, and she wore a lace-fine gold choker. Her red sari was embroidered with golden thread, and half-a-dozen bangles chinked as she waved to us. As soon as he saw us, Raj swiped the white crown off his head and the photographer stood up, looking a bit exasperated. "Hey guys, cheers for coming."

"Congratulations man," said Buzz, shaking Raj's hand.

"Yeah, congratulations mate." I shook his hand and nodded at Priyanka; "Congratulations," I said, thinking about kissing her or shaking her hand, but in the end doing neither.

Lucy kissed them both. "Wow," she said to Priyanka, "you look absolutely amazing."

"Hey Bhenchod, cheers for coming," said Raj, slapping Gordon on the back as Priyanka gasped and slapped his shoulder.

"Please, please," said the photographer, pushing Raj and Priyanka together.

"Aw man," said Raj, "it's been like this all day. I feel like a prick." He flapped his ivory veshti and tugged at his silk shirt and made a small bowing gesture. "You want poppadums?"

"Don't worry about that," I said. "We got married in skirts."

"Please, please, my friend," said the photographer. "With the crown, please." He patted his head and Raj dutifully replaced his crown and stood there as the camera clicked. "Now in front of Torana."

"Nah, come on chief, I gottae introduce my friends, yeah?" He gestured for us to enter the hotel and Lucy went first, stilettoing the steps one at a time. At the reception desk, a young woman in a blue suit squeezed out a smile, and an older woman grabbed Raj, brandishing the receiver of the public telephone. "Raj putt, talk to your aunt." As she passed the phone, she held his arm and asked, "Have you seen your uncle from Chandigarh?"

Raj shook his head and held the phone to his ear. "Namaste." He pulled the receiver away and grimaced, as though the person at the other end was blowing a whistle.

"Sorry for him," said the woman. "Indian relatives. I am Raj's mother. You're very welcome." She looked at Lucy's naked legs. "What a nice dress. We've just finished eating. Please, the bar is through there. Get yourselves drinks and join us." She patted Lucy's arm and called to another woman who was talking to the girl behind the reception desk. "Have you seen Raj's uncle from Chandigarh?" The woman smiled and shook her head and Raj's mother turned back to us, pausing to breathe. "Look at his father; he should be here, helping me." She pointed through a garland of marigolds, into the function room where a podgy man with a metallic tie grinned and waved a tumbler of scotch. "Rajiv!" shouted his wife, "Come here and meet Raj's friends!" Raj's dad turned and pointed towards the bar.

The public bar had big armchairs and small spotlights on its ceiling. Where the hardwood floor met the carpet, Kit was clearing a table. She was wearing a tight black polo shirt with the hotel logo stitched over her heart. She'd quit Benny's after we broke up and this job, looking after the Corso Rostóva bar, was probably an improvement. "I was wondering when yous'd get here," she said, smiling when she saw us.

"C'mon," said Gordon, crashing onto a chrome-legged bar stool. "I'm fuckin parched, by the way."

This made Kit laugh as she set down an armful of glasses. "If you carry on like that, you'll no be getting served."

Above her, *Sky News* was playing on a plasma TV screen. The pictures were from Genoa: an aerial view of a black bloc smashing and burning a shop-lined street; Graffiti slogans sprayed on walls: "We are everywhere", "The future is unwritten"; armoured cars careering through crowds of rioters; an overturned armoured car with flames leaping through the driver's window; confused-looking police standing beside a burning barricade; a tornado of smoke. "Get into the bastards," said Spocky.

"Man," said Buzz, "that looks heavy."

As Kit poured our drinks, I couldn't help thinking she looked good; the acne on her cheeks had faded or was covered with foundation, her bust stretched the buttons of her uniform so I could see the bridge of her bra, and her lips were painted a glossy pink she never wore when we were together. She finished pouring our drinks and helped herself to one of Gordon's Marlboros. I tried to catch her eye but she was complimenting Lucy on her turquoise dress, making Lucy laugh and blush. "It's too short. I'm scared to sit down!"

"Well, it's the same length it was when you put it on," said Spocky, without looking away from the television.

Then Raj staggered into the bar. "Fuck me," he said, slumping onto the stool beside Gordon.

"Here," said Kit, passing him a bottle of Budweiser.

The door to the kitchen swung open and crashed closed and a man in a misfitting suit strode towards Kit. He threw his hands out, pissed off about something. "Come on! Do you think I make you shift manager so you can stand about smoking? If you want to smoke, wait for your break. You smoke on your time, not mine, yeah?" Kit stubbed her cigarette out and scrubbed an invisible spill as her boss strutted towards reception.

Gordon glowered at his back. "Ah'm gonnae have that prick."

"Good," said Raj, dropping his head into his hands.

Buzz slapped him on the back. "Cheer up, dude."

"Buzz man, that's easy for you to say."

Through the large French windows I could see Priyanka posing for more photographs in front of the setting sun. A bindi sparkled on her forehead, her lips were painted deep red, and her eyes were big with a thick border of kohl. "Raj mate, I've got to say, if my evening promised what your evening promises, I think I'd be grinning like mad."

"Yeah? Maybe you would. But then you havenae spent the afternoon being force-fed sweetmeats. Nobody's thrown flowers at you or made you stand on a fuckin rock. You havenae spent the afternoon walking around a fire, and you didnae spend last night praying to some freak with the heid of an elephant." While we were laughing, an old man in a tan-coloured shalwar wandered into the bar, seemed to forget what he'd come in for, and started to wander out again. But when he saw Raj, he paused and pointed his walking stick. He made a machine gun sound and when he stopped and we were looking at him, smiling, not quite sure how to react, he spoke. "Moral responsibility," he said. He spoke with a certain weight, this old guy, like Nelson Mandela or someone, but though we listened, expecting the sentence to develop, that seemed to be it. "Moral responsibility," he said again.

Eventually, Raj said, "Yeah, nice one man."

The old guy nodded and pointed his cane. "Moral responsibility. Do you do what you do?"

"Who was that?" asked Lucy as he wandered away.

"My uncle from Chandigarh. I think he's a bit mental."

"I wish I was there," said Spocky, still staring at the screen. Everybody looked up at the TV and, as if he'd said something he'd meant to think, Spocky quickly added, "Sorry Raj, I don't mean— Obviously—"

"Dinnae worry about it," said Raj. "Fuck me, I wish I was somewhere else too." He pointed at the television where five armoured policemen were beating a body on the tarmac. "I even wish I was that guy!" Then he saw his mother bustling towards us.

"There you are, Raj putt. What on earth are you doing through here? They need you to do the first dance! Everybody is waiting. Where is Priyanka? Have you seen your Uncle from Chandigarh?"

"He went that way," said Raj, and he was about to point out Priyanka when his mum turned and clip-clopped towards reception. Raj picked up his Bud and led us through the foyer, where three twelve-year-olds were rapping and beat-boxing. A plump woman lunged at him, kissing his cheek, putting her hands on the side of his head so her bangles slid over her wrists and stuck on the fat of her forearms.

The function room was decorated with white flowers and bright balloons with ring-curled ribbon tails, and at the far end, patio doors opened onto a lawn where a tent had been erected. The guests were gathered around circular tables. Some of them were standing, singing a bhangra song and clapping their hands. You could see the aftermath of dinner: stray grains of rice, crumbs of roti, and napkins wrestled into grotesque positions.

Raj nodded towards a solemn couple seated behind a table of Sikhs. "Priyanka's parents," he said. "Miserable fuckers." Meanwhile, Raj's dad waved a cigar as he sang a solo part that made everybody fall into their chairs laughing. (Raj's relatives were definitely showing more enthusiasm for this union than Priyanka's, but then they hadn't paid for it. Also, if you're a Hindu and your son makes a living selling beefburgers, I suppose you're in no position to criticise his bride.)

You need to understand that a year had passed since I'd broken up with Kit, and in all that time the closest I'd got to a date was eating lunch with a French anarchist in Prague. Spocky had Lucy, and Raj had Priyanka; meanwhile, Buzz, Gordon, and I had set up a Subbuteo league. But at the table in the centre of the function room, amidst three friends, sat an Asian girl in a glittering silver crop top. I thought, maybe, she smiled at me. "Hey Raj, who are they?"

"Them? How the fuck should I ken? Priyanka's friends, Priyanka's cousins, my cousins, how do you keep track? Yo Rahul!" He grabbed the shirt sleeve of a guy who was wearing a chunky zirconia ear stud.

"Hey veer mera," Rahul said, slapping Raj's back.

"Who are the girls?" said Raj, pointing with his eyes.

"On your wedding day? Man, I'm disappointed in you, Raj. I mean, it's not enough you marrying my sister, yeah, you wanna get with all my cousins too?"

Raj laughed and pointed at me. "No, it's for my friend Wayne."

"Wayne mate," said Rahul, placing an arm around my shoulders as Priyanka entered the function room to cheers and applause. "They're my cousins, yeah? They've not got boyfriends or nothin, but they're from India, you know? *Dey no speak anee English*," he said in a *bud-bud-ding-ding* voice. "If you wanna get wi them, Wayne, you gotta speak to them in Punjabi, innit?" Sensing my interest was waning, Rahul squeezed my shoulders tighter. "It's easy man; go over there, yeah, and say to the one you like best, 'Hey kuthi, mere tuttay choosla.'"

"What does that mean, like?"

"It's like... 'Hey beautiful... I gladly choose you.'"

"Yeah?"

"It doesn't translate too good but it makes sense in Punjabi, innit?"

Raj nodded.

"How d'you say it?"

"Hey—kuthi—mere—tuttay—choosla."

"You're not winding me up, are you? I'm not about to ask them for sex or something?"

"My cousins?" said Rahul, disgusted by the thought.

"It's straight up, Wayne," said Raj.

"Hey—kuthi—mere—tuttay—choosla?" They both nodded.

I practised as I walked towards the girls and they must have seen this strange guy muttering to himself because they stopped talking and made cartoonish *this is a bit weird* faces. I stood opposite the girl in the sparkly crop top and, feeling a great sense of inter-cultural exchange, prepared myself to speak the password. "Hey—kuthi—mere—tuttay—choosla."

"You what?" she said. "What did he say?"

"It sounded like—"

"Are you tryin tae be wide, like?"

"Sorry, sorry! Your cousin Rahul, he said—" We all looked at Rahul, who was doubled with laughter.

Then the DJ came on the PA and said, "Okay. How's everyone doing? Welcome, yeah. Alright, we're ready to start a bit of music and we want the happy couple to get up here and kick off the dancing."

I used his announcement as cover to escape back to Rahul and my friends, who were breathless with the hilarity of it.

"She's from Glasgow!" I said.

Rahul slapped his thigh. "'Hey bitch, suck my balls.'" Gordon put his arm round me, knuckle-rubbing my scalp. Raj and Priyanka shuffled onto the dance floor, as Shania Twain crooned "Looks like we made it."

Soon everyone was at it—Raj's dad thrashed the air, wiggling his hips in a compromise between Bharatanatyam and *Saturday Night Fever*. Rahul's cousins swayed in a circle. Rahul said to Lucy, "Oye sohniye, you want to dance?" and she blushed and took his hand. Rahul's father muttered to his wife. Spocky left the function room alone.

Later, drunker, once people had danced until they were tired, drunk more and danced some more, made friends with strangers and fallen out with people they loved, Buzz and I retreated to the public bar and hit balls around the pool table, bouncing them off cushions with little expectation that they would ever encounter a pocket. Most of the wedding guests were in the function room and there was nobody behind the bar. Beside the French windows, Spocky and Lucy sat by themselves, absorbed in some serious subject. Meanwhile, Buzz and I debated whether we would sleep with various celebrities, none of whom were particularly likely to ever proposition us.

The Brahmin had identified the twentieth of July as an auspicious date for Raj and Priyanka's marriage after consulting his almanac and giving due consideration to lunar cycles and the betrotheds' names and horoscopes. But he hadn't considered the fascist inclinations of the Italian police or the determination of those who would have stormed the Zona Rossa. He could not have foreseen the battles on Via Tolemaide or the assassination of Carlo. "Look," said Buzz, pointing at the television above the bar. "Fuck." It scrolled across the bottom of the screen: "G8 Summit latest. Confirmed: At least one protester killed during violent clashes." The FTSE 100 Index had closed on 5,566.9. The pound was down against the dollar. "Spocky!"

"Fuck," he said, seeing the pictures as he crossed the room.

"Oh my God," said Lucy.

A small boy ran, giggling so much that spit covered his chin, as the plump woman with the bangles smiled in weary pursuit. On television, the police shot tear gas from a helicopter. Lucy said "They'll still only talk about the anarchists' violence."

Spocky shook her arm off. "It's the bourgeois media, isn't it?" He said it in that dismissive voice he sometimes used when he talked to me. Christina Aguilera appeared on the television, smiling at the cameras in a long silver dress.

In the foyer, I used the pattern on the carpet to navigate a straight line. The reception desk was closed and near the entrance, on leather sofas, Raj was lounging with three of the cousins in front of whom I'd earlier disgraced myself. "Wayne mucker," he said, "how's it going?"

"Not good, mate. Someone's been killed." Raj craned to see the function room. "No," I said, "in Genoa."

"Aw shit, you're kidding?"

"It's on the telly in the bar."

I walked past him towards the toilet, but I must have taken the wrong door because the corridor was too long and I realised I was amidst the bedrooms. I was trying to find my way back when I saw a couple kissing. It's funny because I recognised Gordon first and I thought *Go on son* because he hadn't been with a girl since Julie. I was happy for him and then I realised who he was kissing. Kit stopped kissing him and looked at her feet.

"..."

"Carry on," I said, but walking towards reception, I thought there was a chance that I might cry.

Sitting on the steps, by the fire door that joined the public bar to the car park, I noticed how bright the moon was and wondered if that was something foreseen by the Brahmin. It was one of those nights that smell of barbecues and lawn cuttings, when sounds slip through open windows and you wish you had a balcony. I heard someone say goodbye— "See you. Thanks for coming."— car doors clicked, an empty keg of beer ground across a gravel path, and through the open doors I heard the wedding noise: the laughter, singing and clapping, *"Shavaa! Shavaa!"* and Robbie Williams' "Angels." Then heels tapped the concrete behind me and Lucy said, "Mind if I join you?" She bent over and set her glass of sparkling wine on the uneven concrete, holding its stem until she was sure it was stable. I shuffled along the step and she sat next to me, in the yellow glow of the nightlight. She folded her hands between her legs and pulled her knees towards her chin, dropping her clutch bag next to her ankles. I followed the bag past her thighs, past her calves, past ankles criss-crossed by the black straps of her shoes, to her carmine-red painted toenails.

I took my Lambert and Butlers from the breast pocket of my shirt, and when I passed her one, she put the end in her mouth and waited for me to light it. Meanwhile, Robbie Williams stood aside so that John Travolta and Olivia Newton John could sing "Summer Nights." Lucy sipped her drink. "So, are you alright?"

"You heard then, did you?"

She nodded. Had she known about Gordon and Kit already?

"Aye, I'll be grand."

"Yeah," she said. She placed her hand on the back of mine and I opened my fingers so that hers fell through the gaps and our hands were entwined.

"At least the DJs stopped experimenting with Cornershop and the Asian Dub Foundation—that was getting embarrassing."

"Yeah, it's karaoke classics all the way from here," she said. Then she sniffed, said "Sorry," pulled her hand free of mine, and wiped smudged mascara tears from her cheeks.

"Lucy, hey, what's wrong? Come on, it's only *Grease*; it'll be over in three minutes."

She laughed and held her hand against her nose. "Sorry," she said, scrabbling for her clutch bag.

"Dinnae greet, Lucy. Come here." I put my arms around her and she cried onto my shoulder.

"He says he doesn't want to be with me any more..."

"That's not true." Her hair was soft against my cheek and she smelled of coconuts and talcum powder and long lazy bubble baths. "It's just tonight, Lucy, with that guy that got killed. Everyone's a wee bit upset. It'll be better tomorrow."

But she kept crying into my neck. "I can't do anything, I can't even dance..." The music cut dead and the function room jeered and the PA system screamed with static. "We're finished, Wayne. I know it. We're finished."

★ 13 ★

Back me up on this: when Kit (my first—and only—serious girlfriend) started dating Gordon (my flatmate and friend-ever-since-school), surely that was a relationship I should never have *seen*? Surely their relationship should have developed off-screen, like sex in a black and white movie? Instead, Gordon got sacked and couldn't afford his rent, Kit fell out with Deanne, and since that was sort of my fault, there was nothing I could say when Gordon invited her to move in. "I ken it's a wee bit difficult, but it's no for long," he said. "I promise, mate. We've got plans."

And they did. Kit was left to lock up the hotel bar and one night they emptied the safe. You knew something was wrong as soon as they entered the flat: Gordon held her shoulder bag against his stomach and when I said the colour suited him, he didn't tell me to fuck off or to suck his balls, he tipped the bag upside down and it was full of banknotes. It was like a mass parachute jump. The notes tumbled out of the bag all scrunched up, and then they spread flat and floated to the carpet.

Why did Kit and Deanne fall out? Well, a year earlier, in the summer of 2000, I used to go to a nightclub called "Underground." Underground was called "Underground" because it was in a basement, not because they played radical beats mixed by a DJ from Brighton. You didn't go there to hear speed garage or chemical breaks; there was no drum and bass with the Tribal Vibes Collective or euphoric trance sessions with DJ Lovevibe. Underground boasted "An eclectic mix of chart and party classics"; it was like being trapped in a family car journey with your dad and your wee sister fighting over the cassette player. They played Aqua, Boyzone and Celine Dion. Erasure, 5ive, and Geri Halliwell. On quiet nights they made us listen to Idlewild and James, Kylie, and Lulu. On student night they played the Manics, Nirvana, and Oasis. They always played the Proclaimers, Queen, Rod Stewart, and Tiffany; and every night they sent us home with the inevitable, completely fucking ironic, "Time of My Life."

You went there to complain about how shite it was. There were hands above bobbing heads and girls pouting, grinding their hips, and boys doing big box, wee box, animated by strobe lighting.

The DJ muted the chorus but nobody sang. "Here comes the foam!" The dancers screamed and raised their hands. The foam spurted—*Pfff*—like an old man blowing the head off his pint.

And that was when I saw Deanne.

She was giggling and twisting in a cloud of smoke.

She looked slaughtered. Falling over. Handbag swinging from her shoulder. Arms above head. Pinpricks dotted on her armpits. Foam in her hair. She waved and swayed. "Aaaaagh! Wayne!" she said. "What the fuck are you doin here?"

"Y'alright?" I said.

"Is Kit no here?"

"Nah, she's staying at her Nan's house."

"She's daein what?"

"At her Nan's house!"

She swigged my drink and kissed my cheek. "Who ye here wi?"

"The boys from work."

"You gonnae dance?"

"Who's got David?"

"He's at my ma's. I'm fuckin wrecked!"

"Aye, me and all."

"Are you dancin?"

"I dinnae dance."

"Fuck's sake, come on!" She held my wrists, manipulating my arms like a puppeteer. "Cheer up!" she said, and fixed her breasts.

"D'you want a drink?"

She tapped her ear.

"D'you want a drink?"

She pulled me towards her mouth and her breath was warm. "I want a fuck."

"You're mad, Deanne!"

She pushed me back and dabbed her teeth. "You want some speed?"

I shook my head.

She smiled at me. "Choose life," she said, dancing closer, biting her lip. Ruffling her hair, the way that strippers dance in films.

Lights swung and flashed and when they strobed, Deanne appeared, then disappeared. And every strobe revealed one glimpse. Her top made wet and tight with foam. The fake tan marks, coffee coloured around her arms. Her lashes bunched with mascara. A butterfly, still on her back.

She placed her arms around my neck, and rubbed her body against me. She turned around, grinding her bum against my crotch, and spun and smiled, dancing real close, guiding my hand to the hem of her denim skirt. She laughed a bit as my hand moved under her skirt, feeling the weight of her buttocks. "So Wayne," she said, "your place or mine?"

She still kissed like a Labrador.

In the morning, there was all that uncertain intimacy, because neither of us was sure how much of last night's complicity had survived. A weather forecaster talked on next door's television, and a flat football slapped against an outside wall. The condom was in a tissue on her side table.

"When's Kit back?"

"Dinnae ken. When d'you have to get David?"

"Two hours ago! This is a fuckin nightmare."

"I know."

"Cheers."

"Dinnae get me wrong"

"I ken."

"I mean, I enjoyed it."

"Aye, me too but—"

"Exactly."

Then our hands were scrabbling on the floor for yesterday's underwear, and we were dressing in bed beneath the bulging duvet. The hesitant morning kiss. The *if we had more time* look. Then the hairbrush tugging, jean buttoning, morning post mortem: "It was a once off." "She must never find out." "Nobody got hurt." "We were drunk." "You only live once."

After that morning, Deanne and I talked in memorandums—about visits from the housing officer or David's social worker, about who finished the milk or the toilet roll—like a conversation between Post-it notes.

And Kit? We didn't break up like a vase or a mirror or a china cup; we split like a piece of wood. We cracked at first. We fractured until you could bend us and make us creak; then we snapped and splintered, until there were only fibres between us,

Kit had told me she and Gordon were entering a new phase in their relationship, but I hadn't expected this. When Gordon tipped the bag upside down, the banknotes fell brown and crumpled on the carpet. When they covered his feet, he swung his legs, like a wee boy kicking though leaves. "We took it aw! We fuckin chored the lot, man!" Perhaps I now know how he was feeling, but at the time, I don't think I said anything. If I did, I said "Fuck," or something like that. I watched Kit unhook her coat from behind the door and stuff it into her bag. I watched Gordon crash into his room. For a second, he stood and looked, and then he started banging doors and tugging drawers and throwing clothes onto the bed.

I remember Spocky in a white T-shirt and square tartan boxer shorts, pulling the legs of his glasses behind his ears. He'd been sulking ever since he'd broken up with Lucy, and he wanted to complain about the noise.

"They've cleaned out the safe at the hotel!"

"Well shut up about it! Why don't you invite the neighbours round and tell them over nibbles?"

I could see how this getaway would look to someone else, I could even see how it would look to me in retrospect, but the nowness of the thing, the sense of participating, was missing. Even when we were downstairs, as the taxi shuddered in the cold, as I kissed Kit goodbye, I turned to Gordon and I said "Take care of her, aye?"

That wasn't my sentence.

In the morning, I lay half-awake, unsure if these events were real. Monday was behaving as it should: our fridge murmured in the kitchen, and a toilet flushed on another floor. Pipes hissed, a door opened and slammed, keys jangled and office shoes tapped down the stair, one heel dragging loose across the stone every fourth step.

When I got up, I saw the money they had left me, and I started to panic (even the pettiest thieve imagines that between investigating Republican paramilitaries, Russian Mafiosos, and Colombian drug cartels, Interpol makes time to pursue the villains who nicked the Phil Collins CDs from Woolworths). It was five past nine, and somebody must have noticed the money was missing. They must have phoned 999. I imagined helicopters, forensic searches of the countryside, closed borders. It was only a matter of time before a SWAT team swung through the windows firing tear gas. I took the money and Kit's hotel shirt, and I fled the scene.

All the time I'd lived in Dundule, I'd never visited the museum—it's funny how you don't do that stuff in your own town—and it seemed the place where I was least likely to meet anyone I knew. In the lobby, where the town's new slogan, "Seize the initiative," was painted over pictures of smiling school children, there was a plan of the Brandonside Redevelopment. There was a "before" picture of the rubbish and graffiti at the foot of Breast Mountain, and there was an architectural "after" model of the proposed transformation. In the model, smiling figurines sat on green felt lawns, strolled between lollipop trees, and licked ice creams on the steps of a plastic "Technology Centre."

I walked through "Prehistoric Puzzles" ("There's no evidence of Roman settlement in this area, but had the Romans visited

Dundule then they might have left behind a pot like this one") and entered "Medieval Mysteries." There, I watched a multi-sensory exhibit of a medieval settlement, in which men with beards sawed wood with a jerky clockwork rhythm. You could hear the bark of medieval dogs and even smell medieval air. It smells of shite, medieval air; in fact, this seems to be the thing we know most certainly about the past—it smelled of shite.

But what I wanted to tell you about was "The Age of Industry" room, where two blackened miners crouched in the dark. A tape recording said "Well, if you ask me that cage didn't look too safe." "Never mind that, just make sure your lamp doesn't go out." And a group of Spanish school kids—why would they come here?—leant on each other's shoulders, trying to take the weight off their tired legs. The next case described the construction of the railway line. I saw a polished-up hip flask and a rusty pick. The board said "Many of these 'navvies' were Irish men who came to Scotland to contribute to industrial development after the failure of the Irish potato crop. The work was hard and dangerous and many men died before the project was completed." But in the photographs, they are holding up their picks and smiling— not forced Pan American smiles because there's a camera pointing at them; they are smiling genuine, involuntary Duchennes. They are smiling with crinkled eyes and upturned mouths, with pride and a sense of achievement, as if to say "In spite of everything, we have built this and it will endure for a thousand years." "In spite of everything, we have carved the future out of rock." Now, run through to the "Age of Enterprise" exhibits, and see how much has changed. Look at the mannequins, in their shirts and ties, with their no-hands headsets and painted grimaces.

The police got me at seven the next morning. They woke me and I answered the door in my dressing gown. They were looking for Kit and Gordon.

I said, "They're no here," and added, "I don't know where they are."

"Where were you last night?" said the tall one, holding his cap under his armpit.

"*Last* night?" I said, assuming they meant the night before.

"Aye, last night, son. We called round about six?"

"Oh, last night I was in the pub." That would have been enough for Columbo. He would have smoked a cigarette and when he was about to leave, he'd have stopped with his finger on his temple and his foot in the door, and he would have said, "Oh, just one more thing, Mr. Foster. How come you knew what night the crime took place on before I told you?"

These cops just shuffled inside and lowered themselves into the couch, jiggling handcuffs, adjusting stab vests, turning their truncheons to the side of their hips.

Thirty seconds after they left, the phone rang. It was Gordon. He and Kit were in a bar on 42nd Street, New York. I could almost see him, Bud in hand, at a payphone near the window, across a road on which yellow taxis sat bumper to bumper, horns beeping in the sunshine.

But in their room, where nobody had turned the light off since they left, where an ice-cream tub was half-filled with small change and a football book lay facedown, everything was stopped. It was like Satis House or the ruins of Pompeii, and you had the feeling that something awful had happened here. A jumper and a pair of jeans lay twisted on the floor. A dress had snagged on a cupboard door. Gordon's shirt was discarded on the bed, one arm dangling off the edge.

In a box of dusty forgotten things, I found a plastic rose with a green stem and black petals, and, underneath it, a half-filled photo album. There was a picture of me in a denim jacket that I no longer owned. There was a photo of Kit and Deanne in front of the high flats that dominated Westbridge before they built the motorway. I've kept this picture. They look about thirteen, propped on BMXs, each with one foot on the ground. They're squinting into the sunshine, dimpling beneath matching perms. It looks a rare hot day.

Three months passed before I next saw Kit and Gordon. By then, they were flat broke. They were living in London but had come back to tell me about Deanne. Someone had found her hanging from the kitchen door beam. Kit said, "Her telly was on, ken? And there was six fags left in a packet on the table. Does that no seem weird?"

We were in the kitchen. The fridge was doing that shudder thing it did—a loud *brrrrrrr* as though it had just realised it was cold. I felt I should ask for more detail: what did she hang herself with? Who found her? Where was David? Who was the last person to see her?

Instead, I kicked the base of the bunker and kicked it and fucking kicked it until the chipboard crumbled and the bracket swung loose and the wood crashed onto the tiles.

Deanne's funeral was on the first really cold day of the year. We stood outside the church, stamping our feet and rubbing our hands. Someone said "Aye, well, she's gone tae a better place," dead sure about this, as if discussing that young left-back who was transferred to Everton. "Fuckin, it cannae be any worse than Westbridge!" and we laughed a bit too loud then, caught ourselves, sighed, and shook our heads. "Terrible thing."

I sat beside one of the old dears—the ones nobody can place, who shuffle away when the last sausage roll's gone. "Such a bonnie girl," she said, settling herself. "And leaving that wee boy. It's an awffy business. You wonder, don't you, what demons she must have had insider her, to make a girl do a thing like that." It was the white bouquet you couldn't stop looking at: the chrysanthemums arranged to spell "mum."

Outside, the cemetery was glazed white with frost and the sky was pure blue—if you were religious you'd say God had lacked the heart to paint it—and way overhead, so high I knew it wasn't stopping, an airliner crossed the fading jet trail of another plane, brushing an icing sugar X. The undertakers puffed steam as they lowered the coffin, and wee David made explosion noises. I watched him blowing his cheeks fat and then blasting his breath out so his lips vibrated. He held a plastic Buzz Lightyear by the ankle, swinging it horizontal through the air.

★ 14 ★

You can lose concentration when life seems quiet. It's like you're reading a book, skimming through the dull bits, and suddenly there's a new character trying to kill the protagonist, and you have to flick back to work out where he came from. Lucy was awarded funding to study a PhD in London. She left Dundule in September 2001, less than a fortnight after we lost Kit and Gordon.

Spocky wouldn't go to her leaving party, but I turned up with Buzz. Lucy answered the door wearing a white angel shirt-dress, which had loose sleeves and a skirt that was layered with ruffles like an expensive cake. Her thick wedge heels made her walk tall, stretching her legs straight with every step, so you could see the white backs of her knees.

Her flat had high ceilings with detailed cornices, big bay windows, and exposed floorboards that were varnished amber. In the living room, a dozen people were scattered around nibbles—some standing, some sitting—all talking at a volume, and with an etiquette, that made it obvious that this wasn't the sort of party we'd anticipated. As Lucy introduced us to her flatmates, I looked at the carrot sticks and vol-au-vents, the canapés, the olives balanced on little puff pastry pedestals, and I had a sense of having been ambushed. "Rachel, Annie, these are friends from my old job: Wayne and Buzz." Annie was a bespectacled girl, fussy and bookish and beak-nosed, like anthropomorphic representations of owls in children's stories. She shuffled from foot to foot and eventually asked, "Are you studying?"

"No," said Buzz.

Annie nodded and looked lost. "Lucy, this guacamole's delicious."

Well, drink followed drink, followed drink, followed drink, and more people arrived, standing awkward like they were being photographed, smiling and bowing as they were introduced and offered hors d'œuvres, asking vague questions about Lucy's PhD, and listening, nodding, as she explained about post-structuralism and deconstructing the contemporary categorisation of sexuality. At this point, they'd look a bit wary and say, "So it's mainly a theoretical thing?" or they'd murmur a name or two—Foucault, Derrida, Judith Butler—as their eyes bounced around the room, searching out the people with whom they wished to talk. They'd say, "It sounds fascinating," or they'd chuckle and say, "At least it puts off getting a job for a few years!" and then they'd slink to another group.

Then, as the party loosened up, I noticed how the ricochet of conversation seemed to avoid us. You could hear how all these groups were joined to each other: how Annie said, "He did not!" and shrieked and covered her mouth; how the guy in the suit leant away from the girl in the flowery dress and said, "Who's that?"; and how it spread and passed on. "So, Lucy, have you read his stuff on Hegel and Bataille?"

"So, how do you know Charlie?"

"Are we smoking inside or outside?"

"Who knows Charlie?"

"It's one reading: Derrida's 'Différance' is just Hegelian dialectics properly understood."

"Miguel? Miguel honey, pass me that ashtray." Round and round, somehow avoiding us, as if we were two ghosts whom nobody could see.

I don't know why I did it, but at some point, without asking, I let myself into Lucy's room, and I fell asleep on her bed. When she woke me, she placed her hand on my forehead, and she said, "Are you alright, Wayne? Everybody's gone home." I remember looking up at her cleavage and noticing her lashes and saying something awful like, "Are you an angel?" I was half-asleep, but it was still an awful thing to say. Lucy looked really bored and said, "Maybe she's born with it, maybe it's Maybelline," and her tone shook me awake. I pushed up on my elbows and saw 4:25 on her alarm-clock radio. I saw the half-packed boxes and the bare walls. "Sorry, you should have woke me."

"You looked too peaceful." I swung my feet off the bed so that I was sitting next to her, and I reached into my back pocket for cigarettes. The packet was squashed flat but I reshaped two fags and passed one to Lucy. She leant over me to click on her bedside lamp. It felt strangely intimate sitting beside her dresser; there was something erotic about the smell and the shine of her beauty products—Babyliss Total Freedom hair straighteners, Rimmel Extra Super Lash Mascara, Lancôme Foundation, a star-shaped crystal phial of Thierry Mugler's Angel Perfume.

"Half-four—fuck. Was it a good party?"

"Apart from one of my guests passing out on my bed, yeah."

"Aye, sorry about that."

She laughed and lit our cigarettes.

"You almost packed then?"

"Almost."

"I'd get out of Dundule tomorrow if I could."

"I only moved here because it was inland." Lucy had told me before about the village where she grew up, where the fishermen came ashore in stinking orange overalls and thick wellingtons, cleaned themselves, drank until they were sick, and then left again.

"You never go back, do you?"

"Where, Kinraddie? Christ no. What's to go back for? Incest and wicker men?"

"Family?"

"Oh God, we don't get on. We haven't spoken since I left."

"Seriously? What d'you do?"

She took a long draw on her cigarette and looked like she was balancing whether or not to tell me, and then she smiled and flattened the ruffles of white material on her lap. "You know how I was a really geeky kid?"

This was something else she'd told me and something I struggled to believe: the way she described herself as a child—the ankle-length green skirt, the train track braces, the bowl cut and acne—was irreconcilable with the Lucy I knew.

"Well, the worst bit was that my dad taught at the school. In the morning, he'd drive me up the coast, but after school, he'd stay later and I'd get the school bus home. I had one friend, Donald, and, oh God, he was even geekier than I was. He was like the boy that biology had cursed. I mean, he had everything wrong with him: greasy hair, glasses, freckles, spots. He was interested in botany, especially seaweed. Anyway, I used to sit next to him on the bus home, and of course the other kids would throw crisps in our hair, spit on our backs—" She saw me looking for an ashtray and passed me a plastic cup. "Donald and I lived on the same stretch of nine houses and we got off the bus together. Instead of going home straight, we used to go and sit down by the sea for fifteen minutes or so. He'd tell me about the seaweed—seriously. I can still remember the names: dabberlocks, oarweed. Once he tried to make me eat oarweed with butter and pepper. I think that was our idea of dating. We never *did anything* but I didn't tell my parents."

"How old were you?" I said, flicking my ash into the cup.

"I would have been fifteen. Donald was a year younger."

"It's hardly going off the rails."

"Tell that to my father. You know he wouldn't let me watch *Scooby Doo* because he said it celebrated the occult?"

"Serious?"

"He was an über-strict Christian. He banned *Neighbours* because he said it was smut. He withdrew me from sex education; I mean, how embarrassing is that?"

"Jesus."

"Exactly. And of course the more you repress something, the more exciting it becomes—"

"Like all those priests that diddle kids."

Lucy looked unconvinced by the comparison but continued anyway. "So, one day, when Donald and me were sitting down by the sea, on the rocks, talking about London—we always used to talk about how we were going to move to London, isn't that strange? We were holding hands and I— I started to move our hands up his leg, like this." She placed her hand on her thigh and nudged her skirt towards her waist. "We didn't say anything, just stared out to sea. And when I touched him, he gasped and shuddered. And I thought it was the most amazing thing, you know? It was like I was doing a science experiment, like I was completing the circuit and the bulb was lighting. And I sort of kept doing it, like to test the relationship between pressing and illumination. I'd touch him and he'd gasp. And then, I don't know why, I suppose because we both wanted me to, I unfastened his trousers." She kicked her shoes off, curled her toes, flexed her feet, and laughed. "And his dick, right, was pointy and curved, I swear. I've never seen one like it since, thank God, but at the time, I thought they were all like that. So I— you know." She mimed a wanking gesture. "And after a few seconds... *spurt.*"

"Not what you want, is it?"

"But the worst bit was that he reacted like I'd done something really bad, you know? He stood up, stepped backwards and looked at me, shaking his head like— Then he—he was still doing up his trousers—he turned and clambered over the rocks. I tried to wash my hands in this rock pool and there were all these hopping beasties and I really thought I was going to be sick."

"So, what happened? Did your folks find out?"

Lucy looked at the ceiling where a halo of light was projected through the top of the lamp. "The next day he did what you'd expect of a no-mates fourteen-year-old who's just been tossed off by a girl in the year above; he told the world. I think the whole school probably knew before the end of registration. And word reached the staff room."

" "
...

"Yeah. On the bus home, Donald sat with the other boys and had his back slapped until his glasses fell off, and all the girls were throwing things at me and gesturing hand jobs, and this one girl, Kiera Campbell, had a tub of yoghurt left over from lunch, and she squeezed it so the yoghurt spurted over my skirt and blouse." Lucy sniffed and her lashes folded and stuck together, and I thought of a butterfly with waterlogged wings. "Some of the boys joined in as well, thrusting their crotches at me, asking how much I charged. Best days of your life, schooldays." She tried to laugh, snorted, wiped the back of her hand across her face. "Sorry," she said. Her cigarette had burned to the filter and she dropped it into the cup. "So I waited at home, terrified. The house was always silent; the only noise was an old grandfather clock that sometimes chimed thirteen strokes. Or its pendulum used to stop and start on its own. Honestly, it was so creepy. That afternoon, I counted thirteen chimes and I thought, This is it. I'm going to walk up the cliffs and—" She leant across me and the displaced air made me tingle. She was pulling tissues from the box beneath the lamp, blocking the light so the room darkened and a haze of lamplight glowed around her, but it felt like she was whispering in my ear. "But he came home early," she said, sitting upright again. "I heard the creaking on the stairs, the footsteps. My father used to quote from the bible a lot, and he started shouting, roaring, stuff like... 'A shameless woman shall be counted as a dog! But she that is shamefaced will fear the Lord!'" The tissues were stained black with mascara, but Lucy was starting to laugh. "'Withhold not correction from the child; for if thou beatest him with the rod, he shall not die. Thou shalt beat him with the rod, and shall deliver his soul from Hell!' And then of course he started to beat me, but not like he normally did. This was frenzied, hysterical, you know? He slapped me until he was breathless, and then, when he was finished, for the first time ever, I shouted back at him. She snorted a laugh. "I said he should get Old Pooty round and any other village elders, and they should have a stoning. I said that we hadn't had a burnt offering for a while and it was about time. I said— I said stuff like that and all of a sudden I wasn't afraid of him."

"Wow." I didn't know what to say. My erection was pressing against the seam of my jeans, and I felt bad getting turned on while she was recounting her miserable childhood. There's something stupid about a hard-on, the way it's so sort of happy with itself, stuffed with self-satisfaction, like a man determined to make a speech at an inappropriate moment: *Excuse me, excuse me. I just want to say a few words.*

"D'you want a drink, Wayne? I could do with a drink."

"Aye, me too."

"There's loads left over in the lounge."

"Wait here," I said, "I'll get something." I pushed off the bed so my back was turned by the time I was standing.

Annie was carrying empty glasses to the kitchen, and when she saw me she faked a smile. The living room had the smell of afterwards; the ashtrays were full, empty wine bottles stood shoulder to shoulder on the mantelpiece, and pistachio shells covered the tablecloth. The surviving snacks had been pushed onto one dish and covered with cellophane, and a single green olive sat on a paper plate. I took two plastic cups and a half-full bottle of Tia Maria and I didn't think to knock. I barged in and Lucy was bent over, pulling red satin pyjama bottoms past her knees. I said, "Shit, sorry."

She pulled them over her bum. "You're okay." With her back to me, she reached for her pyjama top, and her shoulder blades looked to me like tiny wings. She was yawning as she turned and fastened the buttons across her chest.

"Tia Maria?" she said. I shrugged, poured two half glasses and raised a toast to London. "To London," she said, tapping her cup against mine before pulling her hair free of her collar and shaking it down her back.

"Annie's on a domestic mission through there."

"She enjoys it, loves playing mum." She placed her cup on the side table and floated back on the white sheets, so her hair fanned out across the pillow and a gap opened between her pyjama bottoms and top. She lay there with her eyes closed and I wished I could think of something to talk about except her fucked up childhood. "So, you've never made up?"

"Hmm?"

"With your dad?"

"No, I stopped going to school after that. I was sitting my Highers that year and I studied in my bedroom. Then I turned sixteen, and after my exams, I left."

"Did he try to stop you?"

Lucy yawned. "My mum cried, I remember that. She cried and checked we were alone; then she gave me some money. And then, the most beautiful sight in Kinraddie: the bus south." The rest of the story, you already know. It's the plot of every High School drama: the geeky unpopular kid takes off her glasses; the ugly duckling becomes a swan.

After another drink, Lucy rolled onto her front, pulling herself onto her knees and flexing her back. Was it a deliberate thing? Did she want me to think of— Or was her back sore? Did she want me to rub her back? Was she saying she was tired? Did she want me to leave? "Oh God," she said, "it's after five."

"Sorry, sorry, you must have loads to do tomorrow."

"I'm sorry, Wayne. Christ, I'm knackered."

"Sorry, I better get going and give you some peace."

"Don't be daft; you're not walking home at this hour. You can crash here."

"You sure?"

"Of course." She slid under the sheets, leaving them folded open. I had a funny nicotine-rush feeling and took a second to balance myself. When Lucy saw that I wasn't moving, she patted the mattress, smiling to herself, perhaps aware of the roles we were now playing. Then I started undressing as fast as I could, feeling clumsy as I pulled my shoes and socks off, shaking and fumbling with the buttons on my shirt. We lay on our backs, on opposite sides of the bed, and she yawned again and said, "It's all a load of rubbish, you know?"

"What?"

"The Bible."

"Aye?"

"Mmm hmm. There's so much that doesn't make sense. Like, how does God make day and night before he makes the sun? And who does Cain marry? His mum? And when's the last time you saw a talking donkey outside of Numbers?" I moved closer, enjoying the coldness of the sheets. Lucy's bed smelled of coconuts and talcum powder, and her pillows smelled of hairspray. "But you... You can't get away from it, whether you believe it or not. You can't expunge two thousand years of Christianity from our understandings of the world, of sex, of ourselves. You can't escape from all the shit we've internalised."

"Suppose."

"That's the thing with sex," she said. "You can't have sexual liberation. Not really. You can't separate sex from the effects of power. Don't you think?"

"I don't know."

"What would be left? Without guilt and shame, without repression and unattainable desire, we'd be...." Lucy's eyes were closed and her breathing was slow.

"We'd be what?" I said.

"We'd be... copulating like frogs."

"They seem to enjoy it."

She stretched her legs under the covers. "Of course, some of it's just sick."

"Some of what?"

"The Bible."

"Aye?"

"Yes," she said, and it was the first time I'd heard her sound childish. She rolled her back to me, but as she did so, she held my hand and pulled my arm around her. It had surprised me the way she'd said "yes," in that cutesy voice, and I asked, "Like what?"

"Mmm?"

"In the Bible?"

"Oh. Let's see... Well, Judges is pretty sick."

"Yeah?"

"Mmm hmm. Like, this guy gives his... *concubine* to a mob, and they gang rape her, and abuse her, and she dies, which isn't very nice. And Jephthah kills his daughter, which isn't very nice either." I shuffled into the warm space behind her and burrowed my knees into the curl of her legs, worried and excited to think she could feel my erection pressing against her bum. "And," she said, "Moses orders the abduction of every Midianite virgin... Tamar has sex with her father-in-law, Judah... Lot gets pissed and fucks his daughters..." Then she rolled over so her lips were almost touching mine, and she whispered, in a very different voice, with the pause and the breath and the timing of a seductress, "It's really no wonder I turned out such a pervert."

And she was so *sleepy*! As we were kissing, her body went passive, and she rolled onto her back, into the dark shade on the far side of the bed. When I stroked her thighs, she murmured, "That's nice," but her eyes stayed shut. Then, as I started to touch her, she smiled and sighed and half-asleep she said, "There's... condoms. Under the bed. If you want to fuck me."

I felt a surge of excitement, as though all my fantasies had been added up, stuffed inside me, *making* me wrench her pyjamas to her knees, making me climb on top and push her legs apart. And yet, no matter how turned on you get, there's always some weird thought that tries to spoil things. I know I should have been concentrating on the moment, but the way she lay beneath me, all sleepy with her legs open, reminded me of a documentary

I saw once: it was about fairytales, and how, in the original version of Sleeping Beauty, Sleeping Beauty was raped.

Spocky was standing in front of the TV, as though at any second poised to turn it off. "You stayed at Lucy's?"

"What's going on there?"

"America," he said.

"What's happened?"

"I don't know. I just turned it on. You stayed at Lucy's?"

"Yeah," I said.

"..."

"What is this?"

"I don't know. Buzz phoned. He said, 'Are you watching TV? Turn the TV on.'" I moved forward so I could see the screen better. "Plane crashes into World Trade Centre." The camera was zooming in and out. You saw the towers and the blue sky and the smoke and the camera zoomed into the smoke and out again. "Did you and Lucy—" And that word "Live" dominating the screen. Unbelievably comic book somehow: they said that a plane had hit the tower and you could really see a plane-shaped crater. Then you saw the second plane dip and level and curve on its wing. "Did you—" It came from the edge of the screen and pointed its nose at the tower. You knew it was going to hit the tower, I think. You didn't have time to make that thought conscious, but when it hit the tower, it was what you expected. It almost seemed to go through the tower. You imagined some crazy stunt where it came out the other side and kept going. *Live?* You felt you had to respond but didn't understand what was happening and didn't want to be duped. You thought about that *War of the Worlds* radio hoax. The camera zoomed in, then out. You saw the blue sky and the fire and the smoke. They said it was *live*.

Thinking backwards, and still with a cautious scepticism, *if* it was real and *if* it was live, then you'd known about it before the people in the tower. And, for the first time, you thought about the people in the tower and the people in the plane. *If* it was real, if the planes were full, if the towers were occupied— If— People would have been killed, hundreds of people would have been killed and— there's no way they'd— they don't even show real *sex* on TV.

"Is this—"

" "
...

" "
...

"Hold on," I said. I switched channels.

"Wait, what happened there?"

I knew how to tell if it was real—if the BBC were showing the same thing then it had to be real because they were in competition with ITV and wouldn't— "World Trade Centre on fire: two planes have crashed into the World Trade Centre in New York, setting it on fire." The camera zoomed into the smoke and then back so you could see the towers and the blue sky, and then it zoomed back further, across the Hudson River, so you could see the Lower Manhattan skyline, the Goldman-Sachs HQ, the Woolworth Building—things you recognised.

★ 15 ★

More than a year later, in October 2002, Spocky and I stood out-side King's Cross Station, resting our boxes of leaflets on the taxi rank railing. Since arriving in London, we had studiously avoided conversation and eye contact. This was not unusual: soon after the Lucy incident, we had learned to avoid each other. We kept to our rooms and made our kitchen runs when we heard the toilet door lock. If I heard the kettle boiling while I was in the bath-room, I'd sit on the edge of the bathtub, until Spocky's bedroom door clicked shut, then I'd flush the toilet as if I'd just finished, and hurry back to my room. Even when Spocky said he was mov-ing out, I never told him what had happened.

Now, I was studying the kiosk vendor: he listened to a cus-tomer, ducked out of view, folded a newspaper, spoke, ducked out of view, passed something, and listened again. Two transport cops looked on. Buzz was struggling with an internet printout map, turning it round and round ("So, if we came out here, and that's that junction there, then the Camden Centre should be... No, hang on"); he and Spocky had travelled to London on the overnight coach, and they had met me on the station forecourt— I had taken the early train so I wouldn't have to travel with Spocky—rolling their shoulders and muttering, both irritable as card pyramids.

"I think we need to cross the road," said Buzz.

Spocky scooped his leaflets with an "*oooomph*," but I hung back a few paces, pretending to wrestle with my box. When I caught up with them on the halfway road island, I stood to the left so there was a woman with a pushchair between me and Spocky. I could see that he was talking to Buzz, but their words were obscured by a siren from near St. Pancras. When we reached the far side of the road, Buzz said, "Wait here while I piss," and pushed into Burger King.

I set my box on the pavement as Spocky kicked a bottle cap against the wall. The cap bounced, landed on its rim, and rolled, in a slow curve, across the pavement and into the gutter. After a moment, Spocky followed it and stood, box rested on the railing, gazing back at the station. I moved up to the window and peered through the reflected daylight. At the front table, a family ate with their heads down, their ketchup-fingered burger wrappers scrunched into balls. Behind them, a manager in a short-sleeved blue shirt escorted a homeless guy towards the door, guiding him, tracing an imaginary force field around his coat.

This is how the Anarchist Bookfair goes. At midday, you want to celebrate the libertarian tradition in all its diversity. After half an hour, you remember that anarcho-primitivists are mental. At one o'clock, you tell your mate, "If it's not class struggle, it can fuck off and play in the traffic." At three o'clock, you remember that Situationists are annoying, autonomist Marxists are boring, and platformists are Trotskyists in disguise. By five o'clock, it's only your old mates Dave and Jim who are even worth talking to. And at seven o'clock, you remember that Jim sprays everywhere after he's had a few, and Dave has an annoying habit of quoting Malatesta.

Fuck the lot of them.

There are weird people everywhere: girls with bullrings through their noses and dreadlocks thick as anchor ropes; boys with tall, flopping Mohicans; bookish men in raincoats; the Spartacist League—even crazier than the year before. People are reluctant to lower their political guard, so they ignore your leaflets, or they pause, suspicious, as if you're a circus performer who might squirt them with water.

No Way are you coming back next year.

"Fuck this," I said, "let's go for a pint."

"That's a poor level of commitment," said Lucy—no, if you're wondering, she hadn't fallen in love with me and we weren't now a couple. She had left Dundule as planned, and though she sent me e-mails with her news and smiley faces and exclamation marks to point out the jokes, this was the first time I'd seen her since that night.

Buzz waved his leaflets. "Aye, fuck this."

It has to be said that Spocky, who had escaped into the council communism meeting, was the only one of us with an activist work ethic. We probably would have left then had someone not crept up on me. She put her hands over my eyes and said, "Police, freeze!" I spun round, pushing her away—it was a *her*. She said, "You do not recognise me?"

Of course I did.

"You manage to stay off the railway tracks then?"

Her hair was in a black bob with a dyed red fringe and her voice was different—almost London sounding—but the little nose, the eyes like melted chocolate!

"You do not talk any more?"

"Fuck, it's good to see you. Why— How come you're here?"

"I live in London now."

"Wow, nice one." I was still smiling.

They were collecting donations at the door, shaking the buckets with a loud *rattle-thud-rattle-thud*. Someone shouted, "Manette, Manette!"

"Here, fuck off, cenit? I am talking here, yeah?"

Then I said—I've no idea why—"Are you still vegan?"

"Course I fuckeeng am."

"So am I." And it's not such an awful idea, is it? I could feel Buzz looking at me, screwing his face up, about to contradict me. He got as far as, "Man that is—" before Lucy kicked his heel. "This is Manette," I said. "She rescued me in Prague. Manette, this is my fellow worker Buzz, and this is Lucy, who used to work with us too."

Someone said, "Excuse me folks, we've found something like a suspicious sort of package thing, and people are thinking that maybe we should, like, get outside, just while we check out what it is."

"So, what is your leaflet?" asked Manette.

"Hey Manette, we're going outside cause they've found this fuckin weird thing—"

"Okay, fuckeeng go! Putain."

"Here," I passed her a leaflet. "It's an appeal for solidarity with industrial action we've got planned at Benny's."

"This is you? I have seen the website."

People started to move past us. Some were laughing, some going in the opposite direction, some making cartoon explosion noises. Someone said, "Ted Kaczynski hasn't got out, has he?" and people laughed. "This never happened at Conway Hall!" Others didn't know if they were really supposed to leave and stood at the side, holding papers, looking puzzled.

She turned the leaflet to see if there was anything on the reverse. "For how long you are in London?"

"Going back Monday."

"You want to do an interview tomorrow? My comrades and I have a website; you know enrager dot net?"

"Aye, sure."

"If you want, you come to mine, we do the interview? Maybe I give you something to eat."

"Brilliant, aye."

"Yes?" She put her backpack on the floor and bent over while she found a pen. She wrote on our leaflet, against her hand, and then gave it back to me. "Okay, this is my phone number. You need to get the tube to Highbury and Islington. You change onto the overground there. I write it down for you, okay? If we say, four o'clock, five o'clock? Something like this. Call me from the station; I come and get you." Then she joined the shuffle towards the door. "Hey Rob, you hippy wanker! I can't believe you plant a fuckeeng bomb just cause you hear they put whey powder in the crackers!"

Rob waved and shouted back. "I thought you done it cause they were selling instant coffee!"

"No justice, no peace!"

Then we were in daylight, among the juggling clubs and diabolo, the sound of a ghetto blaster and a drum, the empty cans of Super and the smell of marijuana. All around me, people were laughing and recognising their friends, sitting on the road and lighting cigarettes, and somehow, once again, I lost her in the crowd.

The next day, we met outside a greengrocer, where the pavement was scattered with big leaves, and a cauliflower lay bruised against the wheel of a car. Beneath a green awning, two Middle Eastern men sat in deck chairs, surrounded by crates of ginger and aubergines, fragrant bunches of browning coriander, and triangular piles of peppers and mangoes. Behind them, the dusty back of a tall fridge overlapped the doorway, and through the gap I could see shelves stocked with wine and beer.

"Welcome to beautiful Hackney!" said Manette, pointing at the glittering shards of glass that frosted the pavement beneath a vandalised bus shelter. The daylong gloom was easing towards evening; half-lit neon signs glowed dim above kebab shops, and the smell of charcoal reminded me that I'd told Manette I was vegan. Two kids rode past on small BMXs, knees up, muttering to each other from under hoods. A drunk staggered out of a pub and stood for a moment, checking he had all his limbs with him, before patting the side of his denim jacket, swaying on the spot, and meandering in the opposite direction. As we turned left down an Edwardian terrace, Manette nodded towards graffiti on a cracked limestone wall. "We have Turkish Tankies round here, eenit?"

We stopped at a gate that was stuck half open, beached on the stone pathway. A few tiles had fallen in the small patch of long grass, and the wheelie bin was decorated with a circled A and a squat sign. Against the wall, there rested an old bike. Its seat was missing and its front wheel was bent like a Salvador Dali clock face.

The door swept up junk mail as it opened. In the hallway, there were two rideable bikes beside a dusty piano. Towards the stairs, there was a small bookcase: Ackelsberg, *Free Women of Spain*; Hegel, *The Phenomenology of Spirit*; Tressell, *The Ragged Trousered Philanthropists*; Dauvé and Martin, *The Eclipse and Re-Emergence of the Communist Movement*. "Leave your bags here; we can take them up in a minute. Salut! Petite chatte, ma princesse! Comment ça va?" She squatted to stroke a little cat who had big brown eyes and a silly boa of white fur. "This is my cat I had since ten years. She been in this country a year and a half and she still don't speak fuckeeng English." The cat looked at us and yawned. "Oh, mon amour, tu as faim?" She kissed its nose. "Hey fuckeeng you foreign wankers?"

I followed her into the kitchen.

"Manette, ciao bella."

"You do not feed my fuckeeng cat?"

"Ah minchia, for me this cat is spoiled."

"Fuck off. Bastardo fascista. Nothing is too good for my kitten." She opened the fridge and removed a packet of smoked salmon.

The man stood up to shake my hand. "Welcome to our squat."

The cat meowed as Manette sliced the salmon into small pieces and scooped it into a silver-coloured bowl in the corner. "Federico, this is Wayne from Benny's Resistance Army."

"You feed your cat smoked salmon?"

"Fuckeeng right. Nothing is too good for my kitten, eenit?"

"She is checkout girl at Tescos," said Federico, settling back into his chair.

"*Girl*? I give you fuckeeng girl, you misogynist Italian wanker. When we need shopping him or Hristos come to the store, queue up at my till, and I pretend I do not recognise them. Then I pass all the expensive things over the scanner and beep the fuckeeng toilet roll and shit. They pay me seven pound and we eat like kings."

"That's quality!"

"Grande, nothing is too good for the working class."

"Where is Hristos?"

"Upstairs, I think he is in a sulk. Either that or he is making a bomb."

"Putain! What is wrong with him now?"

Federico shrugged. "Mah... the usual. It is raining. Gris won't fuck him. There is not enough struggle..."

Manette walked into the hallway and shouted "Hristos! Hey Hristos!" The cat yelped and trotted out of the kitchen and Manette returned with a shrug. "Bon. Scottish wanker, what you want to drink? You drink wine? Red? White?"

"Aye, whatever."

"You want to try this Côtes du Rhône?"

"Aye, sounds good."

"You want a glass, Federico?"

You could hear someone pounding down the stairs. "Mmmmm... Maybe a little to taste."

She threw the corkscrew at him as a stubbly man in a red vest and flip-flops appeared in the doorway. "Ei capo! Hristos Malaka, Come va?"

"Ciao Federico, tutto bene?"

"Bene Hristos, bene."

"You want something to eat, malaka?"

Hristos shrugged and sat opposite Federico. "What you are cooking?"

"Vegan slop," said Federico, popping the cork out of the wine.

"Fuck you."

"Maybe a little to taste," said Hristos.

"Sorry," said Federico, "you did not meet before? This is Wayne from Benny's Resistance Army."

"Ah, the syndicate," said Hristos, stretching across the table to shake my hand. "Hristos."

Federico found clean glasses and poured the wine.

I passed a cigarette to Manette but Hristos shook his head and Federico preferred to smoke his Lucky Strikes.

"Hey Souvarine, you been fighting the fuckeeng bus shelter? Chaos in the city, eenit?" She held her first and last fingers up like a metal-head at a gig.

"Fart on my balls."

"Aw, Hoffendahl, you are sad? Gris still not fuck you?" Manette was talking with her back to us, dicing onions.

"Salute," said Federico, raising his glass.

"I am fucking pissed off."

"Awww, bébé, pourquoi?"

Hristos sighed and started to skin up. "In this country, our class is defeated. There is no spirit in the people, no fight."

"Hristos, my friend, is not just this country."

"Óhi, is different in Italy. Is different in France. Listen, next year Greece has the presidency of the EU, yes? You come for the manifestation and you will see how is anarchism in Greece. But in England? That book fair yesterday, it piss me off. Why is it that in Britain there is so many fucking pacifist and hippies?"

"Aha," said Federico, slapping his hand on the table. "This I can explain. In Sicily we say something like: 'If you plant corn you don't expect to harvest peppers.' You see? It is like this. Activists, they organise some event—meeting, manifestation, whatever— and they want people to turn up, see? But they have only so much money so they can make only so many leaflets. So to make the most use of these, they give the leaflets to the sort of people they imagine will come to the event, you see? They give a leaflet to a girl who is a punk or to some fucking hippy. They do not give it to the worker, the mother, the OAP, the man in a suit. Then, you see, when the punk and the hippy come to the event, and the others they do not, this prove the punk and the hippy were the sort of people likely to come. You plant corn, you get corn."

"Is an interesting theory," said Hristos.

PEACE, LOVE & PETROL BOMBS

"It's fuckeeng stupide!" said Manette, tossing the contents of the saucepan.

"Olé!"

The pan sizzled and the room smelled of fried garlic and onion. "I will tell you why this is. It is the fault of all you fuckeeng insurrectionists—"

"Minchia, I'm a Marxist!"

"You are a fuckeeng ultra-leftist intellectual wanker. I mean Bonanno in the corner. Ravachol over there."

"Fart on my balls."

"Johann fuckeeng Most and his mates. All you activist know that capitalism is stupide and that the revolution would make it all better and you think if you can explain this to people then they will be active in "the movement," or the riot, the insurrection, whatever it is you want. Only the anarcho-syndicalists—"

Hristos threw his head back and laughed. "Here we go. Only the syndicalists what? Join the government?"

"Understand that this thinking is all wrong, is fuckeeng stupide. Because people know that, as the individual, them "being active" will not bring about the revolution or anything else. I mean, the people cannot decide as a block, en masse, no? And for the individual it only make sense to go into activism if you think you get some other benefit, like you make new friend or something."

The little cat had reappeared and was licking its paw on the kitchen step as Federico laughed and stubbed his cigarette out. "Is this why you struggle—to make friends?"

"No, you fuckeeng asshole, it is because my desire for a full life is so strong it make me do crazy things that do not make sense even to me."

"Stinyássas," said Hristos.

Hours later, when I was well fed, half-pissed, and slightly stoned, Manette said she would walk me to the bus stop. The rain was heavier now and the pavement glistened yellow in the streetlight. At the corner of her road, where a large puddle had formed, she reached through a privet hedge and dropped a coin into a Styrofoam cup. "That fuckeeng old guy, he always sleep behind this bush. He never speak, I don't think he can, and he fuckeeng smell. But it's sad, you know?"

The only other person at the bus shelter was a big black woman in a blue hospital uniform, who shuffled from foot to foot and shook her keys inside her jacket pocket. I watched the raindrops hit the bus shelter, merge with each other and zoom across the glass. Eventually, I said, "You got work tomorrow?"

"Yes, the fuckeeng early. All day at work then I have to go to the anti-war meeting. I will be exhausted."

"Shite, sorry; don't let me keep you up."

"Ah no," she made a dismissive gesture with her hand.

"You're lucky there's so much going on in London."

"You think?"

"In Dundule, three men and a flag constitute an upsurge in class struggle."

"Well, if you want to move to London then you know we have a spare room."

"Aye? We've got contacts at loads of stores here; we could do with someone based here. You know, like, help organise stuff."

"Yes? Well I am sure you would be welcome. The room is not really a room; it is more like a cupboard. But it sit there empty, and you do not seem too much of an asshole."

"Cheers."

"And there is no rent; we pay some bill but it is not so much."

A man walked past, wearing his umbrella low like a hat, and then the bus appeared as a light in the distance. "Fuckeeng Hell, normally you have to wait forever." We watched the bus approach until we could hear its engine. "Well, thank you for the interview."

"No, thank you for everything, all the food and bevvy and that."

"Bien sûr, nothing is too good for the working class." Manette walked forward, held my sleeve, hesitated. Then she rocked onto her tiptoes and pecked my cheek. "If you want the room, you let me know, yes?"

"Aye, definitely."

"You can e-mail me: princesscasamassima at yahoo dot com."

"Princess what?"

"Or just phone me, or text, whatever." The nurse walked to the curb and held her arm out. The bus slowed and indicated, windscreen wipers wagging as I stepped inside. "Stay away from trains, okay?"

Reader, I moved in with her.

★ 16 ★

The night I moved in, after dinner, Federico did the dishes, and Hristos tried to explain modern Greek history. "Next year you come for the manifestation, you will see—in Greece the police are not allowed on any university campus."

"Blah blah fuckeeng blah."

"This come from when we overthrow the American junta. Papadopoulus."

"If Greece is so fuckeeng wonderful, why you live here, eenit?"

"You know about the insurrection at the Polytechnic of Athens? They send the tanks and the soldiers into the Polytechnic and they kill many of the students. This was November 17th, 1973. Is why the November 17th group are called this."

Federico was at the sink with a tea towel over his shoulder. "Minchia Hristos, you notice I do not have to tell every person who come to the house about the Movement of '77? Or the FIAT Hot Autumn or the Ronde Operaie or—"

"This is history. In Greece we still have the student movement. We still have the working class militants."

"Ignore him, Wayne; the closest he come to the working class is when he burn their fuckeeng cars."

"Si, but is closer than he comes to Gris, I think." Federico smiled and tapped his palm with the top of his fist.

"Every year on November 17th there is the commemoration of the massacre, and for the anarchists it is a chance for revenge against the police. Always we make the fight; always we have the molotovs."

"Mais non! Quelle surprise!" She laughed and poured more wine and Federico covered his glass with his hand in case she tried to force some in.

"I make the best molotovs. Is almost sad to burn them."

"Yeah yeah, you fuckeeng toto. Wayne, you know the joke of the two Greek anarchist? They are making petrol bombs and one of them say, 'What we throw these at anyway?' And the other guy he say, 'What are you, a fuckeeng intellectual?'"

"Fart on my balls."

"How many Greek anarchist does it take to change a light bulb?"

"Two," said Federico. "One to buy a new bulb and one to burn the hardware shop."

"Malaka, where is my lighter?"

Federico ran water round the sink and dried the work surface with the tea towel. "Hristos, my friend, capitalism is a social relation; it is the extraction of surplus value from labour. The proletariat is at once the expression and the negation of the existing society. This is why—"

"Where is my lighter?"

Manette lit two candles and threw the lighter to Hristos.

"Minchia, you cannot burn a social relation. For me, the problem is not the conditions of labour or even the distribution of wealth; it is the alienation of our lives in a world where activity is dictated by capital. This is the problem."

"Tomorrow this will be the problem," said Hristos, pocketing his lighter as he stood up. "Tonight I go to bed... Jerk off, think of Gris..."

"I don't want to fuckeeng know!"

"Si, si, Hristos, you are right. It is late and we should leave these lovers."

"Fuck off."

"You have wine, hashish, candles; you want some music?"

"Fuck off you fuckeeng Italian wanker!"

"I sing for you? *Nessun Dorma! Tu pure, o Principe—*"

"I fuckeeng kill you, Federico!"

Hristos made kissing noises as he shuffled out of the room and Federico followed, still singing and tapping his palm with his fist.

"I kill you in your fuckeeng sleep, malaka. À demain! Sorry about those assholes." She finished her wine with two big gulps, stood up, and opened a cupboard door. "What we drink next? You want absinthe?"

Manette didn't have to work in the morning and long after Hristos and Federico had gone to bed, we stayed at the table, drinking and smoking, until the candles were rooted in the empty wine bottles, and we could hear birds singing. Maybe it was the fear of what to do next that kept us there.

When I got up to pour a glass of water, Manette lit a cigarette in the candle flame and stood beside me, her back against the sink. "In France we say: if there is a good atmosphere in the room then the candles burn brightly."

We were only a foot apart, and the way she was looking at me, I knew what was about to happen. I don't mean I was conscious of it; I knew it the way that sometimes, when you listen to a CD, a song finishes and you can already hear the opening bars of the next tune, even if you could never recite the tracks in order. This was how she looked at me. It was a look that belonged in an old film: a symphony look that made me swallow and close my eyes.

This was the kiss. You know those kisses? When we kissed like that, it seemed that history was speeding up.

Those first nights she clung to me as if we were sharing a parachute. She kept me so warm; she woke just to check I had enough covers and she said I always slept with my left shoulder exposed. She asked about my scar and I told her about when I was stabbed. She said, "Scars are wonderful things," and she showed me where she had tried to cut her wrists as a teenager.

"Why?"

"I don't know; it was another life."

"You must have some idea."

"Not really. I cannot feel like this person, think like this person, or know this experience any more than the next asshole. But, I have this mark here and it mean there is some... something like... continuité. Probably not continuité, but maybe some connection at least. This is why I think scars are special."

"Suppose." Sometimes I remember when I got stabbed and it feels like it happened to someone else.

"Tattoos are similar but I think never quite as good."

I asked her about the scar on her cheekbone.

"I try to cover it with my hair now."

"You shouldn't; it's pretty."

"You are not some fuckeeng S and M weirdo, are you?"

"No!"

"This is from very long ago. Most of it I only know from what other people have told me, but I'm sure I remember my rabbit. I think at one point I said I would never leave the farm in case something happen to him. I was just a fuckeeng toddler. Then one day, after dinner, I was doing the washing up and... I used to wear this... pinafore?"

"Aye."

"It was too long for me so that it would trail around my feet. And my fuckeeng father, he said we had just eaten my rabbit. I ran out of the flat and trip on this pinafore and I hit my face on the stair. When the neighbours find me, I was hiding in this bush where I liked to go. They hear me crying and see me all covered in blood and they think this is why I cry, but I cry because while I was crawling under the bush, I have caught my bracelet and it snap. And I was so proud of it. It was plastic trinkets on a thread, and the thread snap and the neighbours find me crying over these plastic jewels in the dirt. All covered with blood."

"What did they do?"

"I don't know, Petit Fantôme. I suppose they took me to my parents. But I don't remember any of this. When I think about it, the thing with the bracelet, this was in Paris, so maybe it was nothing to do with the rabbit. Maybe that was earlier. Who fuckeeng knows. But the scar says, 'This was you.' The scar says that I was once a child."

"Why d'you call me 'Petit Fantôme'?"

"You have never heard of *Le Petit Fantôme*?"

"No."

"The little ghost? It was my favourite story when I was a child."

"So why d'you call me that?"

"Cause you so fuckeeng white! In Scotland, do you live in darkness?"

I laughed and kissed her cheek. "What's your first memory?"

She shrugged on the pillow. "What's yours?"

"I think I can mind being in a pram. Just the sunlight coming through the trees. Like I'm in the park or something."

"Yes, this is my first memory also."

"And that one?"

"Is where I got my appendix removed, you wanker."

I kissed her tummy. I wanted to fuck again already.

Most nights, most towns are only quiet for a little over an hour. Until four, the clubbers and partygoers are meandering home; after five, the streets are busy with joggers and delivery-staff. Leaving her at 4:05 was the hardest thing. I suppose I didn't tell her because I knew she would want to come—maybe Federico and Hristos too. I imagined her breaking the windows. Hristos throwing petrol bombs.

The night feels so fucking cold when you should be in bed. From streets away, I heard the vibrations of a taxi, its doors closing, the rise and fall of its engine. The only other noise was my footfalls and the rattle of spray paint. It wasn't raining, but the air was so wet that I could feel it on my face. A taxi burst through the night, *shooshing* surface water off the road, blustering with light. Far away, a siren echoed the darkness.

I found Benny's without checking the map. A mail van passed. I thought I heard footsteps, so I kept going, walked on past. Round the block, still not sure what to write. I wanted to write something I'd never written before. Something that meant everything we thought all scrunched up in a few words.

The second time, I heard nothing. I checked the cars were empty. Looked around. Metal shutters covered all the other shopfronts. There was a light on across the road. I could hear a taxi, but it was getting quieter. I tied my scarf over my face and pulled my cap down, shaking the paint. *Rattle-rattle-rattle*. So fucking loud! Once I'd started, I didn't look round, like how a sprinter doesn't look over his shoulder. I wrote red letters on the windows, over the door, across the whitewashed wall:

FUCK THE ECONOMY
THE WORLD IS OURS

It felt like I'd been painting for hours. As I was drawing the BRA tag at the bottom, I already knew that this wasn't what I wanted to say. I threw the spray can into a bush. This wasn't it. There were vans on the road, too fast to stop. I picked up a rock and threw it—thumbs up for the camera. I was running when it hit the glass. Into the night, running like a puma. *Da-da-da da-dadara, Darada ra-d-da, da-da-dara, Here comes Johnny, Yeah!* I was running so fast that I forgot to be out of breath.

I creaked open our bedroom door, but Manette was already awake. She was resting against the headboard, in a T-shirt that said "Barcelona 36." She threw her book on the floor. "Petit Fantôme! Thank fuck! Where have you been? Come here."

I sat on the bed with my back to her and pulled off my Sambas. "Just went out to leave a message for Benny's." I was smiling such a big stupid smile that I was glad she couldn't see it.

"I was fuckeeng worried for you," she said, kissing me behind the ear. Then she grabbed me by the collar and pulled me backwards. It was a stronger tug than I'd have thought her capable of, and I sprawled onto the covers with my head on her lap. "You listen to me you fuckeeng Scottish cunt!" She grabbed my wrist and gave me a Chinese burn, twisting my skin really hard. "You ever fuckeeng do that again, you ever fuckeeng leave me that way again, I fuckeeng kill you, you fuckeeng wanker!" She was digging her nails in, and I was wriggling, trying to get loose. Then she had a hold on my ear, twisting it, like adults do to children in old stories.

"Ow! Dinnae! Fuck off!" It was really fucking sore and I had no idea why this was happening.

"You fuckeeng asshole, you ever do that again, I swear I break your fuckeeng legs!"

I elbowed her in the stomach, just a nudge to get her off my ear. Then she was on her knees, punching me on the side of the head, in the face, on the arm. "You ever fuckeeng leave me like that again, you cunt, you fucker!" I was curled on the bed, head in my arms. Then the blows stopped.

"Manette?"

Through my arms, I watched her light a cigarette. She slapped the lighter on the bedside table as if it was the decisive hand in a dead-serious game of cards.

"What the fuck was that for?"

She was panting, watching the smoke swirl in the lamplight before disappearing into the dark corners of the room. "Because I fuckeeng love you, you wanker! You stupide cunt! I fuckeeng love you!" There were tear trails on her cheeks. "I love you Wayne and I want to protect you and I don't want you to ever leave me that way again."

"I'm sorry," I said, and pulled myself next to her. I asked if I could take a cigarette.

"Of course you can! You do not have to ask me for things like this."

"Sorry."

"Stop fuckeeng saying sorry!"

"Sorry."

She laughed and then we smoked for a minute. "Oh, Petit Fantôme, you are bleeding." She pointed at the bedclothes and then saw the blood on my lip.

"Shite, sorry."

"It was me that has fuckeeng punched you, you wanker!" She placed a finger on my lip, to check if it was swollen or to shut me up, and then she kissed me, soft as sleep.

Ever since I moved to London, I've suffered a recurring nightmare. The police are chasing me, and though I'm not aware of having committed any particular crime, I know that I mustn't be caught. A description of me statics over a police radio, and I start to power-walk, head down. In Piccadilly Circus, above the Coca-Cola sign, below the golden arches, there is a giant picture of my face. It starts to flash.

I jump on a bus, but as soon as I sit down, I can see the driver watching me in the mirror. The bus stops and he won't tell me why. We're waiting at the side of the road and he won't open the doors. When I force them, he shouts at me and I run and keep running until I'm at the train station. It's not King's Cross. It could be Waterloo, or maybe Liverpool Street. It's filled with people, so many it makes me dizzy. I'm no longer watching from inside myself but can see the scene as though I'm in a film. I can see myself through CCTV cameras. I can see different angles. I can see distant shots where I look lost amidst all the people in the concourse. I can see zoom shots, where my face is so big that I can see every eyelash. I can see all of this on the monitors in police-busy security rooms.

It's not yet time for my train—I never know the destination of this train, though I know I need to wait for it—so I order a coffee and sit in a quiet spot. There's a green rucksack under the table. I take it to the counter and I say, "Someone must have left this." The barista thanks me. He is a Spanish boy with curly black hair. He is about to put the rucksack away when a white man, a customer, says, "I heard a security announcement; we're to look out for anybody with a Scottish accent acting strange." The barista drops the bag and steps back.

I run up the escalator, pushing between people. I run into the underground, taking the stairs two at a time. Without looking, I know I've lost my travel card and all my money, so I hurdle the barrier. The security guards shout and chase me. Behind them are the men who have followed me on CCTV. We're all running down the escalator, pushing through other passengers. I can see us on the cameras. I go left then right, up stairs, down stairs, Piccadilly, Bakerloo, Westbound, Northbound—

My arm itches. I pull up my sleeve and there's something glowing orange under my skin. When I peer into it I can see someone watching me. It's a tag, some sort of tag. I start to rip at my arm with my nails. I want to cut my arm off; I'm looking for something that can cut my arm off. I want to throw myself in front of a train, anything to get the tag out.

Of course, at that point, I always wake up. The first time I had this dream, I never even made it to the train.

I was running down the escalator, they were just behind me, and then Manette was shaking me and whispering, "Police, Wayne, police."

And in the passage from one reality to another, I realised the police were not on the escalator, or at least *I* was not on the escalator. Instead, Manette was leaning over me, already dressed, pressing her finger against her lips. "Shhh, Petit Fantôme, shhhh."

"What?" The light was bright through the curtain.

"Police... Hello? Police..." They were shouting through the letterbox and their voices came into the hall and climbed the stairs, so that at first I thought they were at the door to our bedroom. Manette was smoking and she never smoked before breakfast.

"What's going on?"

"Outside," she said. "Look." She pulled the corner of the curtain an inch to the side of the frame. "Careful."

The road was crawling with them, swarming with them, black and yellow like wasps. "How the fuck?" I said, rolling out of bed, tugging my jeans on, looking for yesterday's socks.

There was a knock on our bedroom door. "Hey, Manette?"

She opened the door as I buttoned my jeans.

"Minchia, have you seen my glasses? What the fuck is going on?"

"Wayne fuck up Benny's last night."

Federico shrugged. "But who knows he is here?"

"Where the fuck did I put my shoes?"

"Oh, Petit Fantôme, your lip is swollen!"

"Eviction?"

"This place has been squatted for years."

The beating on the door started again, but it was louder this time. "We have to show this building is occupied," said Federico.

"I'm not answering it, not after that thing at Lockheed Martin."

I was pulling my trainers on as Hristos thudded down from the top floor.

"Hristos malaka."

"They must have got us on camera."

"Minchia Hristos, what have you done?"

"After the meeting last night, me and Carlos, we fuck up the Army Recruitment place. I am going out the bathroom window and over the wall."

"That is stupid, Hristos."

"Then you stay, make them espressos."

"Hristos, wait for me," I said.

"I come with you, Petit Fantôme."

"Police... Hello? Police..."

Hristos ran to the bathroom, dodging through the doorway.

"Someone has to answer the fucking door!"

"You fuckeeng answer it then."

I hadn't tied my laces, but I followed Hristos.

"I can't find my glasses."

"You don't need your glasses to answer the door. Petit Fantôme, wait!"

The window was ajar and Hristos stood on the toilet seat, peeking through the lace curtain as Federico ran down the stairs, shouting "Vaffanculo stronzo!"

We queued behind Hristos, Manette brushing her teeth, saying something incomprehensible through a foaming mouth.

"How's it looking?"

The front door opened.

Manette spat into the sink and dropped her toothbrush. "Go on then, you asshole."

Hristos pushed the frosted glass into the morning. He swung one leg over the edge and looked for a foot hold.

We could hear the police talking to Federico. They said something about homicide.

"Homicide?" said Manette, looking at Hristos.

His head was through the window but his arse was still in the bathroom.

The door closed. "Minchia. Hey, malakas! Hey!" Federico ran up the stairs, arriving pink-faced in the bathroom doorway, smiling and shaking his head.

"Well?"

"You sons of bitches! Is not for any of you."

"I think I am stuck," said Hristos from outside the window.

For a few seconds, we were laughing. "So, it's alright?" I asked.

"No, not really," said Federico. "You know the old tramp, the homeless man who sleep across the road?"

"Yes," said Manette, "in the hedge."

"They find his body on the road."

"No."

"Si."

"Shit."

"Yes, is very sad. They think it is a murder."

"Shit. What do they ask you?" said Hristos, clambering back through the window.

"They just try to move the car outside. They think maybe it is ours."

"That's it?"

"Yes."

"Not much of a murder inquiry."

"No," he said.

"Fucking gourounea."

"Minchia, I make some coffee."

After Manette and I moved to France, I only once returned to the squat. By then, it was almost two years since the tramp's death, but his bedding was still there, melting into the earth beneath the hedge. Privet saplings grew through his blankets, and a refuse sack was stretched between branches, torn and separated from whatever it had once held. The puddle at the roadside had also remained, swollen around a blocked drain. I watched the rain drops throw rings on the surface as the wind gusted and a squashed Marlboro Box sailed for shore. But when I reached my former house, though I recognised the wheelie bin with the circled A and the squat sign, and the bike with one bent wheel, the windows and door were covered with the sort of metal guards that the council use to keep crack-heads out of abandoned properties. I stood for a moment, amazed that this could have happened without me even knowing about it, and then I threw my hold-all on the wet ground and dialled Federico's mobile number. "The number you have called is not recognised. Please check the number. If you need help, please call the operator on one hundred." Instead, I called Lucy. She answered the phone, saying her full name, proper official sounding. "It's Wayne," I said.

"Oh my God, how are you? Where are you?"

"I'm in London. I'm in London and I need some help."

★ 17 ★

In June 2003, Manette and I travelled from London to Thessaloniki. We arrived on a train from Belgrade, which creaked and hissed, straining to stop at the platform. Doors swung open and from different carriages a dozen people emerged into the morning heat. Two men jumped from the first carriage, laughing as they ran down the steps free of luggage. A family passed laundry bags from the train and cursed the broken handles, holding them underarm where the checked canvas had split and pots and children's toys nosed into the sunshine.

It was cool in the station building—fans motored; a man in a long winter coat picked cigarette butts from the dark slabbed floor—but outside, Thessaloniki sweltered in the morning sunshine. Bus drivers in big sunglasses leant against their vehicles, and nine policemen loitered by a small office. The police looked up as Manette threw her rucksack into the shade, but they slumped back into conversation as she unzipped the top pocket and tugged out her guidebook.

I sighed and leant my rucksack against the wall.

"What," she said, lifting her sunglasses onto her hairline, "you know the way?" We had slept on trains the previous two nights, and dots of stubble had reclaimed her armpits. "Fuckeeng shut up then." Beyond the buses, through the haze, cars paused at traffic lights. Engines revved. Now and then a horn sounded. Manette folded the book, trapping the page with her finger, and then she lifted her rucksack and walked into sunshine that hurt my eyes.

"You sure?"

"You want to study the map?" She must have been exhausted; during the night, I had slept on her lap, and so I wouldn't wake, she had cupped her hands over my ears whenever the train had roared through a tunnel.

In Platía Yardhari, the leaves of trees looked lush above the scorched yellow grass, and the smell of roasting vegetables mixed with the background pong of stalled sewage. There were posters, pasted to walls and stuck on electricity boxes, with pictures of masked figures throwing petrol bombs, and a caption in English: "We promise a warm welcome for the leaders of Europe."

Flanked by tall pastel-coloured buildings with balconies at every floor, Odhós Egnatías is a wide road with three lanes on either side of the central reservation. We crossed to the shady side, where a waitress struggled with a parasol, and her colleague dragged metal chairs scratching across the pavement. Manette stopped to read the menu, but it was all in Greek. "Are you hungry?"

I shook my head. "Need some water but."

"We should eat also."

We walked in silence for a few minutes before Manette pointed ahead. "Look, Petit Fantôme, up there, that must be the..." She turned the page in her guidebook. "The Arch of Galerius."

"Oh aye?" I dropped my rucksack in the shade and my T-shirt stuck to my skin. Around the arch's abutments, bikes rested against green railings, and English tourists walked this way then back again, studying carvings that had softened with time. When we pulled our rucksacks on, we both laughed and grimaced as cold sweat licked the length of our backs.

We walked another fifty yards until Manette stopped at a street kiosk. She checked her guidebook and mouthed the words to herself as she stepped to the counter.

"Oríste?"

"Dhío neró parakaló," she said, pointing.

"Dhío? You want two?" said the man, holding up two fingers.

Manette nodded and passed a note as the seller looked in his money belt for change.

On the far side of the road, audible between cars, Avril Lavigne sang on a crackly radio, as workmen fixed corrugated aluminium across the windows of Benny's Burgers.

"Look, Benny's," I said.

"They fuckeeng expect us then." When the sun hit the unpainted shutters, the metal glowed as if on fire.

From the third floor of Aristotle University there hung a black banner as big a penalty box, on which was painted "SMASH CAPITALISM" in giant white letters. Loudspeakers played "A Las Barricadas" through an open window and out into the noise of the street. But once we were on the campus, behind the Theology Department, it was all soft-paced and calm. In a square of grass criss-crossed by concrete paths, topless men finished constructing a stage, while others stretched on the yellow turf, or sipped water in the shade beneath trees, holding their arms out when ever they felt some breeze. Manette fixed on a man in a white vest, who was smoking a roll up at the entrance to the refectory. She crept up behind him, placing her hands over his eyes. "Arrette, Police!"

He kicked his chair back and spun round. "Manette, Salut! Tu va bien?"

"Ça va malaka?"

He put his arms around her waist, swinging her feet off the ground as he kissed her cheeks.

"Comment va Paris?"

"Plus de la même chose: grève à la SNCF; grève dans les écoles."

"Sounds about right. I fuckeeng miss it, you know?"

His hands still held her shoulders with an easy intimacy that made me think that at one time they had been lovers. Eventually, Manette introduced me and Alex clasped my hand as though we were about to arm wrestle. "Come inside, please. You can leave the bags here."

The room was empty except for a scatter of chairs and a giant drum of water. Alex pulled a can of Amstel from the drum and the water lapped the sides and the cans bobbed like rowing boats. "You want beer? They take all the refrigerators so we keep them cold like this. They take everything from this building, all the computers, everything. But in the Law Building, across there, we have Indymedia Centre, and this is also the base for the medics."

"Wow."

"Yes." We sat with our beers: Manette and Alex sat on plastic chairs; I sat cross-legged on the cool tiled floor. Alex was in his mid-twenties with dark hair almost as short as his stubble. He had the build of a medium-weight boxer, but there was something quiet about the way he sat. "They learn that we will squat this building and they plan to build gates and hire private security. So we go to the Dean of Theology and we say: One way or another we occupy this building. Either you give us the keys and we stay here, look after it, and next term you still have the building; or, we fight your security, we smash our way in, we break everything, and we burn it before we leave. After this, he give us the keys. Anyway, welcome. Stinyássas. To a hot summer." We tapped our cans together and drank. "So, how you come, by plane?"

"Nah, train. We met some comrades in Belgrade yesterday, then came down overnight."

"Is good this way, I think. No problems at the border?"

"Nah, no search or anything."

"And the Serbian comrades, they come also?"

"They cannae get visas, can they?"

"Po-po-po. This is very important. Tomorrow night—tonight is big party, we have bands playing, we drink, we have fun—but tomorrow night we make manifestation for solidarity with the sans-papier, you know?"

"That's tomorrow night?"

"Yes, yes. Is not us who organise this, but is our friends from Athens. We make the manifestation in the suburbs, where is the homes of many Albanians and other immigrants, so is very important that we do not make the fight then. Not because we are pacifist, but because we do not want to damage the neighbourhood of our Albanian brothers and sisters, you see? Then next day we make the main manifestation, and where we find the police in the most number, there we attack. With the sticks, with the stones, and with the fire."

In the afternoon, we explored the university and the streets outside. It was summer vacation; bushes grew unpruned and weeds squeezed between paving stones. Political slogans and posters advertising long-passed demonstrations covered the walls. The university buildings were concrete with big windows that reflected the sun, and in-between these modern blocks there were half-excavated Roman remains: the base of a column, an engraved flagstone, a knee-high wall. Near the Law Department, beneath a sunshade suspended between two trees, a man in shorts cooked stew in a big pot, and behind him two women descended a grassy slope, weaving between tents, clambering over guy ropes.

In the evening, we bought red wine and plastic cups, and we sat on the grass with Alex. On the stage, a punk band hacked through a sound check. Then they shrugged and jumped onto the grass, leaving their instruments leaning in the sunshine and the square quiet except for the hum of a Vespa. I watched the riders approach, their shirts billowing as the girl held the boy round the waist. They stopped outside the Theology Building, and everyone looked as they removed their helmets.

"Hey Stavros!"

"Alex, malaka!"

As those around me returned to their conversations, I lay on my back and let the sun shine orange through my eyelids.

I fell asleep like that, and when I woke the sun had gone and people were standing up, pointing and shouting, as a crowd—maybe fifty people—rushed past the Theology Building. They had a road sign on a metal pole, and they were whooping with wild energy.

"You are awake," said Alex, slapping me on the back.

"Look," said Manette. "Hristos!"

"You know these malakas?" asked Alex, rolling a cigarette.

People ran from the tents, chanting *"No justice, no peace! Fight the police!"* They swarmed around the steps of the Philosophy Building, and Manette held my hand as we ran towards them. She called out to Hristos, but the crowd was too loud. There was something of the medieval siege about it; the metal pole, still with the no-left-turn sign attached, was being used as a battering ram. It swung backwards and forwards, held by more hands than there was room for. Then the door crashed open and the crowd cheered and surged forward. I could hear smashing before we were all inside. As we ran through the corridors, a punk hit light bulbs with a stick. Someone let off a fire extinguisher. Near the front door, where a noticeboard had been ripped off the wall, a man in a black vest sprayed big letters: "We don't forget. We don't forgive. Carlo vive."

We didn't realise how many people were in the university until the immigration demo. Then they streamed from every building. There were thousands of us—four, five-thousand of us—squeezing through the university gates, hoisting flags. Some wore bandannas but most didn't. Some had cameras swinging from their necks and others held cans of beer. Some were running at the side of the march, spray painting the wall of a church. You wanted to scramble to the highest point so you could see it all.

Then, at the crossroads, we saw riot police in the side streets. They were dressed in green uniforms and white helmets, and they held their shields to their chins. Young anarchists ran forward to throw bottles. They stood in the road, swearing and taunting, until their friends put arms round their necks and pulled them back. Sometimes, the police ran forward, shouting and gesticulating, until they were restrained by their colleagues. It was getting hotter and hotter. When the march roared as one, the noise left you feeling winded. "BATSI! GOUROUNEA! DO-LO-FONÉ! BATSI! GOUROUNEA! DO-LO-FONÉ!" Cops, Pigs, Murderers! Cops, Pigs, Murderers! Louder and louder, until you heard it with your whole body and your insides shook.

In the evening, the sun slipped behind the Theology Building, and the darkness seemed to grow out of the shadows. A smell of petrol settled over the university, and we talked so quietly you could hear the chink of empty bottles and the lawnmower buzz of cicadas. "I have heard," said the American guy, pausing and looking behind him, "that there was a meeting in the Philosophy Building, a meeting of insurrectionists, who say they plan to kill a cop in revenge for Carlo."

"Fuck," said the English guy.

"This is the shit I'm talking about, man!" Welsh Rob stretched his legs out on the Labrador-coloured grass. "This is what I'm saying to you; half the people here are fucking crazy. Look," he said, whispering now, bird-like the way he pecked around for danger, "there are guys staying here who have outstanding warrants for fucking serious shit. I mean, straight to jail shit. Do not pass go, do not collect two hundred pounds shit. Membership of banned organisations, kidnapping, explosives, arson. Decades in jail shit, right?" A Vespa tore through the quiet, and the engine grabbed a breath as the driver changed gears. "And these guys are going out tomorrow, carrying hand guns—"

"You are fuckeeng scared, Rob."

"Yeah, I'm fucking scared. These guys are carrying pistols because they don't plan on being taken alive. That's too much heat, man."

"You sound like a fuckeeng scared hippy."

"If someone shoots a cop, they'll gun us down. Forget rubber bullets, they're gonna—"

"Nobody shoot a fuckeeng cop. No wonder you so scared; you believe every rumour you hear. Listen, the last time I am at Hyde Park, an old man tell me that the fuckeeng world end on Friday."

"So?"

"So you believe every rumour you never leave the house, eenit?"

"Look," said the English guy, pointing at a stripy gecko on the wall of the Theology Building.

"I'm not a pacifist," said Rob. "I was with the black bloc in Genoa, but I'm staying away from that shit tomorrow."

Manette stood up, kicking the pins and needles out of her legs. "As long as you have my fuckeeng dinner ready when I get back. I go to find Hristos." She threw her cigarette away and walked towards the Philosophy Building.

"And you?" asked the English guy. I shrugged and ran after Manette.

"Fuckeeng hippy wanker. As long as I know him he is crying about police brutality, but as soon as anyone start fighting back, he fuckeeng run away." The Philosophy Building was guarded by a man in an unbuttoned sleeveless shirt, who sat on a broken wooden chair, chewing gum and tapping his palm with a short club. Inside, our feet crunched on broken glass. The paint fumes made you feel drunk, and the slogans were hard to read because so many lights were broken. "By any means necessary." "The Future is Unwritten." "Ultras AEK." "No War Between Nations, No Peace Between Classes." The shadows, and the people in the shadows, and the closed doors, carried the suggestion of an ambush, so I found myself looking left and right, as if crossing a road.

Climbing the stairs, I stopped on the landing, and through the window I watched the square below: the intense conversations, Alex's comrades wielding sticks beneath the lights of the Theology Building, the rest of the campus black and quiet, and, beyond that, the city. You could hear the noise of a dog barking in the distance.

At the top of the stairs, at the end of a corridor where the air was thick with petrol, a man stood in boot cut jeans, wearing his Ray-Bans folded over the V of his polo shirt. "What?" said Manette.

"Is nobody can come in here."

"We are friends of Hristos."

"Sorry, is nobody can come in here."

"Well, fuckeeng tell Hristos Manette come here to see him."

A female voice said, "Nikos, ti néa?"

"Eva, you know where is Hristos?"

"Ékso, méh Yiorgos."

"Hristos go out, sorry. Maybe after he come here." Fumes tumbled through the doorway, intoxicating, like the runaway train smell of diesel.

Thessaloniki, 20th June 2003. I choked through a cigarette, and then I stretched and joggled my arms, like a sprinter waiting for starter's orders. When you sleep on concrete, your body is so many hard bits: elbows and wrists, hips and knees. Manette spat toothpaste into the dusty ground, and, all around us, people rolled their shoulders and pressed their backs. A man washed his shaved head under a bottle of water and then hooted and shook himself like a dog. Meanwhile, the sun climbed over the Law Building, shooting up the morning.

When they had finished their coffee, Alex and his comrades tried on gasmasks: police-issue modern respirators with full face visors, or World War II relics with round eye holes and long snouts.

They fitted motorcycle helmets and hit themselves, shaking their heads like boxers. They strapped shin-pads to their forearms and distributed red and black flags tacked onto sticks shaped like base-ball bats. Manette accepted a flag, swung at a rose bush, and then rested it against the wall. She tied a bandanna tight over the bridge of her nose, laughed, and punched my arm. "You ready for some sport, Petit Fantôme?" A girl with ski goggles round her neck tugged a brush through her hair. A Spanish boy, talking through a decorating mask (the sort of thing you'd wear to sand a floor), asked if I knew where he could get ball bearings for his slingshot. Two guys fought a sword fight with sticks. There were girls with T-shirts wrapped round their faces jihad-style. Guys who'd got too hot in their balaclavas had rolled them up so they sat on top of their heads. There was a Greek girl, in low cut jeans, bikini top and a bandanna, leaning in the shade, holding a petrol bomb.

Midmorning, a rucksack went on fire, and a toxic smelling smoke rose in front of the Philosophy Building. The rucksack's owner beat the flames with a long stick, looking somewhere between guilty and amused, while all the time the sun climbed higher, and I waited, just wanting it over now.

There were 500 people in our bloc, formed into a tight rectangle and enclosed by flagpoles. We left the University when the sun was directly overhead, burning up Odhós Egnatías, blistering the tarmac, swelling cracks in the concrete. There were no cars. No pedestrians. Running bare to the horizon, where heat waves swayed and mottled the air, the highway carried a road movie's invitation to adventure, and it filled me with a reckless sense of freedom.

I didn't feel trapped, though there was now no option but to be carried with the bloc; instead, I felt a sort of anticipation. I said to Manette, "I want to do this!" I wanted the proximity, the immediacy. I wanted to stand toe to toe with a cop and fight it out. He'd hit me with his truncheon and I'd swing back with my stick and this seemed real, it seemed—

Then the insurrectionists, thousands of them, spilled onto the road behind us. They smashed traffic lights and street signs. Men in black hoods pushed a supermarket trolley filled with molotov cocktails. They bumped it down the university steps, landing it wheels askew. Then they charged, struggling to steer straight. A helicopter swung over the flats, gargling a circle above us. Windows smashed. The insurrectionists shot fireworks at journalists on rooftops. They attacked the offices of the Communist Party, breaking through the door with an axe.

But we held our formation. We turned right and climbed the slope. From behind me, I heard the *whoosh* of petrol. Looking back, I saw flames jumping two stories high from the Communist offices. We marched between lines of parked cars, until we reached a crossroads where the police surrounded us. We stopped, and they stood still, so we faced each other, just metres apart. There were some with batons and shields, and others with knapsacks stuffed with gas grenades. Some wielded big guns, and others held pipes fed by cylinders mounted on their backs. And my sense of freedom slipped away, replaced not just by fear, but by a familiar powerlessness. I watched a Greek girl load her slingshot and fire a pellet that bounced high off body armour, and I waited, huddled inside myself, knowing it had to kick off. Yet somehow it didn't. The bloc rotated and shuffled down a narrow street, an extreme left turn that led back to Odhós Egnatías.

And from there, looking towards the university, you could see petrol bombs cartwheeling, luminous orange against the black smog. You could hear the battle—the explosions, the clatter of axes tearing into metal shop fronts—but all you could see was this fireworks display of molotovs, gas bombs, and phosphorescent flares, arcing against the black sky. Then shouting and pushing spread from the back of our bloc, people ran, explosions fused into one big noise, and in five seconds everyone had disappeared. I was gasping, trying to clear a space in my lungs by inhaling more gas. I no longer knew which way to run, so I stood there. I held my stick. I felt a tug on my shirt. Manette shouted, "Allez quoi! Fuckeeng run!"

When we stopped, bent over, skin burning as we pressed our chests, I saw that behind us, the road was clouded with gas and smoke. It reminded me of the way clouds look from aeroplanes. There were men with gasmasks running out of the cloud—some carrying captured police equipment—while others were running into it, throwing rocks and petrol bombs. There was a shop on fire and a girl vomiting watery puke. There was a man sitting on the road, naked except for shorts and a bandanna, bleeding from a wound above his eye.

"You okay, Petit Fantôme?"

"Aye."

"You look even whiter."

"I want a cigarette."

"You can't fuckeeng smoke with that in your lungs."

"Can I have some water?"

She took off her rucksack and passed me the water, but before I could drink, people ran past me, and though I couldn't see what they were running from, I followed until we stopped in a big square. The gas drifted from far away, and to my left, a tree was on fire. A boy with red eyes was groping and crying "Parakaló!

Parakaló!" Manette led him by the arm to one of our medics. A guy in cut-off trousers hacked the tarmac with an axe, smashing it into pieces we could throw. Everywhere, people were coughing and spitting. Then someone shouted "Batsí! Batsí!" and I saw green uniforms at the far corner of the square. We edged forward, firing slingshots, hurling rocks and bottles, gas canisters, a foot of lead pipe, a broken wing mirror. "Petit Fantôme, look," said Manette, running across the road. Men in motorcycle helmets were ripping axes into the aluminium shutter of Benny's Burgers. I wanted to write something, to claim the destruction for the workers, but before I could find my paint, a burst of fire had filled the crack in the shutter. As Manette ran back to me, the sweat glistened on her chest. Then she veered and accelerated, her rucksack bouncing on her back, as the sky disappeared and the gas canisters exploded. I was just a second behind her, carried in the stampede. "Sigá sigá!" As the panic pushed one group to the right and the other straight-ahead, we realised what was happening and reached for each other with our eyes, helpless to prevent this separation.

An hour later, I hid in a bar, and the proprietor, a woman with varicose veins and a brown contoured face, must have noticed the white CS powder stains on my trousers, or my red eyes, because she smiled at me and changed the television to the news from which I had just escaped. The streets looked quiet now. Police patrolled in gasmasks. Fire crews hosed smouldering shop fronts. A bush remained ablaze at the roadside, and a litter bin burned in the middle of the highway. The air was hazy with smoke and spray and steam. A group of children edged into the frame, wanting to see the aftermath of what they'd watched on TV. They were dressed to imitate the anarchists, with their T-shirts pulled over their faces, wielding our discarded sticks with both hands. When a cop pretended to run at them, they dropped the sticks and scattered.

They cut back to the studio. The TV was muted and I was alone in the bar so the only noise was the fan on the ceiling. As the TV started doing replays, showing the highlights, I decided it would be safe to smoke. It was strange to sit there and see what had really happened. The gas wasn't as opaque as I remembered, and I seemed to have overestimated how many of us there were at certain points. For example, in the footage of the destruction of Benny's, filmed from a rooftop or maybe a helicopter, there were only a dozen people on the screen. Nobody running. No police. I couldn't see Manette, or myself, and I began to wonder if we'd been there.

Then a map came on the screen, and there was some sort of analysis, with arrows showing the movements of demonstrators and police. It was like something you'd see on Match of the Day. "This is early on, Gary. Look at the position the anarchists are in; I mean, defensively, it's cavalier." Then more highlights, petrol bombs, an injured cop. Then the scene from the leftist demonstration: the street congested, the tightly organised blocs trying to press towards the railway station, away from the fighting. Behind them, thick smoke rises into the blue sky, and the helicopter circles overhead like a buzzard. Then an arrest: someone beaten to the ground and pinned on the pavement.

When they showed him without his mask, I saw it was the English guy from the university, Simon. I wanted to help him, to do something. And that, of course, is exactly what the spectacle precludes.

★ 18 ★

Emerging from the metro at Kléber, I found a thick fog had settled over Paris, so that clouds of light hung in the air, and at first
I didn't know where I was. The fog had brought a hush to the
city, and I realised that on previous visits, I must have followed
Manette without noting the route. I considered asking someone,
but I didn't know the French for Greek Embassy— l'embassie de
Greece?—and, besides, why would anyone, except a Greek who
has lost her passport, know where the Greek Embassy was? So
instead I guessed, and walked, until the Arc de Triomphe loomed
out of the fog, which definitely wasn't the right way, and where,
in any case, the road was blocked by scarved-and-gloved specta-
tors, straining for a view of— Of what? A procession. A procession of donkeys and children, a wooden cart, men holding flam-
ing torches, all shuffling ghost-like through the fog. I stood and
watched for a minute. Then I returned to Kléber, wondering
what it meant.

We had moved to Paris in late September 2003, when the
hunger strike was just starting and afternoon temperatures still
averaged over thirty Celsius. That was at the end of the French
heatwave, the one that left ten thousand pensioners dead and so
many bodies unclaimed that morgues overfilled and refrigerated
trucks were hired to store the extra corpses. But days had passed,
then weeks, until November came, and winter settled over Paris,
and the hunger strike continued, and the pace of bad news accelerated. We heard that our comrades, Simon and four others

arrested in Thessaloniki, were coughing blood, suffering from severe weight loss, guarded at gunpoint by hooded anti-terrorist commandoes; they had to refuse water for two days in order to go to the toilet in private. We started to hold demonstrations in front of the Greek Embassy, sometimes ten, sometimes forty of us, shouting "*libérer nos camarades,*" spattering the Embassy walls with paint. Two days earlier, the CRS had made us gather on the opposite pavement, shaking our banners at the dark windows of an empty building, chanting "*Police partout, justice nulle part,*" until the inconsequence of our protest became unbearable, and Alex threw a rock at the windows. Then they sprayed tear gas and we ran to the metro, making for it like rabbits to a warren. Would I soon see Alex and Manette running through the fog?

But wait—there was something I recognised: a cardboard woman showering in the window of a chemist. It was near here that we left the main boulevard, but did we turn right or cross the road and turn left? Rush hour traffic was flowing down Avenue Kléber, so I turned right, just because it was easier. Yet there was something familiar about that street; even the name, Rue Paul Valéry, I thought I recognised. I quickened my pace and arrived, disappointed, on Avenue Victor Hugo. A Japanese-looking businessman was doing a scuttle run, tugging a wheeled suitcase behind him, and I had a crazy impulse to ask if he knew where I could find the Greek Embassy. I remembered, one time when I really needed to catch a train, running around the vicinity of Gare du Nord, shouting with growing panic, "Où est la guerre? Où est la guerre?" and maybe that's a better question: Where is the war?

During my time in France, we used to drink at a bar in Montmartre, where an old dog that we all called "Compañero" slept folded in front of an electric heater. The bar had been opened by a Spanish CNT militant, an exile from Francoism, who had decorated the walls with black and white photos of Durruti, and framed prints of the Paris Commune. Because the communards had positioned cannons at the top of the hill, where later, after the repression, the government built Sacré-Cœur Basilica, the bar had been named Les Canons des Montmartre, and this name had never changed. The photographs had also stayed, but the son of the original owner had hung his own pictures, mainly rock memorabilia, until the walls were covered. The effect was strange: Zapata was grinning at Syd Barrett, and El Quico appeared to be arguing politics with Sergeant Pepper's Lonely Hearts Club Band.

When Manette stormed in from the embassy, she almost stood on Compañero. Rather than admit I'd got lost and wandered around Paris, I told her that I'd decided not to go. I told her the protests were pointless.

"Our comrades, they fuckeeng die in prison, and you sit in here like a— We try to make the occupation, we have to fight with the CRS, and where the fuck are you? And is not only here, you understand? In Greece— ask Alex about Greece. Hey Alex?"

He turned around, lifting the drinks, pretending he'd just received them, but in a way that was unnatural, too quick or too slow, as though he'd realised we were arguing and had decided to hang back.

"Tell this fuckeeng malaka about the solidarity in Greece."

"In Greece, now, the situation is very tense." He sat opposite me, telling me things I already knew—the rioting during the commemoration of the November 17th massacre, the incendiary devices left in banks and government offices, the occupations at every university—but he told me these things with the intensity of someone sharing a secret. "The comrades occupy *many* buildings: the Ministry of Health, the union of the journalists, the General Secretariat of Youth. They *occupy* the radio stations *and* they take over the microphone and make a speech *to favour* the hunger strikers, you understand?" He sat, looking older than he had in the summer, with both hands wrapped around his beer, as though it was a mug of something that could keep him warm.

When someone opened the door at Les Canons, Compañero would lift his head ten degrees, just enough to inspect the new arrival, and if it was someone he approved of, he would drag his tail, slowly, as though it was an enormous mooring rope, from one side to the other. He looked up at Christophe, but seemed too weak to move his tail. Maybe it was Christophe's expression; he normally smiled a big rusted pillar-box grin—you could never decide if it was friendly or sinister—but his face remained serious as he approached our table. He kissed Manette and shook our hands. "Regarde," he said, pushing a computer print out into Manette's hand.

They swore a lot as they read the paper but I stopped trying to understand and watched the three of them from a distance. Manette had guddled the ice cubes from her drink, and now, as they melted, they skated back and forth on the wooden table. When she finished her drink, Christophe stood up with a clatter of boots and stool legs. He was in RASH (Red and Anarchist Skinheads), so he dressed like an extra from *Romper Stomper*, in red Doc Martens that knocked on the wooden floor as he crossed to the bar. That was when I read the print out:

The health state of the 2 hunger strikers (that have been denying food for 67 days the former and 52 days the latter) is EXTREMELY DANGEROUS.

Apart from all symptoms due to the long term lack of food, SOLEIMAN DAKDOUK [Kastro] has a destructive appearance of the pituitary of the anus, while SIMON CHAPMAN has a zero blood pressure while standing. As it is obvious, this state may lead to unpredictable consequences for their health (irreversible harms) and their life AT ANY MOMENT and it is ABSOLUTELY NECESSARY that they will be transferred to an organized state hospital.

When I'd finished, Alex drew a wad of leaflets from his bomber jacket and slapped them on the table. "Fuck! Look! Look at the pictures!" I had seen the photos many times before: Simon arrested wearing a blue bag; Simon sitting on the curb as a riot cop places a black bag of molotovs at his feet. There was something in the sincerity of Alex's frustration that, like old Compañero, had the quality of a friend. Maybe that's why, when Alex said he was leaving, I decided to go with him.

It was so smoky in Les Canons that on exiting there was no sense of stepping into the fog; one big cloud seemed to continue on either side of the door. As we started down the slope towards Pigalle, I asked, "What d'you think's gonnae happen?"

"Please, not so fast."

"With the hunger strikers, what will happen?"

He paused, in a way that implied the great importance of what he was about to say. "Is like this: if they die then all of Greece will burn. This they cannot risk. *But,* if they let them go then, after everything, it is us who have won. And the police, the government, they do not let this happen. So, I think, tonight, or tomorrow, I think they force them."

"Force feed them?"

"Yes, I think so."

Then a car threw its doors open, spreading itself spider-shaped across the road. Men jumped out and I thought—no, I didn't think—I *reacted* as if it was a mugging. I balanced myself, ready to fight, but nobody hit me. They slammed Alex against the shutter of a closed shop, and as he struggled, the metal buckled and crashed, making a noise that filled the street. They pushed him into the car with his arms handcuffed behind his back while a third guy pulled a pistol from a bum bag below his belly. He held the pistol at head height, pointing it at the sky. Then he also climbed into the car. The doors slammed, and I was alone: the car had gone, Alex had gone, the men—

I was left in the middle of the road, feeling invisible.

I knew I had to go back and tell the others what had happened—what *had* happened? Why hadn't I stopped them? Or rather, how had the scene passed by without affecting me? Why had nobody hit me? I should have jumped on the bonnet or something. *It all happened so quickly*—that's what witnesses say on detective shows, the rubbish witnesses who aren't any help.

You know in ghost stories and horror films, how animals can see spirits that are invisible to humans? Well, when I re-entered Les Canons, Manette and Christophe were knotted in conversation, but Compañero lifted his straggly tail and dragged it from side to side. Even when I stood at the end of their table, Manette and Christophe didn't notice me. "Guys," I said, and then they looked uncomfortable, as if in opening the door I had admitted a gust of cold air.

"Hey you," she said. "Why you have come back?"

"It's Alex. Alex has been abducted. Arrested. Abducted."

"What?"

"Manette, en Français?"

"These guys, they were in a car, they jumped out, pushed him in the car and—"

"Manette! Qu'est-ce que c'est?"

Manette translated for Christophe and he jumped up and ran to the door. "Rien," he said when he came back.

"You think they were cops?"

"Plain clothes cops, aye. Well, presumably."

"They show no identification?"

"No."

"Why you do not stop them?"

"I—How? I mean, there wasn't really—"

"You should have got us"

"There wasn't time."

"Okay. Okay. Bon. Let's think. Before you forget, write down the registration."

"The registration? I didn't get it."

"Okay, so we have no idea where— Okay," she said, touching my shoulder.

"It was white, I think."

"Don't worry." She peeled the plastic wrapper from Christophe's cigarettes and dropped it in the ashtray. "We phone all the police stations, try to find out where they hold him. We phone the legal group. Then tomorrow we have a solidarity demo."

"A solidarity demo for a guy arrested for doing a solidarity demo? If we get arrested for doing that, who's going to do a solidarity demo for us?"

Manette translated this, adding something of her own, and a private laughter bounced between them. I was still standing and every part of my body needed to be manoeuvred with conscious effort. I clenched my jaw, bent my knee, and put a hand in my pocket. Then they stopped laughing and the silence grew until they were looking at me the way you would look at a postman who, having delivered a package, inexplicably remains standing on your doorstep.

"Alright, I'll try to leave again."

"You be careful, okay?'

"Aye, that's a point. Maybe we shouldn't go out on our own?"

This hadn't been Manette's point, and she looked at the table before answering. "If you are scared then stay with us. We finish these drinks and then we go up to the house of Christophe, drink some more beer, listen to music."

The plastic fag wrapper melted in the ashtray with the acrid smell of burning tyres. "But you'll miss the last metro."

"Then I fuckeeng come home in the morning, okay?"

"Aye, of course."

"Thank you," she said, but in a sarcastic voice, the way people say, "Sorry for breathing."

Outside again, old buildings kissed across the narrow street. Soft ladders of light slipped through the slats of shutters, and I stood on the pavement, thinking that Paris in November is surprisingly cold. Did I go back to the window because I already knew what I had lost?

She was talking to Christophe with that total concentration, that almost predatory determination. She talked the way she made love: so oppositional she sort of locked into you, until all boundaries dissolved, until you lost yourself in the intensity of the combination.

★ 19 ★

They buried Manette's mother on 15 August 2003, when the mé-téo said Paris could hit forty Celsius, and flies flickered around us, making the old people tut and swat as the earth piled higher. It was the only time I ever saw Manette in a dress.

Afterwards, back at her mother's house, the patio doors were pushed open, and Manette prepared food as her relatives loos-ened their collars and lit cigarettes. Outside, the heat bent the air, and the parasol lurched from side to side, swooning with each shake of the table. When a man wedged stones at the base of its pole, the other men of his age made a joke of congratulating him, which helped them to gather, to introduce each other and shake hands. These men—with grey hair at their temples and round paunches and faces creased but not wrinkled, who have, or look like they should have, dependents on either side—were the first to abandon their funeral clothes. They cast off ties and some even changed into shorts and polo-shirts. Then they stood in a circle, smoking in the waitful quiet, while in another group, the old people gathered in the shade, fanning themselves, so that the skin beneath their arms swung morbid and white.

When it was time, I helped Manette serve the food (bread and cheese, sliced tomatoes and basil leaves, olives, cous cous, and bean salad in a crystal bowl), and one of the men made a joke, perhaps at my expense, which hung with the smoke from their extinguished cigarettes. Then the men were up, walking inside with hands on each others' backs, as grass-stained children ran to the table, and their mothers stood on the yellow grass, faces taut in the sunshine. Then the men were back, circulating bottles of wine, peering at the labels through reading glasses, pointing and shrugging and smiling as each bottle uncorked with a hollow tuneful noise. They poured and sniffed and tasted, and then they looked at each other and said, "Ah oui, c'est bon," or "*Aah* oui, c'est *bon*." Meanwhile, the old people struggled over their food, content with the achievement of eating.

Finished in the kitchen, Manette stood beside me, drinking a glass of wine too fast. She asked if I was okay, as if it was *my* mother we had just buried. "Look at that bitch," she said. "Why is she looking at the fuckeeng salade like this?" She meant her aunt—the sister of the deceased and don't you forget it—who was staring into the bean salad, as if she'd just found two Band-aids and a pubic hair.

Later, when most people had left, we gathered in the living room, at the table below the chandelier, in the stream of an industrial-sized fan, and one of the old women sat beside me, holding my arm as she said things I couldn't understand. I listened and smiled. Sometimes, Manette leant over to answer questions or to translate a sentence such as "She says it is a hot day for a funeral."

The Aunt was conducting the mourning, and there were so many things to be seen and remembered—photographs, scrapbooks, favourite songs. There she was, hair curled, smiling in the light grey sunshine. There was her father: a fat man laughing on an Algerian beach. There was her first husband (Manette's dad): a big man with a boxer's nose. There was a wee girl in an orange

Then we stopped on Pont Neuf and smoked Gauloises. After a moment, she said, "Petit Fantôme, last night I speak with my aunt and uncle."

"Aye?"

"You know how my mother was made rich by her last marriage?"

"Right."

"Well, there is a flat in my name."

"That's brilliant."

"You think I should accept it?"

"Of course you should accept it." She shrugged and leant over the side as a boat-full of tourists waved up at the bridge. "You going to sell it?"

"Petit Fantôme, I miss Paris. I have been away so long; maybe it is time for me to come home."

"You want to live in it?"

"I do not want to lose you."

"You're no going to lose me! If you want to live in Paris, I want o live in Paris."

"Petit Fantôme, do you see this building? We call it the onciergerie. Is where they kill Ravachol."

"Yeah?"

"You'll have to learn French."

"Bien sur," I said. "Je etudies tres fort toutes le jours." She kissed my ear and looked into the Seine.

ight they grabbed Alex, I returned to the flat, where the cat the windowsill, making a pneumatic purr. I shook some s into her bowl, but she didn't move, so I stood by the

raincoat, squinting at the brightness of the future, with her index finger pushed knuckle deep into her mouth.

"Who's the wee girl?"

Manette shrugged and I wondered if it was her. "This," she said, turning the page, "Was her third husband." The picture was of an old man in a wheel chair. "He owned two businesses."

"Aye?"

"How did you think she has got all this?" She gestured at the house: the chandelier, the garage door that opened automatically, the shiny toilet with a choice of flushes depending on the scale of the job.

Then the man in chinos, who had earlier secured the parasol, entered the living room carrying a box. The aunt covered her mouth, crossed herself, and held her pearls like a rosary. The man in chinos—her husband, I think—rested a hand on her shoulder and stared towards the garden. "Regarde," said the aunt. It was a recipe book. She turned the pages and said the names of dishes, and the relatives, remembering a taste or a time—that boeuf bourguignon, that tarte tatin!—chuckled and made fruit picking gestures, until their laughter turned into a chorus of sighs, and stopped on them, like a car that has run out of petrol. There were old driver's licences and bank-books and a hotel receipt dated June 1983. Manette said it was from her mother's second honeymoon. All these things we store away—a life recorded in letters, holiday snaps, school jotters, and old documents—were passed in a circle, while all the time, below the tablecloth, Manette scrunched a napkin, twisting it, balling it, wringing the bounce from it.

In the evening, I lay clothed on the bed in the room we had been allocated. The effort of watching myself all day, of concentrating on what other people were doing and trying to act the same, of not understanding and speaking through a translator, so that my words, broadcast as if on the radio, always seemed inadequate and misunderstood, had exhausted me. The window was open and birdsong floated in with the release of the day's heat. Maybe I was close to sleep when Manette opened the door. "You alright?" I asked.

She looked so tired. "Look, Petit Fantôme, what I have found. It was mine when I was a child." She held a hardback picture book: an old copy of *Le Petit Fantôme*. She sat next to me on the bed and explained it, holding the book between us so I could see the pictures. "You see, he is always day dreaming at school. Either he dream of what *has* happened or of what—"

"Why does a ghost go to school?"

"Because it is a ghost school. Look, it is in an old ruin. And see, the teacher is a skeleton."

"This is for kids?"

"Yes. Here the teacher is shouting at le Petit Fantôme because always he is dreaming. So then," she turned the page, "as he go home he make the wish that he never dream again. At first it is okay and he is good at the school, but soon he is ill. Then he cannot even leave his bed and—"

"Why does a ghost have a bed?"

"He live in this old attic where nobody go but a child who is his friend. So he does not go to school and the other ghosts are scared for him. So they go to his attic and, look, he has faded so he is almost not there."

"Who's the guy in the cloak?"

"He is the ghost doctor."

"I thought ghosts were immortal?"

"No, he explain to them because ghosts have no body they are only their memories and dreams and without them they do not

exist. So the only way they can save le Petit Fantôme is to tell him all the adventures he has forgotten, and all the dreams he used to believe in. So each chapter they remind him another adventure from his past or another dream of his future, and each chapter he is a little less transparent."

"That's fucking trippy. Kids actually read this in France?"

"I don't know. It was popular when I was a child."

"Yous French are weird."

She cracked the book shut, perhaps upset that I hadn't app[reciated] it more. "After my father has died, it help me."

"I'm sorry," I said. "How did he die?"

"Alone," she said.

The next day, we did the tourist stuff, and it felt good t[o] side, to be moving. We smoked cigarettes in the Jardin [du Luxem]bourg, where old men lobbed metal balls in the air an[d] as they plopped to laughter and cries of "Oui! C'est [?]

"Ah putain!" And then we walked, slowed by t[?] the Latin Quarter, through streets I knew from pic[tures?] eight. We passed the Sorbonne and strolled do[wn?] France, to Notre Dame and the crowds of sigh[tseers?] and hustlers. "You see Notre Dame?" she said, [?] it is still here? During the Commune, an armed [?] they were maybe two hundred, surround th[e?] make preparations to burn it as a symbol of t[he?] religious oppression. But, just as they are ab[out to?] armed militia of artist comrades arrive who [?] is bourgeois, it is also so beautiful and built [by the working] class. So it is here."

raincoat, squinting at the brightness of the future, with her index finger pushed knuckle deep into her mouth.

"Who's the wee girl?"

Manette shrugged and I wondered if it was her. "This," she said, turning the page, "Was her third husband." The picture was of an old man in a wheel chair. "He owned two businesses."

"Aye?"

"How did you think she has got all this?" She gestured at the house: the chandelier, the garage door that opened automatically, the shiny toilet with a choice of flushes depending on the scale of the job.

Then the man in chinos, who had earlier secured the parasol, entered the living room carrying a box. The aunt covered her mouth, crossed herself, and held her pearls like a rosary. The man in chinos—her husband, I think—rested a hand on her shoulder and stared towards the garden. "Regarde," said the aunt. It was a recipe book. She turned the pages and said the names of dishes, and the relatives, remembering a taste or a time—that boeuf bourguignon, that tarte tatin!—chuckled and made fruit picking gestures, until their laughter turned into a chorus of sighs, and stopped on them, like a car that has run out of petrol. There were old driver's licences and bank-books and a hotel receipt dated June 1983. Manette said it was from her mother's second honeymoon. All these things we store away—a life recorded in letters, holiday snaps, school jotters, and old documents—were passed in a circle, while all the time, below the tablecloth, Manette scrunched a napkin, twisting it, balling it, wringing the bounce from it.

In the evening, I lay clothed on the bed in the room we had been allocated. The effort of watching myself all day, of concentrating on what other people were doing and trying to act the same, of not understanding and speaking through a translator, so that my words, broadcast as if on the radio, always seemed inadequate and misunderstood, had exhausted me. The window was open and birdsong floated in with the release of the day's heat. Maybe I was close to sleep when Manette opened the door. "You alright?" I asked.

She looked so tired. "Look, Petit Fantôme, what I have found. It was mine when I was a child." She held a hardback picture book: an old copy of *Le Petit Fantôme*. She sat next to me on the bed and explained it, holding the book between us so I could see the pictures. "You see, he is always day dreaming at school. Either he dream of what *has* happened or of what—"

"Why does a ghost go to school?"

"Because it is a ghost school. Look, it is in an old ruin. And see, the teacher is a skeleton."

"This is for kids?"

"Yes. Here the teacher is shouting at le Petit Fantôme because always he is dreaming. So then," she turned the page, "as he go home he make the wish that he never dream again. At first it is okay and he is good at the school, but soon he is ill. Then he cannot even leave his bed and—"

"Why does a ghost have a bed?"

"He live in this old attic where nobody go but a child who is his friend. So he does not go to school and the other ghosts are scared for him. So they go to his attic and, look, he has faded so he is almost not there."

"Who's the guy in the cloak?"

"He is the ghost doctor."

"I thought ghosts were immortal?"

"No, he explain to them because ghosts have no body they are only their memories and dreams and without them they do not exist. So the only way they can save le Petit Fantôme is to tell him all the adventures he has forgotten, and all the dreams he used to believe in. So each chapter they remind him another adventure from his past or another dream of his future, and each chapter he is a little less transparent."

"That's fucking trippy. Kids actually read this in France?"

"I don't know. It was popular when I was a child."

"Yous French are weird."

She cracked the book shut, perhaps upset that I hadn't appreciated it more. "After my father has died, it help me."

"I'm sorry," I said. "How did he die?"

"Alone," she said.

The next day, we did the tourist stuff, and it felt good to be outside, to be moving. We smoked cigarettes in the Jardin du Luxembourg, where old men lobbed metal balls in the air and cheered as they plopped to laughter and cries of "Oui! C'est moi!" and

"Ah putain!" And then we walked, slowed by the heat, through the Latin Quarter, through streets I knew from pictures of sixty-eight. We passed the Sorbonne and strolled down the Rue de France, to Notre Dame and the crowds of sightseers, buskers and hustlers. "You see Notre Dame?" she said, "you know why it is still here? During the Commune, an armed crowd—and they were maybe two hundred, surround the cathedral and make preparations to burn it as a symbol of the Church and religious oppression. But, just as they are about to begin, an armed militia of artist comrades arrive who argue that, yes, it is bourgeois, it is also so beautiful and built by the working class. So it is here."

Then we stopped on Pont Neuf and smoked Gauloises. After a moment, she said, "Petit Fantôme, last night I speak with my aunt and uncle."

"Aye?"

"You know how my mother was made rich by her last marriage?"

"Right."

"Well, there is a flat in my name."

"That's brilliant."

"You think I should accept it?"

"Of course you should accept it." She shrugged and leant over the side as a boat-full of tourists waved up at the bridge. "You going to sell it?"

"Petit Fantôme, I miss Paris. I have been away so long; maybe it is time for me to come home."

"You want to live in it?"

"I do not want to lose you."

"You're no going to lose me! If you want to live in Paris, I want to live in Paris."

"Petit Fantôme, do you see this building? We call it the Conciergerie. Is where they kill Ravachol."

"Yeah?"

"You'll have to learn French."

"Bien sur," I said. "Je etudies tres fort toutes le jours."

She kissed my ear and looked into the Seine.

...ight they grabbed Alex, I returned to the flat, where the cat ...the windowsill, making a pneumatic purr. I shook some ...s into her bowl, but she didn't move, so I stood by the window, watching Paris as I stroked the cat. Cars glided beneath us, coning yellow light as they cornered, and fog drifted past the glass, as if we were in the final minutes of a flight, at any moment set to emerge from the clouds and see the earth spread beneath us in all its potential.

I poured a glass of amaretto and sat in front of the television, trying to make sense of a film. The doctor was sleeping with two blonde women, who he thought were the same woman. They might have been two physical representations of multiple personalities, or possibly they were twins. Certainly they looked very similar—the same actress, I'm sure—but they argued and pulled each other's hair. At any rate, the doctor seemed to be in love with a third woman, who looked very different. It was, perhaps, a comedy.

Alone in bed, I thought about Alex—had he been beaten?—and I thought about the hunger strikers. Could they sleep? Were they drifting in and out of consciousness or was the pain too bad? Imagine the pain of your body slowly eating itself. A strange thing, when there is nothing inside you, to turn on yourself this way. Most of all, however, I thought about Manette.

In the morning, she came home with good news: Alex had been interrogated overnight and then released without charge. The hunger strike lasted a further two days. On November 26th, the Greek government ordered that all five hunger strikers be force-fed. Though threatened with homicide charges, the doctors refused, and, after several hours of stalemate, our comrades were released on bail. At the university in Athens, the comrades abandoned the riot preparations and celebrated outside the hospital.

We celebrated too—Manette's uncle had given us a bottle of champagne, and this was the time to drink it. Of course I felt relieved, but when the champagne was finished and all the fear and tension had slipped out of me, I felt like I was missing something to take its place. It was as though *I* had been starved of something—of optimism, perhaps—because everything we had done since Thessaloniki, since September 11th, since Genoa, had been defensive. It was a long time since the graffiti slogan "We are winning" had sounded appropriate.

Eight weeks later, when I was ready to leave France, we heard that all charges had been dropped against Simon Chapman and twelve others arrested in connection with the Thessaloniki disturbances. Charges against six others, including one of the hunger strikers, were reduced to misdemeanours, and the courts ordered investigations into a further eight cases due to gaps and contradictions in evidence. But by then I was no longer involved in the struggle. I didn't work for Benny's—I didn't work at all—and all the demonstrations, rallies, and public meetings seemed futile. When Manette went to a protest, I stayed at home. In fact, as the weeks passed, I became as housebound as the cat. I rarely ventured outside, spoke to no one except Manette, and I avoided the news. I stuck my fingers in my ears and said "Na na na-na na" to capitalist modernity.

But the more I stayed home, the more Manette went out. And the more she went out, the less often she returned. As midnight approached and the metro shut down, I would listen to footsteps in the stairwell, and even when I could tell it wasn't her—when the feet had an aged shuffle or a masculine plod—I would continue to hope, imagining she was limping or drunk, until a key turned in a door that wasn't ours. Then I would return to the window and watch the pedestrians. Each of them was cocooned against the rain, each of them was lumpy and androgynous, and each of them was just possibly her.

It was about this time that I started to suffer insomnia. On the nights that Manette didn't come home, I would search her pamphlet collection for something tedious enough to send me to sleep. I would read platformist position papers, minutes from the 1996 IWA congress in Madrid, or the International Communist Current's "Polemic with Aufheben: An attack on the theory of decadence is an attack on Marxism." The winner, however, the most boring thing I could find, was a small book called *Dialectics Demystified*:

Schopenhauer once claimed that:

the greatest effrontery in serving up sheer nonsense, in scrabbling together senseless and maddening webs of words, such as had previously been heard only in madhouses, finally appeared in Hegel. It became the instrument of the most ponderous and general mystification that has ever existed, with a result that will seem incredible to posterity, and be a lasting monument of German stupidity.

Perhaps, therefore, G.W.F. Hegel retains an unwarranted reputation as a 'difficult,' thinker, that is to say, as a thinker best left to the specialist scholar. In fact, Hegel's thought in general, and his dialectical view of history in particular, is logical and self-explanatory, and easily comprehensible to any intelligent man. .

Like Kant, Hegel observed the 'gap' between the noumenal and the phenomenal, that is to say, between the intelligible and empirical; for example, in self-reflection, where the self *qua* object of consciousness is displaced from the self *qua* subject of *énonciation* (i.e. in the thought, 'I am,' the 'I' is always already removed from the 'am'), which is to say that the thought of being is never exactly coincident with being. But for Hegel, the distance between the noumenal and the phenomenal is not an epistemological problem, but rather the basis of our capacity to become other than we are, to be 'self-moving': 'What is implicit in man must become an object to him, come into his consciousness; then it becomes *for* him and he becomes aware of himself, explicit to himself.'

This becomes even clearer when we recall the first thesis of 'presuppositionless logic' in his *Science and Logic*, where one tries to think the utter indeterminacy of *being*, but recognises (and the reverse is also true) that the thought of pure being, as it is thought, invokes its inherent reliance on the thought of *nothing*, which is to say—to put the case another way—that to think of being without presuppositions is to think of a thing so indeterminate and inchoate that it is not in fact *being* but, rather, being's transition into nothing and back again to pure being—i.e. *becoming*.

The basis of dialectical movement really is this simple: at one level it is the process of abstraction that proceeds to negation and is positively resolved through the speculative principle of *Aufhebung*. At a world-historical level it is the movement through which *Geist* (mind/ Spirit) successively negates itself, and redefines itself through a speculative integration of these dialectical opposites, a sublation that preserves difference while abolishing antagonism. In other words, *Geist* 'determines itself out of itself to be the *other of itself*', which is to say...

And sleep, merciful sleep.

On Christmas morning, it hailed. Our breath condensed around the corners of windowpanes, frosting the glass, and the wind blew the hail stones into the corners and crevices of buildings, dusting doorways and windowsills polystyrene white. Manette (don't ask me why) bought Christmas presents for everyone, even the cat. She said that usually the cat appeared insulted by anything she was bought, but this year Cat sniffed her new mat, padded forward, and, slowly, with the arthritic movements of an old person climbing into a bath, lowered herself onto the mat and purred.

On Boxing Day, Manette found Cat lying on the living room floor, convulsing in a puddle of urine. She looked like a smashed egg. We wrapped the cat in a bundle of towels, and I carried her downstairs. She was so thin, beneath all that fur. I could feel her lungs lifting her ribs and collapsing under their weight. On the way to the vet, Cat stretched, clawed the air, and died.

"Wayne? Can I tell you something, even if it makes you upset?"

"Of course."

"You've got to promise not to get angry."

"..."

"I'm seeing someone else and I do not want to stop." She said it staring at the floor and only looked up when I didn't say anything. Why did she decide to tell me that afternoon? Was it something to do with having buried cat? This is what I think (and I've thought about this so long): I think we usually wake up with more or less the same memories and beliefs as we had the day before, and this reassuring consistency is what we come to call our self, and if there's a major change in our circumstances or beliefs, we adopt phrases that expresses discontinuity—some people are reborn as Christians or they start new lives in Spain; I was a different person at twenty-four than I was at seventeen; when I'm depressed I'm not myself. I have thought about this a lot and—

"Who?" I said, because it was the most obvious question to ask.

"I can't tell you."

"Who?"

"Non."

"Fucksake, who?"

"…"

"Who?"

"Christophe."

"Skinhead Christophe?"

"Yes."

"No."

She nodded.

I laughed. "Christophe?"

"Christophe."

"You're joking. Tell me you're joking."

"Why do you say this?"

"Have you seen him?"

She shrugged.

"Have you seen the fucking state of him?"

She shrugged again. "I am sorry. Petit Fantôme, I am so sorry."

You know when you stub your toe and you have time to think *that should hurt,* before the shock passes and you realise that it does hurt? Well, after dinner, her gaze went aimless, and I said, "What you thinking?"

"Nothing." She lit a cigarette. Sometimes she had this way of acting, like a character in a film noir. You could hear the gasp of her lighter, the intake of smoke, and these things seemed to highlight the silence around her.

"Come on, what you thinking?"

She waited until the smoke had dispersed. "I bought this shampoo bar, and I can't find it anywhere."

"That's what you're thinking?"

"Well, you fuckeeng asked."

"That's all you can think about just now?"

She flicked her cigarette and looked at her watch.

"You know the worst thing about this? It would have been so hard for me to leave you."

"Petit Fantôme—"

"If I was leaving you, it would have broken my fucking heart."

"Petit Fantôme, don't be upset."

"Why? Because it's boring for you? Because you've heard this shite so many times and now it's just boring?"

"Do we have to do this, Petit Fantôme?"

"Yes," I said. "Yes we do."

"Come on; let's have something nice for dessert?"

And then I kicked the chair in front of me. I kicked the chair as hard as I could, and it screeched across the tiles, holding its balance on two legs like a stunt car, before falling to the side and crashing against Manette's hip. She looked so angry I thought she was going to hit me. Instead, she set the chair upright, lifted her coat, opened the front door, and clicked it shut behind her.

On my last day in France, the air had that slight freeze that makes the light soft and the sky silver, and we rode the metro out to Père Lachaise cemetery, where, without needing a map, Manette led me between the gravestones, past the grungy kids that hang around Jim Morrison's tomb, first to the Communards' Wall, and then to the crematorium. There, we climbed the stairs to Makhno's memorial, and I stood apart from her, drinking from a bottle of amaretto, studying the carving of Makhno's face. Manette waited a minute, blowing on her hands; then she said, "You want to see Proust?"

Here's something funny: you know how normal people fight over the evening she spent with Greg from work or where he cuts his toenails? Well, that stuff's small change. People like us are used to dealing in more serious currency: discrepancies in life expectancy between social classes, areas of rainforest the size of Wales. Political activists pretend their disagreements can be located in structural frameworks of oppression, in world-historical contradictions, in *isms*. As we walked towards Proust's tombstone, I said, "Is it true you started seeing Christophe because he's a wannabe bureaucrat?"

"Wayne, please don't."

"In a reformist union—"

"Petit Fantôme—"

"Slithering between exploitative relations like Vaseline and—"

"Petit Fantôme, why you are being like this?" She had stopped walking and now she turned to face me. "You are not the centre of the world, Wayne. You know this?"

We were standing about two metres apart, within view of the main cobbled throughway, on which a trilby-hatted man, holding flowers, supported an elderly woman by the elbow. "But you said you loved me."

At this point, Manette's whole countenance changed; her head dropped, she walked towards me (six precise steps that hardly crunched the gravel), touched my elbow, and looked up. "I know," she said. "I did—I do—I always will. Stupide."

"Then why?" I asked.

"Petit Fantôme, you knew we would not be together forever."

"Did I?"

"We have both changed and—"

"I've *changed*?"

"Yes. You never do anything anymore."

"Like what? Wander about town waving a flag? D'you think if there had have been twenty-one people at the demo instead of twenty then we would have achieved a critical mass? D'you think we missed the revolutionary moment when I was watching the PSG match on TV?"

Manette read the blunted inscription on a horizontal tombstone. Dead leaves blew around our feet.

"Seriously, how long are you going to keep kidding yourself? There are a handful of us here, a handful there; sometimes we gather together and we number a few thousand—it's *nothing*."

"You talk always about activists as if they make the revolution. They keep the ideas alive, that is all. The working class make the revolution. We are six billion."

I laughed and shook my head.

"Okay. So what do you think make you so fuckeeng special? You think you are the only student who is trained for some stupide job? You think you are the only low paid worker who want something better? You think that everyone else is too stupide to imagine the future?"

"That's exactly it," I said. "I can't imagine the future."

"Ah. Just now feels like defeat? Maybe. Then in five years, ten years, twenty years, something will happen—some stupide war or pension collapse or environmental crisis or recession—and it's a spark, and every student being trained for a stupide job, and every bored worker, and every unemployed person, and everyone who is without papers, and all the people who must work longer and longer for less and less pension, and are isolated, and are taught to hate themselves, they will look at the world of capital, and they will be in the streets, millions of them, and they will imagine the future."

I laughed again. "You've never been to Dundule, have you?"

"Maybe. Maybe it start in Paris. Maybe it start in Athens. Maybe it start in rural China. But it will start. And it will spread and spread."

"You really believe that?"

"Yes," she said. "The future is unwritten. You believe we all keep taking our anger on ourselves, on each other? Some stupide gang fight? Another stupide suicide? What is your alternative? You find a girl and somehow, despite everything, you make each other happy forever?" The sun had emerged behind her; already low in the sky, it lasered through a tall white mausoleum, stretching the shadows of gravestones. "No, you do not believe that," she said.

★ 20 ★

I took the Eurostar to London Waterloo and then travelled on to Hackney, hoping to surprise Hristos and Federico. When I reached our street, the tramp's bedding still lay under the hedge, though it had been two years since he had died. It's a strange feeling, isn't it, to return to a place where you've been before: everything is at once familiar and radically changed. I recognised the wheelie bin with the circled A and the squat sign, and the bike with one bent wheel, but the windows and door were covered with the sort of metal guards that the council use to keep crackheads out of abandoned properties. When I dialled Federico's mobile, his number wasn't recognised. So I dialled Lucy. "It's Wayne," I said.

"Oh my God, how are you? Where are you?"

"I'm in London. I'm in London and I need some help."

"…"

"I need somewhere to stay for a few days."

There was a pause, long enough for two breaths. "Of course. Where are you now?"

"I'm in Hackney."

"Hackney?"

"Aye."

"Well, I'm on my way to a gallery; you want to join us?"

"I'd love to."

"I'm with my partner."

"Great."

"Okay, can you get to Whitechapel in an hour?"

Lucy's partner was a girl. Yeah, I expected a bloke too, but she was definitely a girl. And I do mean a *girl*; she looked about fifteen. She was as tall as me but thin and flat chested, like her hormones had gone crazy and she was developing at all different stages. Her face was freckly with a long nose and thin lips and eyes that were almost on the side of her head, where a rabbit has its eyes. Now and then she would pout her bottom lip, directing her breath upwards, blowing where her hair fringed her eyebrows. We met in the gallery café and Lucy air-kissed me and said, "Wayne, this is Tomasina; Tomie-Cis, this is Wayne." I offered my hand but simultaneously Tomasina offered her cheek, and when I moved to kiss her, she offered her hand. When they'd stopped laughing at me, I sat down and asked about Lucy.

"I'm okay," said Lucy. "How are you?"

"I'm alright."

"You don't look alright. What's happened to your eyes?"

"My eyes?" I said, standing up so I could see myself in the wall-mirror. "No, that's pretty normal; I've been having trouble sleeping."

"How come you're in London?"

"Manette broke up with me."

"Really?"

"Aye."

"How come?"

I shrugged.

"Do you like art?" said Tomasina.

"Not especially."

"Me neither. Shall we go in?"

"Let me go pee," said Lucy. We watched her walk to the toilet, between the tables, the porcelain milk jugs, the matching vases of short-stemmed flowers.

"What?" said Tomasina.

"What? Nothing what. Why?"

"Why aren't you talking to me?"

"I'm not *not* talking to you."

"Oh-kay."

"...So, how did you meet Lucy?"

"Don't you want to leave your bag at the cloakroom?"

"Aye, I will."

"She was my tutor."

"Aye? Wow, that's—"

"That's what?"

"So you're a student?"

"And a model."

"Really?"

"Does that surprise you? Is Jordan your idea of a model?"

"What you studying?"

"Sociology, economics, and population studies."

"What's population studies?"

"No idea; Lucy writes all my essays."

"Cool," I said, and immediately wondered why. I don't say *Cool*; I never say *Cool*.

Lynn Hershman Leeson's retrospective was called "Autonomous Agents," and I liked it. There were all sorts of things to play with, and there were plaques to help you make sense of the exhibits:

"The art of Lynn Hershman Leeson multiplies and refracts fictional identities to the point of exploding any stable notion of self. Her remarkable body of work, produced over more than thirty-five years, provides an artistic mirror for understanding our fragmented sense of subjectivity at the beginning of the twenty-first century." There were interactive video installations and pictures of lingerie models with TVs or cameras for heads or bodies. In "Project Roberta," the artist had created an alter ego, wearing a wig and make-up, affecting a submissive posture, and accumulating all the evidence of a life: a case of personal letters relating to her attempts to rent a room, romantic letters from men praising her beauty, extracts from her diary, and samples of her blood and urine. There was a psychiatric evaluation and an analysis of her handwriting. There were long shot photographs of dates she had arranged through a local paper: Roberta in an amusement park, a man in a Hawaiian shirt and sunglasses. She had an apartment lease, a driver's license, a bank account, credit cards, and dental records. There were even pictures of other women being Roberta, looking at Roberta's picture in a gallery.

"Wayne, Wayne!" Tomasina was bouncing on her toes, clapping her hands. "Try this!"

This was "Agent Ruby"—a computerised face on a glass screen that spoke in an electronic female voice. "What may I call you?"

"Go on," said Tomasina, "talk to her." I felt self-conscious talking to a machine in that wide gallery, but I stood in front of the microphone and said my name.

"I'm sorry, I didn't quite catch that. It sounded like you said 'waaaaah'. Try enunciating."

"Now I'm getting my diction slagged off by a robot."

"Please speak clearly into the microphone."

"Wayne!"

"Please repeat that with more or less context."

"I am Wayne."

"If I was you, I shouldn't worry myself much about that."

"My girlfriend left me because I have no faith in the future."

Tomasina laughed and Agent Ruby said, "Any of a number of games where two teams of opposing players kick or throw a leather ball with the object of scoring points." Tomasina laughed some more.

"I think you're mental, Ruby."

"Is there a twinkle in your eye, or are you just glad to see me?"

"I'm very glad to see you, but I don't think I have a twinkle. I don't feel like I have a twinkle. I feel sad." Halfway though this answer, my voice started to climb, and I realised I was about to cry. Not expecting this, Agent Ruby replied, "Number one hundred and forty five. Number one hundred and forty four." Tomasina looked on in horror. Then, as I started to sob, Tomasina patted my back with one hand while pulling her neck tendons elastic-tight, spooning *come here* gestures with her free arm, and mouthing *HELP! LUCY! HELP!* Lucy crossed towards us, equally distressed, her face screwed up to say *what the fuck?* She was looking left and right, the way she might have searched for help had I collapsed with a heart attack—*do I have to deal with this?*

The girls lived in Richmond, at the end of the District Line, where the houses are all whitewashed with metal balconies and sometimes boast blue plaques to commemorate the birthplace of an eminent physician, or the childhood home of an explorer. Everything in the girls' building—the brass-handrailed stairwell, the cooker with eight hobs instead of four—was on a grander scale than I'd expected. Who needs ceilings that high? Who has friends this tall?

"D'you afford this through modelling?" I asked, dropping my bag in the living room.

"I said I was a professional model, not Kate Moss. I do fashion and editorial work; most of the money's in commercial work. Plastic people from Liverpool with collagen implants. No, this is my dad's. I think he lets me live here as a tax scam."

"Well, it's really nice."

"Yes it is—don't touch anything."

"And what does he think about you two, I mean with—"

"One time they—him and mummy—came round unexpectedly, and Lucy was hoovering, and I told them she was a Polish cleaner."

"They believed that?"

"Of course they believed that. Why would my cleaner pretend to be Polish if she wasn't? And if she wasn't my cleaner, why would she be hoovering my carpet?"

"And how d'you feel about that?"

Lucy shrugged and picked up a magazine.

"Drinks! Something fizzy," said Tomasina, bouncing and clapping again.

I sat on the sofa, as far from Lucy as possible. "So, how's the PhD going?"

"I quit," she said, without looking up from *The Face*.

"How come?"

"I might go back and finish it sometime."

"Why'd you quit?"

"Various reasons: I became disenchanted with the direction of academia in the twenty-first century; I developed alternative career interests; I was sleeping with one of my first-year tutees."

"So I heard."

"Shocking really," said Tomasina, returning with a bunch of champagne flutes. "I mean, preying on youth like that."

"You know what I just realised—"

"You're the king of Bhutan?"

"No. I've not had anything to eat today."

"Jesus Wayne, what do you think this is—the fucking YMCA?" Tomasina was always teasing me like this, but she didn't mean it. When I'd been at their house for a week, and Lucy was sick of me and wanted me to leave, Tomie came into the living room, just after I'd read an e-mail from Manette. Manette's message had been so nonchalant, so *friendly*, and I'd rather have received twenty lines of abuse than her indifference. Tomie saw I was crying and put her arms around me. "It's okay," she said; "I don't understand, but it's okay."

The worst thing about depression (let's name the beast) was the insomnia. Some nights I'd try to drink myself to sleep, then I'd be ill in the morning, and the thing would perpetuate itself. I hate vomiting. There's always a slight pause, when your stomach balances for a moment, pondering the extent of its suffering like a suicidal man on a platform edge; then—*bang*—you expel and expel until you're coughing up bile, and then the bile is gone and you're spitting your emptiness. Then you stand up, shuddering— you know that feeling after you've spewed? Like a tube station when a train has just departed.

"Sorry about that before. With the bathroom."

"Coffee?" Tomasina bounced to the cafetiere, tying her dressing gown tighter and humming "La Marseillaise." "*La la la, la-la, la-la, laah-la-la.*"

Lucy's hair was pinned up with a long needle and she wore a grey trouser suit and thin-framed, rectangular glasses (Lucy didn't wear glasses; she'd never worn glasses). Except for the two stools at the breakfast bar, there was nowhere to sit, and I soon wilted onto the floor. Tomasina looked incredulous. "Okay. I'm trying hard to ignore that you smell of puke and alcohol and that you slept on my bathroom floor, but now you're lying on my kitchen floor. Is this a piece of performance art?"

"Why are you here, Wayne?"

"You need counselling, Wayne, *and*"—Tomasina hummed five bars of a song that I half-recognised, the theme tune to a quiz show or something—"it's your good fortune that Lucy's a sexpert!"

"A sexpert?"

Lucy shook her head to say it was no big deal. "I write a sex column for *Sharp Magazine*."

"Wow, how did you get that?"

"Tomie introduced me to the section editor."

"So, if you want, you can relate some unfathomably tedious though no doubt personally tragic story, while we pretend to listen, impersonating people who care. Then Lucy will tell you what to do." Perhaps this invitation wasn't genuine, but then Cat had never really consented to hear my problems either. So I told the whole story, from how Manette and I met, to when we parted at Gare du Nord. When I'd finished, Tomasina, who had made exaggerated gestures of boredom throughout, pretended to wake up and clapped her hands sarcastically.

"Well? Where's my counselling?"

"Ugh, get over her?"

"Basically, yeah. Look, come on Wayne. Giving advice is futile: it's either ignored or it confirms decisions that have already been taken. You'll do what you want. No, you'll do what you do and then interpret what you do as what you want. But you've got to sort out some kind of independent existence. You need to find a place to stay; you need to find a job."

"Amen," said Tomasina.

"I'm not sure I can."

"Well, you can't stay here."

"I thought maybe for a few days?"

"Yeah, *for a few days*," said Tomasina. "You'll need to cut a spare set of keys."

"Tomie-Cis—"

"If you're last out you need to set the burglar alarm: two-four-six-eight. Don't forget. I've got jewellery that's worth more than your father's house." Lucy laughed and threw a burnt bit of bagel, which arced over Tomasina's ducking head and landed in the sink with a soggy thud. "I'm *joking*, Lucy. Like, where would we be without the working class? I mean, who would buy tinned Spaghetti and Sunny Delight?"

I wanted to play along but couldn't think of anything funny to say. Instead, I asked if I could see the copy of *Sharp Magazine* that was folded back on its spine beside the marmalade.

Lucy said, "This? No, it's embarrassing," but she didn't stop me when I reached for it. It was open at an airbrushed photo of Lucy, in white cotton vest and panties, striking a warrior pose but laughing and wielding a pillow. The headline said "Dr. Lucy Lesjoue defends *your* right to pleasure."

"Lucy *Lesjoue*?"

"I guess Guthrie has the wrong sound."

Tomasina crouched behind Lucy, chin on her shoulder, arms around her like a seatbelt, and she started to croon "Candle in the Wind," coming in at "*They set you on a treadmill, and they made you change your name. Boom, boom, boom-boom-boom*," and hitting big air drums that I don't remember from the original.

The gist of Lucy's argument was that patriarchy has defined heterosexuality around female passivity, and this makes it difficult for women to negotiate good sex within heterosexual relationships. She discussed the ways women have been stigmatised for pursuing their pleasure and noted that in British Law, sex has traditionally been defined as penetrative penis-vagina intercourse to male orgasm. "Historically and institutionally, clitoral stimulation and female orgasm have been repressed." It finished with a personal reflection on her preference for a same-sex relationship and why over the years she had come to prefer sex with women though she still enjoyed sex with men. The products pictured in the margin included a device that was supposed to fit around the penis and stimulate the clitoris during penetrative sex and a rubber glove with stegosaurus-style spikes. "It's really good. I'm impressed."

"God, that photo!" she said, hiding behind her hands.

Cocaine. That made things better. The whole business of it: chopping the lines up, snorting it, the burn, the *whoooosh*, the buzz of it. We were going out—*out* out—something the girls thought would do me good. I was in the kitchen, wearing a suit that Tomasina had given me, enjoying the optimistic smell of hairspray and perfume. We were listening to Franz Ferdinand, and I could see the girls getting ready in the hall. They were jostling for position in front of the long mirror, straightening hair, fixing jewellery, applying lip-gloss and mascara. Then Tomasina skipped into the kitchen, giggling, "Cocaine, cocaine," as she produced a bag of powder from a small wooden box. "Lucy! We do too much cocaine. We must spend a fortune on cocaine. Instead of a smoke box, we should have a coke box. We could put all the money we would have spent on cocaine towards a treat. The Dominican Republic or something." She kissed me on the forehead. "What a difference to see you in a suit! What does he look like, Lucy?"

"What?"

"What does Wayne look like?"

"I don't know... an extra from *Taggart*?"

"Aw! No, he looks... *eligible*." She kissed my cheek again. "Are you ready?"

"I've been ready for an hour."

"Are you sure you don't need to go wee wee?"

"You know that when I first saw you I thought you were about fourteen?"

"Don't feel bad; when I first saw you I thought you were about to steal my handbag. Come on. See that carpet? My dad loves carpets, spends a fortune on them. They always make a deliberate mistake in Persian carpets. You know why? Because only Allah is perfect. Today's thought for the day was brought to you by a coked-out teenager. Lucy? Come on! The world is waiting."

A red rope hung across the doorway in a converse arch, and, surrounding a tall blonde woman who held a clipboard, there was a mêlée of what Tomasina called "D-lists" or "hangers on." All this was alien to me—to get into a Dundulc nightclub you need only prove that you can stand upright without assistance—but Tomasina's modelling agency was on the guest list, and after some talking and pointing, the rope was unhooked.

By this time, I only knew I was out of it when I realised I was concentrating on executing basic movements: entering the club, I placed one leg before the other, negotiating the length of the corridor. But inside, where people sat on Bauhaus-style chairs, nodding to drum and bass or shuffling awkward and self-conscious on the dance floor, I got over the euphoria of having been admitted and realised I didn't want to be there. There was nowhere to sit, so we stood near Tomasina's friends, drinking bottles of Corona, as the club lurched around me, and the dancers appeared in glimpses—a girl with a cigarette, the bottom of a crucifix tattoo bending across a man's biceps—their faces flitting past like something seen from a train.

"Here, Lucy," I said, "what's the best time you ever had?"

"What?" she said, leaning towards me, still nodding with the music.

"The best time you ever had, the time of your life, when was it?"

"I don't know... my first year in London?"

"Remember when we all worked at Benny's and thought we could change the world?"

She smiled with one side of her mouth. "We were wrong!"

"What?"

"We were wrong!"

"I'm not so sure."

"Look around you."

"We were organised. We could have run our own workplace. If everybody had been like us—"

"Well, they're not!"

"What?"

"Most kids. They're not like we were."

"Really? What made us so special?"

"This is a very serious conversation for a nightclub."

"A very what?"

"D'you want a drink?" she said, shaking an empty bottle.

"Wait. Remember how we were always going to doorstep Andrew Duke? We had his home address, remember?" Tomasina passed us on the way to the bar, cheeks flushed from the fullness of the moment. "We could still do it, couldn't we? We could get the whole gang together. Most of us are in London anyway. Maybe I can get hold of Kit and Gordon. Perhaps Buzz would come down from Scotland? D'you think Duke will still be at the same address?"

Lucy nodded. "I'm going to get a drink."

"Wait," I said, feeling the sheen of sweat on her arm. "Do you remember when I stayed at yours?"

"What?" She was half-turned, holding her purse.

"When we slept together. Well, that's the thing: Spocky thinks we did but we didn't. I mean we slept together but—" She shook her arm free and tapped Tomasina, who was trying to find a way to the bar. Tomasina made a question face, and Lucy, lip-writing Co-ro-na, held up her empty bottle. Then she turned back to me, moving in time with the music, almost dancing.

"I just think it's funny that I had always desired you so much and then when we were in bed I couldn't, you know?"

Lucy was smiling, nodding with me, nodding with the music, watching Tomasina prise a corridor through the crowd. Tomasina paused, side-stepped, tilted her ear towards a man, smiled at whatever he was trying to say, and then she disappeared as sabres of light swung above our heads. In front of me, there stopped a woman, whose halter neck top was tied in white bows. As the music coiled tighter, the woman shuffled her bum from side to side, raising her arms, crossing them above her head, waiting, waiting, until the music released and the lights threw stars and the dance floor bounced as one. And that was when I leant towards Lucy and made a sudden, quite unexpected, surprisingly determined attempt to kiss her.

★ 21 ★

"So what did she do?" said Buzz.

"She pulled back and pushed me away, with both hands. Like this. 'What the fuck are you doing?'"

Buzz laughed. "What the fuck were you doing?"

"I don't know."

"It's sexual assault."

"That's harsh."

"You lunged at her, and she had to fend you off. What would you call it?"

"An inappropriate pass?"

"Man, what were you thinking?"

"I really didnae mean it. It wasn't like something I planned. You know?"

"Not really," said Buzz.

It was the day we went after Andrew Duke, the director of Benny's UK. Buzz and I had walked down from Trafalgar Square, and now we stood at the entrance to Parliament Square. "Tomasina said these things happen."

"She should have kicked you in the nuts."

"They both said it was inappropriate for me to stay on at the flat. I said, 'Of course, I understand. I'm sorry.'"

"So you should be."

"I've still got keys. We could hide in their wardrobe and watch."

"And then you moved into a hotel?"

"Aye. I'm in this place near Victoria Station. It's a dump."

"How much is it costing?"

"Forty-five pounds a night."

"*Jesus Wayne!* How the fuck are you paying for this?"

"I'm just putting it all on my credit card."

"Dude, you don't have a job. You're gonna end up screwed."

"Well, it's a good time to get into debt. It's a growth industry. Debt's the only thing keeping the economy going."

"Why don't you come home, man? I'm worried about you."

"I don't think I can." As we waited at the traffic lights, an empty tourist bus stopped in front of Churchill's statue, engine revving. Two policemen stamped their feet beneath Big Ben, looking across to the peace vigil on the pavement.

"Wayne, it's pissing with rain and I really need a pint."

"I want to show you one more thing."

"Don't you want to see Spocky?"

"Spocky hates me—"

"What about Kit and Gordon?"

"I haven't seen them since Deanne's funeral."

Buzz laughed and slapped my back. "At least you won't have to see Lucy."

I stood, looking across to the Abbey, finding it hard to believe that this was where Spocky and I had dug up the grass on May Day 2000. The wind was dragging the rain, whipping lines across the square, and all around me abandoned umbrellas slumped against walls, lying in gutters or stretched on the pavements, spokes twisted and bent by the wind.

Back up Whitehall, past Downing Street and the Cenotaph, into the Wetherspoon's bar: the one that's on your left as you walk towards Trafalgar Square. It was dingy inside and there was no music, just the *chang* of the cash drawer and library-volume conversation. At a table near the door, Kit and Gordon stood up as we crossed towards them, and Spocky, maybe not sure which way to go, kind of crouched, with his arse above the chair but his legs not quite extended. Gordon pulled me in for an embrace, picking me five inches off the ground, but there was something awkward about it. Maybe it was something to do with Kit. She said, "Hi Wayne," in a serious voice that I didn't recognise, and hung her arms around my neck, pressing her bulging stomach against my groin. The thing you couldn't help noticing about Kit was that she looked pregnant. But how do you tell for sure? I felt I should offer my congratulations, but I was worried that the baby could be an impressive beer belly. At any rate, I caught Spocky's eye over her shoulder and couldn't risk appearing to snub him. He was still wearing that black trench coat, or at least *a* black trench coat, and a billowing pair of camouflaged combat trousers. He was going for the state militia look, for the *only in America could he get a gun permit* look. He took my hand, a bit reluctantly, like a politician who's run into Robert Mugabe at an international conference.

Well, there was something of the school reunion about it— "hasn't she done well for herself"; "do you remember the time that"—but it was strange how little seemed worth reporting after two years. Buzz mentioned that Raj was still married but now working for Vodafone (or Orange or Telewest, perhaps); Kieran was still in the job (which surprised nobody); and Kit *was* pregnant, expecting in four months (no, less than that: three months and a bit—three months, three weeks, and about four days). With great relief we toasted the bairn's health, and everyone glanced towards me, the same way that if Kit and Gordon ever got married, the congregation would look at me, holding their breath, when the minister asked if anyone knew of a reason why they couldn't. Then Gordon remembered that Jason Scott was in prison, having been convicted for extorting money from a house-bound pensioner, over a period of months, during which time he tied up the old man and stubbed cigarettes out all over his body.

Nobody knew what to say after that so we sat in silence as the lunching civil servants filled the bar with a school dinner noise of knives on plates. Eventually, Buzz asked if there was a plan. "I mean, what do we actually do when we get there?"

It hadn't really occurred to me that we would need a plan. "We just sneak into Duke's building and knock on his door."

"Yeah, but *then* what?"

"I don't know; hit him with a custard pie or something."

"Do we have a custard pie?" asked Kit.

"Why's everyone asking me? Who made me leader?"

"We gonnae take pictures or what?" asked Gordon.

"You're no gonnae do anything."

"I've got a camera on my phone," said Kit, flicking her mobile open in case we didn't believe her.

"How no?"

"Cause there are warrants out for you?"

"We'll no get lifted," said Kit.

"Aye, cause you're not coming."

Gordon went a bit sulky at this point and folded his arms.

"What's supposed to be the point of this anyway? I mean, what's our objective here?" asked Spocky.

I shrugged. "It's propaganda by the deed, isn't it?"

"Guys," said Buzz, because nobody had a reply to that, "remember that Christmas Eve, how many years ago now?" He started counting back with his fingers.

"Five," I said.

"That long? Crazy. We were all wearing Santa suits, except this guy who was dressed up as a Dalek."

Gordon smiled, remembering this. "There werenae enough Santa suits, that was the problem."

"How was I no there?" said Kit.

"Cause you were working. That was the whole point: it was eight o'clock on Christmas Eve and yous were still at work."

Spocky didn't seem to want to talk about this, and he stood up, perhaps to go to the toilet, coughing into his hand the same way he'd been coughing for six years. And as we sat there, drinking and reminiscing, the certain irreversibility of time, the knowledge that this time of my life had passed, began to scare me. It was like closing a door to which you have no key: you want to hold it ajar while you check you have everything, and when you finally let go, you feel a fluttery panic, a sense of having left something valuable behind.

Later, when most of the suits had returned to work, leaving plates empty except for a few soggy chips or a bit of salad, and the room holding that smell of cooking oil that used to stick to all of us when we worked for Benny's, the barmaid, an Australian girl who seemed irritated by our still being there, stacked our empty pint glasses into a big curving tower. Spocky stood alone, beside the unplayed fruit machines. Behind him, they strobed and flashed with all the gaudy sadness of Christmas lights that nobody took down. It seemed likely to entail enormous effort, but I knew what I had to do. "Alright, Owen."

"Wayne."

"How's it going?"

Spocky reached into the lining of his jacket and leant against the condiment table. He started to roll one of his wiry cigarettes.

"Been a long time, eh?"

"Right."

It was only then, after a few pints, that I realised how much this reconciliation meant to me. I wanted to explain about Lucy. I wanted to talk about friendship. I wanted to say something honest that got at the truth of the matter. "You involved with much politically these days?"

"Not really."

"No?"

Spocky lit his cigarette, blowing the smoke out and reading the back of his lighter before returning it to his pocket. "Have you ever looked at people, actual real people, and realised that pretty much everyone you've ever met is fundamentally horrible? That actually they *deserve* to be sent to Iraq en masse; that actually if half the world died of asbestos poisoning, you wouldn't really miss them?"

"I wouldn't put it like that."

"You wouldn't."

"I mean, I know what you're saying, but isn't that kind of— I mean, isn't the point that the proletariat is the negation of capitalist society, but we're also its consequence; we're—"

"I'm not asking you a theoretical question; I'm asking you at a personal, emotional level—do you *really* care about anyone except yourself?"

"I don't think that's the question."

"It is the question—I just asked it."

"You can't separate one person from everyone else. That altruism and egoism binary—"

"I'm not asking you a theoretical question."

"Besides, you could be like an egoist, couldn't you? Like a Stirnerite or something? I'm not saying I am; I'm just saying you could be, as an example."

"Do you care or not?"

"I know I'm not *a good person*. If that's what you're saying."

"That's not the question."

"This sounds Christian," I said, shaking my head.

"You don't think it's a valid question?"

"I'm not sure I understand the question."

"Do you care about anyone except yourself? It's a simple question."

A bald man in a suit, a late-luncher, was taking a break from his Spaghetti, following Spocky's argument, wondering where it would go.

"You know, what I really wanted to talk about was—"

Spocky held up his hand. "Yes or no?"

"Yes."

"Yes?"

"   "
...

"   "
...

"Listen. I'm not having a great time just now. My girlfriend left me for this guy who looks like an extra from *Romper Stomper*. I cannae sleep—I don't ever sleep for more than half an hour—and recently I've started crying in public. It's weird." I had no idea why I was telling Spocky these things. "I know what you're saying. I'm a selfish person, aye?"

"   "
...

"Is that what you're saying?"

"I'm not saying anything. That's what *you're* saying."

"Are you saying you're not selfish or that you are?" I didn't even know which way up Spocky's argument was supposed to go.

It was like I'd been given some self-assembly furniture with the main piece missing.

"You know the idea of Karma?"

"*Karma*?"

"I think there's something in that. I don't mean reincarnation or fatalism, I just mean that if you're formed by the people around you, then how you behave in regard to them has consequences, not just for them, but also for yourself."

"Sure. Okay," I said.

Spocky's cigarette had gone out and he flicked it onto the carpet. "Men make history but not in circumstances of their own choosing. Right?"

"Right," I said, still unsure where this was going but sensing that Spocky was trying to forgive me for something.

"So what makes men?"

"D'you want a drink?" I said, swilling the last centimetre around my glass. "I might get another drink."

"What makes men?" said Spocky.

"What makes men? The mummy and the daddy lie together and the daddy puts his—"

At this point, Spocky crashed his fist down on a sachet of ketchup with such force that it popped a slash of red across the carpet and up the leg of my jeans. Like someone eating a TV dinner, the bald guy paused with his fork an inch from his mouth, so that a strand of spaghetti pendulumed below his chin. As I struggled for a response, Spocky put his hands to his head and laughed. Then he turned and lurched towards the exit, leaving me to wonder if I'd missed something, or if Spocky had gone completely mad.

An hour later, Buzz and I stood on Southwark Bridge, watching the black barges drifting on the great brown river, enjoying the lonely feeling of being at sea. At one end, looking back the way we had come, you could see the dome of St. Paul's, while ahead of us lurked the industrial shape of the Tate Gallery. Rain washed across the deck of the bridge, and we leant on the railing, smoking cigarettes, with our jackets zipped to our chins.

"So, you don't think Spocky's mad?"

"I don't wanna get involved."

"Buzz, I'm no asking you to take sides between two mates; I'm just asking if you think, maybe, as his friends, we should be worried about him?"

"I'm worried about you."

"Exactly. And I appreciate that. So I'm just asking, having listened to the guy talk gibberish for five minutes, then slam his fist on a sachet of ketchup and disappear without saying goodbye or anything, I'm just asking how did he seem to you?"

"I didn't hear that conversation, so I can't really comment."

"Fucksake Buzz, you're like a politician or something. The guy is talking all this shite—"

"Like what?"

"Like fucking karma, and men make history, and what makes men, and egoism and altruism, and all sorts of shite. Right? Then, totally out the blue, the last thing in the world you would have seen coming, he fucking punches this ketchup."

"You must have upset him. I'm sure you didn't mean to, but you must have."

"Forget that. How did he seem when you were talking?"

It was now dark, but the Bankside lights didn't so much reflect off the water as seem to get stuck and entangled in its depths. Looking east, I saw the tail of a train disappear, pulled into the city, and in the distance, Tower Bridge was lit up, blurred by the dark and the wet. The sky seemed to have layers of depth, miles and miles of cloud, and the aeroplanes looked lost and lonely, their lights blinking as they arced out of sight. After a long pause, Buzz said, "He seemed eccentric. But hasn't he always? I mean, at first, isn't that why nobody liked him? And then, wasn't that what we liked about him most? Isn't that why Lucy fell in love with him?"

"That one still beats me."

"Now you're saying that you're back to not liking him because he's eccentric?"

"I never said I didn't like him. And today he was way beyond eccentric."

"You've got to remember that he's never been a big drinker. He was pretty drunk this afternoon." The wind was swooping along the Thames, so loud we had to shout.

"Maybe I dinnae like him, but it's hardly surprising given he just fucking attacked me with ketchup."

"A few days ago you made some mad lunge for Lucy; if he's crazy..." Buzz threw his cigarette over the edge, and the wind caught hold of it, so that it tumbled towards the river, its lit end disappearing and reappearing in the dark. "I think you and Spocky are both just a bit disillusioned. And today, going to see Andrew Duke, it's like the end of—"

"Maybe we were too optimistic about what we could achieve."

Buzz nodded.

"Maybe. We gave it our best shot. But if most people are happy being wage slaves—"

"But they're not. That's the point. Half the country's on anti-depressants."

"..."

"Self-harm accounts for 142,000 hospital admissions every year. That's just in England and Wales."

"That still leaves a lot of people."

"The Samaritans estimate there's a suicide in the UK every eighty-two minutes. Are we happy? Are we fuck. We're poisoning, cutting, and burning ourselves like never before."

Beneath us, a swarm of seagulls followed a fishing vessel. They swooped and screeched, bright white against the murky water. "Wayne, what are you going to do when you reach your credit limit?"

"..."

"Seriously Wayne, how long d'you think this can go on for?"

The Duke's block had a bar on the ground floor—a real fish-tank of a place with minimalist décor and big glass windows—where we bought two expensive rounds for courage. We had done a bit of reconnaissance, scouting out the entrance lobby and its various obstacles—the CCTV cameras, the concierge—and over our drinks we had decided to wait out of view until we saw a resident enter. Looking up into the rain, with a sort of inverse vertigo, you could see that the lower floors were offices, and that above these, the apartments, marked out by their balconies and potted plants, promised views across the river to St. Paul's or the Gherkin. We soon realised this wasn't the sort of place where people went in and out; nobody was going to nip across the road to visit their neighbours, there wasn't a local convenience store, and now that the office-staff had finished their post-work drinks, the bar downstairs was empty and looked ready to shut. It was one of those buildings with pipes on the outside, meant to resemble the Centre Georges Pompidou (Beaubourg, as Manette called it), but really, when you thought about it, not very different from the sort of building that most of us spend our lives trying to avoid. After we had spent fifteen minutes keeping out of the rain and off the cameras, smoking cigarettes and bouncing on the spot to stave off the cold and the boredom, I said to Buzz that we needed a plan B.

"I agree. Let's go to the pub."

"We should look for a fire escape or something."

"It's stupid doing this just the two of us. I mean, what's the point anyway? It's completely—" Buzz stopped his sentence because a taxi had pulled up and after a few seconds stalling in the cab, a man in a grey suit emerged, holding his briefcase above his head as he trotted across the plaza. "Go! Go! Go!" The man reached the cover of the concourse and slowed so that we had to hold our run for fear of getting to the door before him. As it was, we timed it just right, letting him swipe the pad with his fob and thanking him as he held the door open. We stuck tight beside him as he crossed the lobby. He nodded a greeting to the young concierge, who looked up from a screen, saw the three of us together, and might have assumed we were the other guy's guests. Except you could see from the way his eyes tracked us that something didn't match up. Buzz's jeans were ripped around the arse and frayed to tassels at the bottom, my right leg was smeared with ketchup, and we were both soaking wet. Worse, we were walking in that ginger self-conscious way, anticipating the various signals that would give away our drunkenness, like adolescents coming home after boozing in the park. The concierge watched us, his mouth a little open, but who knows who brings who home and why? Younger relatives at university, rent boys—it was none of his business.

As the three of us walked out of view, the guy in the grey suit glanced over his shoulder, and when the corridor forked, I grabbed Buzz, pulling him to the right. We high-fived before we remembered the cameras and walked on, trying to look relaxed but business-like, following the corridor until it was blocked by a locked glass door. As I started pressing random combinations, Buzz shouldered open an unmarked white door, releasing the hum of an electricity box. "In here," he whispered. It was a service corridor, brightly lit but uncarpeted, stacked with Blue-roll and mop buckets. It smelled of something chemical like Ajax.

I looked up at the roof of giant silver pipes. "What now? Into the air ducts?"

Buzz gestured for me to be quiet and led us, past industrial cleaning machines—vacuums and floor-polishers that filled the corridor like de-activated Daleks—to the top of a short spiral staircase that chimed our descending footsteps. With each step, the light became gloomier and the smell of fermenting refuse grew stronger, until we were holding our noses, breathing through our mouths, and *tasting* the stench. At the bottom, it was dark, except for what light dripped in from above, and I covered my head as a rattling bobsleigh noise started in the distance and accelerated towards us, crashing nearby. Then the lights stuttered and found their glow, revealing a line of skips on a stone floor that was wet with the rainwater that slid under the padlocked mesh gates. "Come on," said Buzz, flapping his hand.

The door at the far end opened into a cement-walled corridor, along which the ceiling lights Mexican-waved with our progress. Then we emerged into the hallway, looking left and right, standing just yards from the lift.

Buzz pressed the call button, many times, like a child impatient at a pedestrian crossing. "What floor?" he said when the doors opened. I reached past him and pressed eight. If our informant was right, Duke lived in number 813. There were mirrors on three sides of the lift and a camera in the top-right corner, so we could watch ourselves being watched. The lift started to climb and a light counted the floors: 2—3—4. "This is stupid," said Buzz. —6. "What we going to do when we meet this guy?" —8.

"I don't know; we'll play it by ear." The doors opened, and we stepped onto the landing. There was a red chesterfield, a ceramic vase of dried flowers and pine cones, and a left-pointing metal plaque engraved "811–820."

"Wait," said Buzz, grabbing my wrist, hard enough that I could feel the speed and strength of my pulse.

"What?"

"Shouldn't we cover our faces or something?"

"Too late now," I said, looking up at the camera as I edged round the corner. I could hear movie gunfire, just audible from behind the door of apartment 811. In a big mirror with an engraved brass frame, I watched our reflections stealth past apartment 812. There was a fire extinguisher behind a glass panel and then door 814. I looked at Buzz. He put his finger to his lips and shrugged. 815. 816. We reached the end of the corridor. We reached the fire escape. We turned back. 814. 812. We retraced our steps to the lift. We turned right instead of left. 801. 802. 803. We counted doorways to 810. We entered the fire stairs and squeaked our trainers on the plastic landing. We retreated, back the way we had come, back to the lift. We saw the red chesterfield and the ceramic vase of dried flowers and pine cones. Outside 811, we heard a helicopter and then a car chase. We saw the big mirror outside 812. We saw the fire extinguisher beside 814.

813 did not exist.

★ 22 ★

During my last aimless days in London, I rode the Underground to the end of each line and then back again. At first I travelled around the central zones, thinking that what I searched for lay overground, but then I decided that the answer resided in the tunnels. I was at Tottenham Court Road, I think, and when my train arrived, I stayed seated and let the platform clear. The train departed and I listened as the echo of its scream limped out from the dark. Quickly, the platform refilled: black people wearing dashikis and kaftans, men in high-vis jackets, school kids with their shirts buttoned wrong and Tipp-Ex slogans on their bags. Behind them, a perfume advert curved around the cylindrical shape of the tunnel: "Freedom in a bottle," it said. The man who sat beside me had one foot in a plaster cast, and a girl's name (Laura? Lara? Lucy?) tattooed on his forearm in time-diluted blue-green letters. On the poster, a girl in a flip skirt rose from the desert, like a stage-angel lifted by a wire. Then I felt the warm air, saw the lights, heard the roar and screech, tasted iron. And for a moment, people crowded and shouldered and reached for handles, their faces, in the yellow light, burning with the expectation of departure. The train beeped, the doors slammed, and I watched the empty track stretch out once more—a squashed Ribena carton, cigarette butts floating in puddles, a sodden converse trainer.

What was the appeal? Maybe I enjoyed the juxtaposition of isolation and incorporation. On the Underground, you are surrounded by others, jostled and shouldered, driven and steered by the crowd; and yet, on the Underground, you are totally, uniquely alone. So I rode the trains to Brixton and Morden, Ealing Broadway, West Ruislip and Stanmore. I explored Upminster, Epping, and Cockfosters. Then, when I was returning from a pub lunch at the extremity of the Northern Line, I noticed the disused old station building at High Barnet. This triggered a new interest. For days I explored the abandoned lines and ghost stations, the secret network of tunnels and staircases that lurks below the metropolis. I rode the Piccadilly Line, scanning for glimpses of Brompton Road, York Road, and Down Street. On the Northern Line, I looked for South Kentish Town, Bull and Bush, City Road. Above ground, I traced the routes of forgotten branch lines. Smoking a cigarette on The Strand, I saw two other men had come to see the former Aldwych Station. Why such fascination?

And then I explored the disused overground lines. In spring sleet, I walked the Northern Heights, from Finsbury Park to Alexandra Palace, and near Highgate, where the yews and birches hang over the pathway, I watched a hedgehog foraging in the trackside grass. I went as far as the restored station at Quainton Road, and I walked the old Wotton Tramway to Brill. Stepping towards the barricaded Robinson Tunnel, the sun set behind me, and my shadow stretched 100 metres long. The embankments were overgrown with brambles and ragwort broke through the stony path and the silence was loud like the silence of deep underwater. If you approach the bars at the mouth of that tunnel, as the sun sets at your back, it feels honestly like the end of the world. Even graffiti artists have ceased to go there. I remember seeing barely legible flaked letters daubed on the left abutment of the tunnel: "SOLIDARITY WITH THE MINERS." And just visible, half-obscured by a hawthorn bush, a faded circled A.

Does even the painter recall this mute gesture?

Throughout all these explorations, I ate and drank as I wanted. I visited a pub at every station and played solitaire while I got drunk. I abandoned veganism and bought takeaway pizzas, roast dinners, kebabs. I paid for everything on my credit card. And then, one morning, sooner than I'd expected, the ATM at Victoria refused me a cash advance. I remember the impatience of the queue behind me as my card was repeatedly rejected. I kept travelling, fare-dodging on the bendy buses, suddenly looking for work. I filled in application forms at a snooker club, a baked potato shop, an internet cafe, a care home, a library. I applied for income support. I even applied to the Oxford Road Benny's Burgers. But it was all too slow. I planned to look up some former comrades, find out about a squat space or a cheap room. I thought about jumping the train to Dundule. I should at least have phoned Kit and Gordon. Instead, I pawned most of my jewellery, including the gold bracelet Manette had given me. And then, on the morning of March 2nd, I returned to Richmond.

There was a coffee-bar on the opposite side of Lucy's street. It had windows that could kick open in the summer, a mocha paint job, and strips of fairy lights criss-crossing the factory art. A girl with blonde pigtails poured my pint while a slouchy boy with rock star tattoos watched on; it was one of those places where the staff are all so gorgeous you're sure it can't be a coincidence.

I sat where I could get the best view across the street. The cloud was high and chalky; there was no mist or fog. Indeed, the biggest problem was buses sticking in the rush hour traffic: I had to peer through one window and out the other and the passengers, sure they were at the centre of something, glowered at my impudence or took it flirtatiously, playing eye-tig until things moved on. But more often the view was open, and I glanced between Lucy's front door and the TV screens above the bar. They were showing Sky News, mute with subtitles that were typed up real-time and full of mistakes. Two middle-aged lesbians were to be married in Multnomah County, Oregon; an unmanned craft, Opportunity, had landed on Mars.

It was only 8:30 and the other customers were all on coffee. Two work colleagues hunched over a laptop, and three boys, sixth formers or first year students, sprawled on leather couches, holding their heads. The waiting wasn't as tedious as I'd expected. In fact, this surveillance felt like a detective game. On TV, there was a panorama of rubble. There were women wearing black headscarves. There were men wearing flip-flops. "Two hundred feared dead after multiple explosions hit Shiite shrines in Baghdad and Karbala." There were women keening, beating the ground. There were bodies wrapped in sheets. There was a man in a football shirt who met the camera's gaze with an expression that said, *What do you want me to do?*

The three boys on the couches were recounting last night, incident by incident, trying to hold onto it. "No, it was you! You asked the guy if he wanted to come clubbing with us!"

"Who the Hell was he?"

"He was just some random."

"I thought Tim was talking to him?"

"Hey, d'you remember Tim climbing up that scaffolding?"

"Oh my God, I'd *totally* forgotten about that."

"And the security guy was like, 'Where you going?' and Tim's like, 'I believe I can fly!'"

There was a little girl, both arms stumped off at the elbows, looking into the camera with a patient, expectant stare.

"And those Canadian girls were saying, 'Don't jump, don't jump.'"

"'We love you, don't jump!'"

"I really can't remember anything after we left Ben's."

The US had declared itself in charge of foreign forces in Haiti, where I hadn't even noticed there was a war. Avril Lavigne had denied calling Hilary Duff a "Goody-goody mommy's girl." The pigtail girl took a break and crossed the street in a funky jacket with a furry collar; it was just cold enough to see her breath. Back in Iraq, and maybe related to the earlier story, a column of men shook their fists and fired automatic weapons into the sky. An older guy emerged from Lucy's stair and paused on the pavement, opening himself to the day.

I saw Lucy and Tomasina leave the house just after I'd ordered my third pint. I didn't want to waste my drink and tried to down it in one, but the chill of it spread into my teeth and down through my lungs, until I had to pause and breathe, and belch up some space. I nearly forgot my bag—a large Nike hold-all, almost empty—and the rock star boy, confused by my sudden urgency, called out, "Okay, well, see you," as I ran to catch up. I felt buoyed by my secret, cutting across the road in two stages, feeling the alcohol surge hit me, starting to enjoy myself. I tailed them like a private eye. But when they strolled into the station, I didn't follow. Instead, I entered a black cab.

The driver finished telling a joke about a Yugoslavian prostitute—"Slobber-down-my-cock-you-bitch"—then he started the engine and pushed forward. The other driver, still laughing from the joke, patted the back of the cab, as if it was a horse that needed encouragement to run.

It was a short drive to Lucy's. Halfway through, the adrenalin locked onto me, and I don't remember thinking much except: *Am I doing this? I'm doing this. Am I doing this? I'm doing this.* I asked the taxi to wait. I ran up the stairs. I unlocked the door and typed *two-four-six-eight*. The microwave was flashing the wrong time and the dishwasher was on, making a territorial hissing noise. I took the mallet out of the hold-all.

I'm not trying to say what I did was okay, but I didn't take any sentimental stuff. I raided Tomasina's wicker jewellery box, tipping the dusty neglected stuff from the bottom two drawers—unwanted presents, misfitting rings and snapped necklaces, bits and pieces she'd gladly have swapped for insurance cash—and the top drawer stuff, the pieces I'd seen her wear, I scattered on the carpet, as though I had dropped them in my rush (a chance of fortune that I imagined would make her smile). I took one pair of hair straighteners but left the other. I took Lucy's laptop because I knew she was obsessive about backing up her files. I took an ipod and a pair of candlesticks. I took the silver cutlery and the antique carriage clock. I took things Tomasina didn't care about. Things her parents owned.

I carried the bag to the taxi and placed it inside. "Shit," I said, "I forgot my phone." Running back upstairs, I thought how funny it would be if the taxi drove away. I collected the mallet, set the alarm, and closed the door. This was the bit I'd been worrying about. One, two, three swings and still the lock held firm. The fourth one cracked it. As I swung for the fifth time, I remembered Jason taking that hammer to Giorgio, hacking his ribs as if he was chopping down a tree. The door swung open, and I followed right through, almost into the hallway. I wiped my prints off the mallet, and as an afterthought, I rolled up the Persian rug. Then I heard a door opening on the floor above, and I ran with the carpet on my shoulder, taking the steps three at a time.

In the taxi, I wanted to say "Drive! Drive! Drive!" because a blue light had started zipping around the alarm box, and that neighbour must have phoned the police. It was a practical joke, I'd say. I'd tell the police it was a prank on my friends: let them think they'd been burgled for a few hours and then give them the stuff back and pay for the door. It was a joke. I was getting them back for— I'd make up a story about how they hoaxed me last April Fool's. I'd give everything back. I'd plead with Lucy not to press charges. No way would she press charges. She'd see that I was desperate. She knew I was depressed. I'd get a caution for wasting police time. I'd say I was sorry.

The driver watched his mirror, waiting for a gap in the traffic. I could hear the *tic-tic-tic* of his indicator, and the alarm—sounding soft through the windows—hitting the sort of shrill note that's supposed to shatter glass.

It wasn't the quickest route, but, even weighed down with all that I carried, I took a masochistic pleasure in walking via Elmore Road. Not much had changed since I left Dundule, and when I emerged from the railway bridge, and I could see Benny's and the Railway Arms, it was easy to imagine Lucy and Kit, crossing the road, teenagers again. I pictured them in red and white striped uniforms, their ponytails swinging from the back of their caps. Through the Railway's windows, I could see Deborah behind the bar and alcoholic Tam crashing between tables. That they remained seemed like pure defiance. The neon B still glowed above Benny's, and I expected to see Spocky or Gordon or Raj, but the boy clearing tables looked up at me, with no idea I'd ever worked there, and carried on bagging polystyrene foams and discarded burger wrappers. Meanwhile, another boy mopped the floor, scrubbing where the cracked tiles (broken by the Teddy Boy's fall), were often mistaken for dirt. I watched as he angled the mop into the water, steering the bucket towards the toilets, veering the slow curve dictated by the wheels, and as the two boys passed, they paused and spoke, their voices lost behind glass, the peaks of their caps just low enough to hide their eyes.

Jerry's shop, below the tenements, at the far end of Lanark Road, with the sign promising "Cash paid for jewellery, antiques, scrap gold and other valuables," and the dusty windows and the wire mesh, was the sort of place where you thought seriously before you entered, where you studied the chain you wanted while mustering your courage, where you stood at the door, breathed deeply, and pushed. Inside, Jerry stood behind the counter, trying to place me. At that moment, the Persian rug slipped from under my arm, tumbling like an Italian footballer who thinks he's been fouled; it unwound with each decelerating roll, until it came to rest, spread flat on the floor. When Jerry recognised me, his face cracked into a grimace. "City Link no good enough for ye, eh? Come on a flyin fuckin carpet, did ye? How are you son? You look like a man who's selling?" Jerry looked like he was dying. His face had that grey-yellow tint you sometimes see in the terminally ill, and as he shuffled behind the counter, I noticed that one of his hands wasn't moving—that one of his arms was prosthetic.

I was unsure how to mention this (how do you lose an arm?), and I was unsure how to inquire about his wellbeing without mentioning it, so I just said, "I've a few things I thought maybe you could have a look at." He sucked the gaps around his teeth, and then, with a habitual ease that made me think the false arm was a recent thing, he tried to rub his hands together.

The office, that sanctum of crime I'd always wanted to see, felt like a reconstruction of something. It had old-fashioned lamps with tasselled shades and green leather upholstery like something from a gentleman's club. And it had a smell of tobacco and sweat—of illegality, if illegality could have a scent—and it was everything I'd always imagined. Jerry studied the jewellery, with one eye crumpling around a magnifier. He said what carat the gold was and if the stones were real or glass. He *seemed* to be honest about it. "Where d'you get a pile of lassie's jewellery, Wayne?" he said, turning a ring on his velvet mat.

"A friend gave it to me."

"Does she live anywhere near here?"

"Nah, London."

"Well, Uncle Jerry is impressed. See your silver here? Complete forty-eight-piece set, original oak case, rat-tail patterned, engraved in period style. See there? It's dated 1928, William Hutton and Sons. Nice that. And this clock, does it go?" He trapped the upturned clock between his elbow and ribs as he fumbled at the base. "Aye," he said. "Now, when I seen this I was excited. See the back plate, here? James Sterling." Beneath the engraving he smudged an imaginary line with one of the dead fingers. "Early nineteenth century, mahogany case, brass ogee feet. See that? Silvered brass chapter ring. Double fusee movement. Four, five pillars. This is a wee Bobby Dazzler. And ken something else? I couldae telt ye this wis worth a tenner. I could of, eh?"

"Aye," I said.

Jerry stood up, shaking so much that he had to steady himself against the chair. It was uncomfortably hot in the office, and in my exhaustion I thought that he or I or both of us might faint. "Right," he said, rubbing his living hand against his dead one, "money, money, money."

I took the train to Glasgow Central, stood in the concourse, and watched the departure boards. And when they announced the platform for an overdue service, I joined the surge of people. In ignorance of the train's destination, I boarded, and sat in the vestibule between two carriages. It terminated in Manchester, where, in time, I let a room and found a job at the bus station.

It's possible that one day I'll repay Lucy. It's equally possible that she'll never know the truth. Maybe Manette and I will become pen pals. Perhaps I'll go back to university: I'll get a career in human resources, fall in love with a girl from accounts, and holiday in Southern France. Maybe we'll have a kitchen with a knife block and a mezzaluna and pictures of Kit's baby stuck on the cupboard doors. I'll work until I'm seventy-five and die of throat cancer on the week I'd planned to retire. Or perhaps I'll be one of those guys who hits middle age and attaches a hosepipe to his exhaust. I don't know—the future is unwritten. I'd like to think that you and I will meet during some as yet unimagined social struggle. We'll stand guard on a picket line or share the weight of a banner. When your hands are up and your head is bleeding and the police are preparing to charge, we will link our arms.

But where are you now? Perhaps you're in the bath and the water has cooled and the bubbles have dispersed. Maybe now is when you'll wash yourself—you'll foam up your armpits, shampoo your hair, duck into the silence of underwater. Or maybe you're on the sofa, next to a full ashtray and a glass of wine you're now disinclined to drink. Yes, you must go to bed. You must set your alarm. You must lay out your work clothes. I'd like to think you're on a train. You'll watch the fields pass until the sun sets, until you see only a reflection of yourself.

ABOUT THE AUTHOR

D. D. Johnston was born in Scotland in 1979. He has worked as a labourer, a dishwasher, a nightclub bouncer, and he was employed in the fast food industry for seven years. While flipping burgers he helped to start an underground trade union, studied for a degree in sociology, and became interested in anarchist politics. He participated in anti-capitalist, anti-fascist, and anti-war protests across Europe, but after being seriously injured in a street fight he decided that the pen is at least as mighty as the flagpole. Since settling in England in 2005, he has worked as a ghost writer and has written short fiction. Today he is a lecturer in Creative Writing at the University of Gloucestershire. *Peace, Love & Petrol Bombs* is his first novel.

ALSO FROM AK PRESS

Jack Wilson is a scrappy city journalist bouncing from one alt weekly to the next, trying to eke out a living in the midst of the economic crisis and play role model to his college-aged son. A chance encounter with a faded Wanted poster in a San Diego library sends Jack deep into the wilds of California's hidden history, in search of outlaw revolutionary Bobby Flash. As Jack tracks Flash through the I.W.W. Free Speech Fights, the Magonista Revolt, and the first red scare, he uncovers the real story of a forgotten revolutionary world—and learns something about the importance of family in the process.

Flash: A Novel, by Jim Miller | $13.95 | 978-1-84935-025-9

Support AK Press!

AK Press is one of the world's largest and most productive anarchist publishing houses. We're entirely worker-run and democratically man-

aged. We operate without a corporate structure—no boss, no managers, no bullshit. We publish close to twenty books every year, and distribute thousands of other titles published by other like-minded independent presses from around the globe.

The Friends of AK program is a way that you can directly contribute to the continued existence of AK Press, and ensure that we're able to keep publishing great books just like this one! Friends pay a minimum of $25/£15 per month into our publishing account. In return, Friends automatically receive (for the duration of their membership), as they appear, one free copy of every new AK Press title. Friends are also entitled to a discount on everything featured in the AK Press Distribution catalog and on the website, on each and every order.

There's great stuff in the works—so sign up now, and let the presses roll!

Won't you be our friend? Both our US and UK offices maintain a Friends of AK membership program, so please email friendsofak@akpress.org or ak@akedin.demon.co.uk for more info. Or visit us online: http://www.akpress.org/programs/friendsofak.

Would you like to contribute a larger sum? Or perhaps sponsor a book? Get in touch!